The baron stood
before them

"Your skills and capabilities will enhance the progress of my ville as we work toward the perfect society. I want you with me, not against me. And of your own free will."

"Do we really have a choice?" Ryan asked. "We're here, surrounded by your sec."

Arcadian considered that. "You may have a point. If you made a break for freedom, we could stop you. The fact that we found Dr. Tanner proves we can sweep this ville with relative ease. But if you choose to run, a firefight would only take out some of my men and lead to your demise."

"So if we say no?"

"Then you'll be held until you say yes. And you will."

There was a steel and ice there that betrayed a will that Ryan knew wouldn't be refused.

"What do you have in mind for us?"

JAMES AXLER

DEATH LANDS.

Arcadian's Asylum

A GOLD EAGLE BOOK FROM

WORLDWIDE.

TORONTO • NEW YORK • LONDON
AMSTERDAM • PARIS • SYDNEY • HAMBURG
STOCKHOLM • ATHENS • TOKYO • MILAN
MADRID • WARSAW • BUDAPEST • AUCKLAND

Recycling programs
for this product may
not exist in your area.

First edition May 2010

ISBN-13: 978-0-373-62602-1

ARCADIAN'S ASYLUM

Printed in U.S.A.

Freedom is not merely the opportunity to do as one pleases; neither is it merely the opportunity to choose between set alternatives. Freedom is, first of all, the chance to formulate the available choices, to argue over them—and then, the opportunity to choose.

—C. Wright Mills
1916–1962

THE DEATHLANDS SAGA

This world is their legacy, a world born in the violent nuclear spasm of 2001 that was the bitter outcome of a struggle for global dominance.

There is no real escape from this shockscape where life always hangs in the balance, vulnerable to newly demonic nature, barbarism, lawlessness.

But they are the warrior survivalists, and they endure—in the way of the lion, the hawk and the tiger, true to nature's heart despite its ruination.

Ryan Cawdor: The privileged son of an East Coast baron. Acquainted with betrayal from a tender age, he is a master of the hard realities.

Krysty Wroth: Harmony ville's own Titian-haired beauty, a woman with the strength of tempered steel. Her premonitions and Gaia powers have been fostered by her Mother Sonja.

J. B. Dix, the Armorer: Weapons master and Ryan's close ally, he, too, honed his skills traversing the Deathlands with the legendary Trader.

Doctor Theophilus Tanner: Torn from his family and a gentler life in 1896, Doc has been thrown into a future he couldn't have imagined.

Dr. Mildred Wyeth: Her father was killed by the Ku Klux Klan, but her fate is not much lighter. Restored from predark cryogenic suspension, she brings twentieth-century healing skills to a nightmare.

Jak Lauren: A true child of the wastelands, reared on adversity, loss and danger, the albino teenager is a fierce fighter and loyal friend.

Dean Cawdor: Ryan's young son by Sharona accepts the only world he knows, and yet he is the seedling bearing the promise of tomorrow.

In a world where all was lost, they are humanity's last hope....

Chapter One

"They say a week in a truck is a long time. 'Specially if you ain't got no shitter, and no time to stop. Me? I say it's how you get to know who your real friends are."

Trader Toms cackled in a wheezing, cracked tone that broke down into a phlegm-ridden cough. Hacking and snorting, he drew up a phlegm ball that followed his trail of tobacco juice into a bucket bolted to the side of the wag. He was still wheezing and cackling, shaking his head and repeating the last four words to himself with a shake of the head when Doc Tanner politely cleared his throat.

"I believe the derivation of the phrase comes from 'a week is a long time in politics,' used by media commentators in the decades before skydark. They used it in much the same way, as it was not unknown for politicians to change their allegiances more often than they would change their underwear."

Toms wiped the tears from his cheeks with the back of a begrimed hand, leaving streaks of dirt in their wake. "Hell, that wouldn't be difficult with me," he breathed, the rattle in his chest making the words seem echoed and distant. "I gotta say, Doc, that's why I like having you around. You may be madder than a bunch of stickies put in sack and beaten with clubs, but you know some seriously old and weird shit. Just like you, in fact."

"Why, thank you," Tanner replied mildly. To be sure, the fat man seated in front of him may have uttered those words in a tone that suggested he meant no insult—indeed, was growing fond of Doc—but the old man still had to bite back the bile and not heed to the temptation of taking the fat man's equally fat head and ramming it into the bucket, so that he drowned in his own spit and phlegm.

Grinding his teeth, he glanced across to where Jak Lauren sat, cradling his 357 Magnum Colt Python as though it were a newborn babe. The albino youth's face was as impassive as ever, but as their eyes met briefly there was a flicker that told Doc he would be backed up all the way.

But no: keep quiet, smile politely, and wait for the big payoff. It had been a long trek across the plains, with the companions unsure of where the next ville or settlement may lay, and their horses were almost exhausted—as were they—when the approaching convoy had become more than a cloud of dust on the horizon.

With no cover, and sapped of their energy, all that they could do was stand their ground and wait to see if the newcomers were hostile. Fortunately—or perhaps not, he mused as he watched the repulsive fat man wobbling on his seat—they had been greeted with nothing so much as deference. The convoy had drawn to a halt at a distance that had indicated no immediate attack would be forthcoming, and the fat man and his two sec lieutenants had dismounted from their wags to approach. This they did unarmed, before declaring themselves and making it known that, if little else, they had recognized Ryan and J.B. by description.

"You can see I got me one hell of a convoy, and I could use extra sec. 'Specially sec that knows what the hell it's doing. And you boys do. Guess the rest of you ain't no useless crap, either, else you wouldn't be riding with One-eye and Four-eyes."

The offensive words contrasted with the artless and disingenuous way in which they were spoken. If nothing else, Doc had to admit, they had been aware of Trader Toms's failing from the first.

With little in the way of food and water left between them, and no real knowledge of the terrain, it had been an offer that couldn't be refused.

Although, as the fat man shifted on his seat, raised one ass cheek and let rip with a fart so loud that it sounded above the whining note of the engine, Doc did ponder that a slow death from starvation and thirst may have been a better option. From the corner of his eye, he saw Jak tilt back slightly so that he could catch the fresh air that blew through an open port at the rear of the wag. As the fecal scent hit Doc, he wished that he had that option.

"You know, Doc, I love all that old shit," Toms continued, with perhaps an inappropriate choice of words, in Doc's view. "I like to try and pick up stuff like old mags, disks, vids… Funny, most people think they're just junk, and they got no worth. Well, mebbe that's right if you're thinking just in terms of food or jack, and mebbe it's right that you put that shit first, 'cause without it we ain't gonna stand a chance. But that old stuff, man, the way people lived and thought before the big one… There's wrinkles in there that can be used. Got a lot of ideas from that. Put me way up the food chain, more than people thought I ever would where I come from."

"A little knowledge can be a dangerous thing," Doc said, conscious of avoiding the irony in his voice while knowing at the same time that it would sail right over the greasy scalp of the trader. "However, the accumulation of knowledge, when applied, can reap dividends. Pay off," he added, seeing the momentary look of puzzlement on Toms's face.

The trader snapped his fingers and slapped a palm against a thigh covered with pants of a cloth so dirt encrusted as to be of indeterminate origin.

"Hell, that's it exactly, Doc. Ain't just what you know—it's knowing who else knows it, and how the two of you can use that if you can't turn it to your advantage on your own. That's what I like about going to Arcady. That baron, Arcadian... There's a man who knows his shit. Backward, forward, sideward and up a bear's ass. Ain't nothing that man don't know. For real."

Doc shrugged. "He certainly does seem to be a most learned man," he murmured. Yes, he thought, and one who prized that knowledge and held it to himself jealously, unwilling to share. He had been cagey around Doc and his fellow travelers. Perhaps that could be put down to a healthy suspicion of those who didn't usually journey alongside a trader with whom Arcadian seemed to do so much business.

But no. There was more to it than that. The baron was a ruler in every feudal sense that permeated these postskydark ages. Knowledge was one of the tools that he used to keep his people under the heel of his boot. Toms may have felt that he was a near equal—if not on a par—with the baron, but in truth he was a cretin in comparison. His learning was small, in real terms, if impressive for someone in this intellectually derelict wasteland. Doc would be the last to say this as a way of boosting his own ego—for where had all his learning got him in this world—but Toms was narrow-minded, and couldn't visualize the uses of knowledge that Arcadian had seemed to have grasped with ease.

Because this was such a strong weapon in his armory, and because it was rarely challenged, so he had been unwilling to enter into the kind of discourse with Doc—particularly—and the others that Toms had tried to engineer. Toms could be ruthless in his business and the protection of his convoy and position. They had seen evidence of this. Despite his almost buffoonish persona, the workers on the convoy respected the way in which Toms had built up his convoy and given them a good livelihood in a world that placed such a thing at a premium.

Yet this was still a man who, when drunk on the potent brew that he carried for the recreation of his crews, could repeat endlessly the reasons why he liked to be called "The Don" whilst doing imitations of the actor from whom he had got the idea, cramming his cheeks with rags, shrugging and gesturing until he almost choked on the rags and his own laughter, falling flat and muttering about "Brando…brandy…" He thought he was so funny, Doc reflected, yet he was a harmless bore.

He couldn't imagine Arcadian getting drunk, let alone having a repertoire of such party tricks. The baron had struck him as a man who could never allow himself to lose control in such a way. He had too much at stake:

much that went beyond the wealth of the ville he ruled. Whatever it may be, Doc fervently hoped that he would never go back and find out.

Even as this thought crossed his mind, and he was aware of Toms burbling on about the conversion of his wags to run on water, not gas—and how he had seen something about this on an old vid, yet the motherfuck tape had frizzed to a snowstorm before all had been made clear—Doc could feel the cold fingers of fear tap at the nerves down his spine.

He looked at Jak. The albino youth's normally impassive visage was curious. Doc shook his head slightly, then turned his attention back to the trader.

"Ah, yes, I believe one of the theories behind such vid wiping is to do with the way that oil companies liked to keep a monopoly on wag fuel. Not that different to now, really…"

It was the cue that Toms was waiting for: "Tell me about it. I did hear tell that the guy Ryan and B.J. ran with—" Doc had tired of the way in which Toms continuously got the Armorer's name the wrong way around, but left correcting it for what seemed to be the thousandth time "—had a lake of gas. That would be cool, to find something like that again, instead of having to pay shit through the nose for what you can get. Then they complain when I have to up my prices because they up theirs. I mean, stands to any kind of reason, man, if…"

Doc allowed him to ramble on, half listening, yet disturbed by the ice that infused his blood.

RYAN CAWDOR and Krysty Wroth were riding in the eighth wag of the convoy, dead center. A fifteen-wag convoy was a pretty big undertaking and, like Doc, Ryan had decided that Toms wasn't quite the idiot that he had first appeared to be. Nonetheless, both Krysty and himself had spent far too long in the lead wag, listening to his boring stories and putting up with the endless bodily functions that made this armored heat-trap seem preferable.

The center wag was under the command of K.T., one of the two sec lieutenants trusted with Toms's convoy. A slim, almost girlish man of indeterminate age with dark circles under eyes that seemed to bulge out of his skull, K.T. was sharp but prone to fits of rage that seemed to come from nowhere. Ryan had wondered if it was jolt-induced when they first met, but had seen little sign of any narcotic usage on the convoy. Brew was okay. Toms drew the line at things that could truly impair efficiency. So it seemed that the sudden irrational fits of pique, and the colorful language that went with it, were merely part of K.T.'s natural state. Both Ryan and Krysty had heard some inventive cursing in their time, but had to admit that K.T. at full throttle showed a facility for stringing together obscenities that would make a deaf man blush. So it was that they were both secretly hoping that the sec lieutenant would blow his top over some trifling matter, as that was what seemed to trigger his temper. Ironically, under true pressure he was calm and collected.

But so far nothing on this leg of the journey—the first hop out of Arcady—had caused the sec man to explode. If anything, he seemed subdued by the ease of departure.

Given only a day's notice of Toms's desire to up and

move on, the two sec lieutenants had marshaled the wag crews in a manner that had impressed Ryan. Not since he rode with Trader had he seen a crew respond so well to having their rest and recreation interrupted in such a manner. They were ordered to prepare for departure a good week ahead of the time that Toms had originally scheduled. When pressed by crew reps pissed at losing valuable drinking and gaudy time, he had said that Arcadian had given him a hint that there was some good business to be done in the ville of Jackson Spire, which was about 150 miles down the road. Close enough to reach within a day on good roads, two at most. Then they could camp while he went about negotiations, and return to their R & R.

Given that the crew reps weren't in the best of conditions themselves, the way in which K.T. and his sideman Lou had gone about their business was interesting to behold. First, the two men had taken the initially pissed reps and dunked them in barrels of ice water to shock them into sobriety. Fishing them out of the barrels and slapping them into line where necessary, they had worked as a team. Lou was almost twice the size of K.T., and his opposite in almost every way. Where the smaller man had a manic stare, a loud voice, and seemed to be made of barbed wire, Lou was a giant who seemed to be encased in a roll of blubber. Yet despite that, and the fact that he had a laid-back manner and a soft-spoken, almost whispering voice, his almost seven-foot body had a hardness rippling beneath the fat that spoke of a layer of thickly developed muscle. And the hard strength showed in the way in which he picked up the complaining reps with one hand, sometimes lofting one in each massive paw before dunking them, lifting them out and handing them over to K.T. Here was where the smaller man's temper and fire came in useful: the crew reps, stunned and shocked, perhaps still a little high from the brew in their veins, had him yelling in their faces, slapping them hard to make them pay attention.

Their orders were simple: go and collect the crews from your wags—you would know better than anyone else where they were. Get them out of the bars and the gaudys. No matter if they were on top of a slut or halfway down a glass. Back here within a half hour.

"Better do it, boys. It's for the best," Lou added mildly when K.T. had finished his tirade.

It was a routine that Mildred, watching at the time with Ryan, had described as "good-cop-bad-cop," explaining at Ryan's puzzled expression about the psychology of the soft and hard.

"That?" Ryan had asked with mild surprise. "That's nothing new. Never heard that expression, though. And never seen it done quite like this."

Yet such was the regard with which the crews held Toms, for all his oddities, that the crew reps were gone as soon as Lou's mild words faded on the breeze, only to return a short while later with their crewmen in tow.

Ryan had doubted that the necessary maintenance and repairs could be made to ready the convoy in time. Half the crewmen were being held up by their fellows, and their level of tiredness, drunkenness and ability to concentrate on the task in hand was—to say the least—dubious.

And yet, harried and driven by the two sec lieutenants, each moving to the crews that he knew would respond best to his particular manner, it wasn't long before the crews were beginning to look like the brew and lust had been riven from their blood. Goaded by the sec men and each other, they were soon fit enough to start the task in hand.

For the next eighteen hours straight they had worked, before resting prior to departure. Ryan and his people had been acting as sec and outriders for most of their short time with the convoy. Toms had told Ryan, as they stood on the melting pavement of the highway on which he had found them, that he knew from stories that Ryan and J.B. were survivors of the infamous Trader's convoy. Since then, stories had circulated about their abilities to fight their way out of a tight corner. So their main purpose in being recruited was to provide additional and experienced sec to augment the force on a convoy that was swelling to the point of being unwieldy.

For the most part, this is what they had done. But now that they were about to leave Arcady sooner than originally intended, they had to earn their jack. They had been promised money and supplies on leaving the convoy, if that was what they preferred. They had also been assured a job as long as they wanted one. The benefits for this were obvious: Toms, while not generous, was an employer who believed that his crews would respond well to being well rewarded. Food was plentiful. Basic meds were stocked. Water was always well tanked. And there was jack for gambling, gaudys and brew when they hit a ville.

But in return, Toms demanded that his crews be ready to respond at an instant. They had to work hard, and turn their hand to anything that would assist the greater whole. So it was that Ryan and his people found themselves pressed into tasks that were alien to their usual way of working.

Yet the manner in which K.T. and Lou had managed the crews after the initial hard-taken tack had been revelatory. Despite the mouth that still could outcurse anyone across the breadth of the land, K.T. had been encouraging rather than scourging, and Lou had used his immense strength to facilitate speed on some tasks that would otherwise have been delayed by the need to find spare manpower for lifting.

Now, as Ryan and Krysty sat in the eighth wag with the sec lieutenant, and he said little or nothing as his protruding bug eyes scanned the horizon before flicking back to the instruments on the dash of the wag, checking the wag jockey's progress, it was as though the stresses of the last day or so had never occurred.

"Taken this stretch of road before?" Ryan asked, wondering why the sec man seemed so intent on the surrounding territory. If what Toms had told them was correct, then Arcady was a regular on their route.

K.T. shook his head. "Shit, no. Trader tells us at the last minute that it's another route out of the asswipe fucker of a ville. Usually take the road heading nor' nor' east, which is an old highway that's been resurfaced in part. Smooth as a gaudy's pussy after a close shave. Sweet, easy route. This pissing road leads who knows where."

"Jackson Spire, presumably," Krysty murmured. It passed through her mind that it was odd that this ville should be their destination, full of trading promise, when K.T. seemed never to have heard of it before. Her hair curled slightly.

"Yeah, probably does. 'Scepting that we've never been to that bastard pesthole ville before. Some ass-end-of-beyond piece of shit that ain't got two turds to rub together, let alone serious trade."

"Then why would it now?" Ryan questioned.

K.T. shrugged. "Why the fuck should I know? Mebbe they got lucky and found some old stockpile on their doorstep while they were fucking each other and their pigs in the dirt. Mebbe they got some blasters and robbed some stupe ass convoy that wasn't looking. Or mebbe Arcadian is setting them up in some way."

"Setting them up? For what?"

K.T. shrugged. "I don't mean like the asshole wants to make 'em take a fall for something. But mebbe he wants to see if they can make something of themselves if they get a helping hand, or whether they'll just piss it away like shithead scum."

"That's magnanimous of him," Krysty murmured. "Kind of good," she added as she noted the puzzled look K.T. shot her.

K.T. sighed. "Weird fucker, that Arcadian. Me and Lou never really get much of a chance to be around when him and Toms are together, and I can't say as I'm too pissed off about that. There's just something about him that really puts the shits up me."

His attention was taken by a patch of undergrowth on their left, and he peered toward it, cursing furiously under his breath as he tried to define if the rustling movement within it was a harmless animal, a possible predator or stickies waiting to attack.

While that occupied him, Ryan and Krysty exchanged looks. Such was the bond that had built between the two of them over the years they had been
traveling that they could almost tell what the other was
thinking.

If Arcadian had some motive for sending Toms to
Jackson Spire, then they would be wise to be triple red.
Maybe the baron was nothing more than a dabbler in
trying to expand his empire than K.T. had half suggested. But maybe he had some motive that was as yet
unfathomable, involving the convoy as much as—if not
more than—the people of the ville.

The eighth wag of the convoy was an old military
vehicle that had, at one time, been used as troop trans-
port. Bench seats still filled the first half of its length
before giving way to an area that had been cleared at
the rear of the vehicle. Here were two mounted Brens,
ancient but reliable, that covered both sides of the road.
Currently they were manned by two of the wag crew.
Ryan and Krysty were due to relieve them in an hour.
Meantime, they tried to rest, knowing how uncomfortable the metal bucket seats of the Bren mountings could
become. But it was far from easy, as Toms was a great
believer in utilizing space to the max: cartons and
wooden crates were piled precariously around them,
barely contained by webbing. These were crew supplies, and were carried in sec wags to keep them separate from trade cargo. It was a reasonable system,
except that it took no account of crew comfort during
rest periods.

"Asshole trees," K.T. cursed, louder than his previous
mumblings. "Makes the land hard to read. You don't

read the land, you don't know what's gonna jump out at you."

Which was precisely why Ryan and Krysty were themselves cursing at that moment. They were trying to get rested so that they could stay triple red, yet thinking that the only thing that was going to leap out at them on benches like these were their own kidneys.

It was going to be a long ride, despite the distance.

"DO YOU USUALLY follow this route?" J. B. Dix asked mildly, taking a look through the periscope attachment that had been welded into the roof of the rear wag. It was a fine piece of work, salvaged from who knew where and lovingly maintained. The welder had been a craftsman, the bearing-mounted swivel allowing J.B. to take a full 360-degree look at the territory through which they were passing.

Despite the mildness of his tone, J.B. felt uneasy. He had picked up from overheard murmurs that this wasn't the usual route taken on leaving Arcady. The scope showed him that the roadsides were dense, impenetrable foliage, almost like a jungle—creeping vines, twisted and gnarled tree trunks with overhanging branches pendant with dark, oily leaves; thick, spiky grasses that poked out of gaps and lined the hillocks on which the trees rose and fell. Dark, ominous rustling from within could be danger, or could be just the movement of the heavy plant life.

This was the territory that had once been known as Missouri. Some of the vegetation he could see would have existed here before skydark, perhaps changed by the mutation of the nukecaust. But most of it was alien—not just to here, but to anywhere that he had ever been. Not least of which was the route they had taken into the ville. There was a sense of foreboding that hung over the old flat-top highway. It may have just been the darkness where the canopy of leaves blocked the sun, or it may have been the way in which the trees seemed to loom, as though waiting for the right moment to pounce.

Someone or something had laid this vegetation along this route. He'd bet on someone, and he also knew who would be his likely suspect. But the question was why? Was it a defense? In which case, why was the convoy being sent to Jackson Spire, which presumably was the only settlement along this old road, and the only place from which Arcady could want protection?

Or had they been sent this way because the foliage was part of an offensive rather than defensive measure? In which case, where was an attack to come from? The why could wait.

J.B.'s question was finally answered. "Not usual to go this way, no. But then, we've never been to Jackson Spire before. No reason to, really. As far as we were concerned, it was a dead-and-alive pesthole, with nothing to take us there. Nothing to trade, and no jack to buy."

The giant Lou stretched himself, his arms rising so that they pushed against the roof of the wag, even from his seated position. He yawned, then pivoted on his swivel-mounted chair so that he faced the Armorer rather than the front of the wag.

"Why? Does it matter?"

J.B. shrugged. He thought it might, but there was no

need to cause unnecessary panic. "I was just wondering. It's this weird shit at the sides of the road. Not what I remember when we came in."

Lou thought about it for a moment, scratching at the stubble on his chin. "That's true enough," he said slowly. "Never seen anything like this around these parts before. Then again, Jackson Spire has a reputation for being rad-blasted, which is part of the reason people like us have avoided it before. Guess it's just rad shit that's done this."

J.B. sniffed. "Yeah, guess so," he agreed.

Of course he didn't. There was an itch at the base of his neck, a sharp prickle that alerted him to a possible danger. If nothing else, he was going to stay triple red and be ready if it came at them.

Carefully, he stepped back from the scope, took off his spectacles and polished them with the hem of his shirt. As he did, he locked eyes with Mildred Wyeth. The doctor had been checking the med supplies that she always carried with her, separate to those of the convoy. It was the first chance she'd had, given the speed with which they had prepared for departure. But as she had listened to the exchange between the giant sec lieutenant and the Armorer, she had paused in her task. She knew J.B. far too well to take his words at face value, and she knew when he was trying to keep something back. Now, as he shot her a glance that was intended to stay hidden from the other crew members, she understood.

The wag that traveled at the rear of the convoy was longer than any others, and had a larger crew. Six people, besides J.B. and Mildred, were in the vehicle.

A radio operator sat at a right angle to the wag jockey. All the vehicles were connected by an old shortwave system that, like the scope, had been salvaged and maintained with care. The whirling, crackling sounds of the rad-scoured ether were an ever-present low-volume background to the business of the wag, occasionally rising above the hum of the engine, sometimes blending with it almost hypnotically, broken now and then by the distorted voices of other wags passing messages.

The wag jockey had a sec man riding shotgun. Currently, an aging and emaciated man named Keef rode there, peering from behind spectacles thicker than those of the Armorer.

Behind these seats were chairs bolted to the floor of the wag. Lou reclined in one of these, and he was joined by another crew member. The final man in the wag crew—unusually, this was an all-male wag—was seated at the rear. A heavy-duty cannon was mounted over the rear axle, its barrel and scope exiting through the space that had once housed doors, but which had been modified to mold steel plate shielding around the blaster.

Around the chairs bolted into the floor were crew supplies, and along the sides of the wag were welded secure cabinets that housed meds and armament. It didn't leave much room for the crew, cramming them close together. Yet, because of the low level of interior light—the windshield and wire-meshed glass on the side doors being augmented by fluorescent-lighting run off the battery—it was still possible for J.B. to convey all he wished to Mildred without anyone else in the wag being aware of what passed between them.

She moved across the floor of the steadily rolling wag, picking her way around the crates and cartons, so that she could take a look at the roadside. When she did, the sight took her by surprise: while inside the wag, having seen nothing of the outside since the convoy started to roll, she had assumed that they would be passing the kind of landscape that she had seen surrounding Arcady. This, however…

"Wow, that is kind of weird," she said in the best ingenuous tone that she could muster. "Can I take a better look?" she asked, indicating the scope and looking toward Lou.

He shrugged, an indulgent smile on his face. "Sure. It is fascinating, I guess."

It was obvious that he could see nothing to worry about, and was amused by the interest that the Armorer and Mildred were showing. Relieved that he had asked no awkward questions, she moved to the scope and took a look at the surrounding territory.

No question. There was something dark and disturbing about the land through which they were passing.

Without comment, she left the scope and returned to her former post. She continued to check the meds, but also found time to surreptitiously check her Czech-made ZKR blaster. J.B., catching her doing this, indicated with the slightest inclination of the head that he acknowledged her understanding.

The convoy rumbled on. The suspension on the vehicle was good, but even so they could still feel the bump and jolt of the road beneath. Looking out at the surface, it seemed unbroken, but it was undulating as they passed over it. Root systems from the trees and bushes on either side had burrowed deep into the soil and spread across the gap between, pushing up the earth but not yet breaking through.

This made progress slower than perhaps J.B. or Mildred would have liked. The sooner they were out of this landscape, the better.

J.B. returned to the scope. To the rear of the convoy, there was nothing except the ribbon of road, the ville of Arcady a distant memory hidden from view by the twist of the road and the canopy of foliage. On either side, all that could be seen were banks of oily, dark leaves and pointed grasses.

Looking ahead, J.B. could see the convoy snaking around a bend in the road. The way in which the vehicles moved erratically across the surface of the flattop gave some indication of how the wag jockeys had to wrestle with the steering, wrenching back wheels that wanted to move with the undulations rather than the will of the driver.

The fourteen vehicles ahead of them were of varied size and shape, some old container rigs, some predark military vehicles. All had been repainted in a variety of colors, the only recurring motif being that the same kind of colors had been used. Maybe, J.B. figured, Toms had found a stash of old vehicle paints and had spread their use among his wags. It wasn't pretty, but it identified every vehicle as belonging to this convoy. Made sense—no coldheart could hijack one of Toms's wags and hide it with any ease.

They traveled with a set distance between every wag. There was little variation, and any wag jockey who strayed too far distant or too close was quick to drop back or to catch up. It prevented them from crashing into each other should the front of the convoy be pulled up, or from being separated and split up if the convoy was attacked from the middle.

J.B. had to hand it to Toms. For such a crude, laughable figure, which he was in many ways, the man had an intelligence that went deeper than was apparent. Which made it all the more odd that he should be taking this route, going to a ville he didn't know, and all on the say-so of Baron Arcadian. From what Lou and K.T. had told them—indeed, what Toms had said when they had joined him on the way into Arcady—Toms had a high regard for the baron, and felt that it was mutual.

J.B. hadn't met Arcadian, but he was aware that Lou shared K.T.'s wariness. Was it possible that Toms's opinion of the baron had blinded him to any possible duplicity or danger?

Trouble was, all J.B. had to go on was a gut feeling. He knew Mildred felt it, too. He didn't know about Ryan, Krysty, Jak or Doc, but if they'd taken a look at the surrounding land, he was sure that he could guess.

All his foreboding came to fruition as the radio crackled to life. J.B. and Mildred exchanged puzzled glances as Toms's voice came over the airwaves.

"Wag One to all wags. Slow to a halt over the next quarter of a mile. There's something we need to attend to. Repeat—slow to a halt over the next quarter mile and maintain distance. Condition blue. No need to fuckin' panic, guys."

The trader's tone had been easy and friendly, with no sign of panic. Yet what could have caused him to call a halt on a empty road, with no sign of the ville up ahead?

J.B., ignoring Lou's questioning glance, spun the scope through 360 degrees once again, staying when facing front. There was no sign of any obstruction ahead, and through to the next bend there was no sign of Jackson Spire—even given that they had only been traveling a few hours.

"What's this about?" he snapped at Lou.

The giant sec lieutenant shrugged. "Fucked if I know. Guess we'll find out soon enough."

Chapter Two

"And then Corleon turns to the guy who's been trying to chill him all the way through, and he says, er…" Toms halted midway through the description and tugged at his beard, his beady, dark eyes darting around and taking a good look at the landscape that passed the windows of the wag.

Doc was relieved, in one way. This had to have been the fifth time he'd had to endure a blow-by-blow description of a scene from an old vid in the past few hours. In truth, he had ceased to pay full attention to what Toms was saying sometime back, and he had a sneaking suspicion that this particular scene was on its second run.

However, the way in which Toms stopped midstory was unnerving. The trader had found—he thought—a willing audience in Doc, and one that had knowledge of these old vids. Doc didn't think it prudent to point out that an interest in one aspect of the past didn't include an all-encompassing fascination.

Still, while Toms was droning on, Doc knew that all was well. For the trader to interrupt himself, something of moment had to be about to occur.

Hawklike, Doc studied the man as he paused, looked, then turned to the wag jockey. There was an unease in his manner, as though he had almost forgotten himself; as if he was about to do something that wasn't necessarily to his liking.

"How far out are we?" he asked the wag jockey, his tone now businesslike.

The driver studied the odometer. "About fifteen miles," he answered. His tone was curious, as though wondering why his boss had suddenly questioned him.

Toms nodded to himself, muttered, "Fuck, nearly screwed it."

"A problem, perchance?" Doc queried.

Toms turned back, looking blank for a moment, before shaking his head and smiling uneasily. Doc noted that it didn't reach his eyes.

"No, not problem. Just something that I nearly forgot to do."

Doc could feel Jak stiffen, even though he couldn't see him. The creeping apprehension that had flooded through him before now returned, and he knew that Jak's sense of danger had also been pricked.

"Something we should know about?" Doc said, trying to keep his tone neutral.

Toms shook his head. "No. Well, kinda. But bear with me, you'll know soon enough," he told him.

Ah, yes, Doc mused, but would they like it?

"WHAT THE FUCK does that fat little shit think he's doing? We've barely got the wags in gear and the prick is making us stop. What was the point of running the asswipe crews into the ground like a bunch of shitheaps if we're going to stop and start like this?"

K.T. banged the palm of his hand on the side of the

wag. Hard. So much so that Krysty winced, wondering how many bones the idiot had broken over the years because of his temper. It was a hard, flat sound in the enclosed space. K.T. cursed again through gritted teeth as the pain hit: not that it calmed him in any way.

"Pull the fucking wag up, then," he yelled at the wag jockey. "Might as well pull out the bedrolls, light a fire and bed down for the bastard night," he muttered fiercely.

"So you don't know why Toms is doing this?" Ryan asked.

"Of course I don't fucking know you shit rag. Think I'd be so fucking pissed otherwise?"

Ryan held his peace, knowing K.T. spoke crudely to everyone.

K.T. grabbed the handset for the shortwave. "Lou, bring it down to zero in three-fifty," he said, visibly controlling his temper. The big man was the only one who could ever put him in his place, and resultantly he was always on his best behavior when talking to him.

"Sure, no problem," came the big man's mild tones. "And you keep it frosty, you hear?"

K.T. grinned. "I'll try."

He turned to Ryan and Krysty, the grin turning apologetic. "Shouldn't have said that to you. Ain't nothing to do with you if Toms goes weird on us."

"That's okay," Ryan assured him. "But is there anything we should know? We're supposed to be sec for you, so if there's any problem…"

K.T. frowned, craning his head out the front window of the wag before answering. When he turned back, he had a puzzled expression. "Y'know, I'd tell you if I could, but I'll be fucked sideways by a bunch of horny stickies if I can see anything weird at all out there. Far as I can see, there's no reason why we should be stopping."

Krysty's hair pulled tighter around her throat, the coils moving in. "No reason" usually meant a real bad reason—just one that hadn't jumped out to bite you on the ass yet.

LOU REPLACED the handset after speaking to K.T., pulling a face that bespoke his own bemusement.

"Guess you'd better get ready," he said to J.B. and Mildred. "Guess we all had." He stood with some difficulty in the cramped interior and moved to the metal gun cabinet bolted to the side of the wag. He took down a carbine and a Browning Hi-Power hand-blaster, checking that both were oiled and loaded before holstering the blaster and throwing the carbine over one massive shoulder. Both weapons were in decent condition.

"You see anything out there that could be why we're stopping?" he continued, directing his question to J.B.

The Armorer shook his head. "Can't see much, for sure," he mused. "But there isn't anything close enough to be visible or to cause too much disturbance to the cover."

Lou chewed his lip thoughtfully. "Then what's the stupe bastard playing at? Last thing we should be doing is just pulling up on an open road, especially with all that cover."

J.B. studied the big man intently. There was little doubt that he was genuine. The sense of impending danger that had infected J.B. and Mildred caused the Armorer to wonder if the convoy itself was the source of apprehension. But if there was an enemy within, then Lou had no part of this. Nor did the other members of the wag crew, who were also murmuring their disquiet.

Was it like this in every wag? J.B. wondered. If so, then what did the fat man have up his hairy-armed and snot-stained sleeve?

The shortwave, up until then nothing more than a constant background undulation with a few crackling bursts of static, burst into life as messages were relayed from wag to wag, synchronizing the slowdown to a halt. At the same time, K.T. and Lou, as sec lieutenants, became focused on sec measures when the convoy had come to a stop. Each wag carried in its crew people who doubled as gear-humpers and sec. At a time such as this, all such personnel were focused on their sec duties. It was agreed that when the convoy had stopped, each wag's sec contingent would exit first, backs to the wags, one on each side of the vehicle, covering both sides of the densely packed verge.

"Where do we fit?" J.B. asked.

"Good point," Lou replied. He spoke into the handset. "K.T., if we deploy the usual people in defensive positions, what should we do with the additional sec group?"

"They're evenly spaced along the convoy, right? I'd say they could act as outrunners, mebbe scout the roadside. What do you think?"

Lou turned to J.B. and Mildred, his expression begging the question. He beckoned J.B. to the handset.

"Sounds reasonable," the Armorer began as he approached. "Ryan, we take it in pairs or go solo?"

Ryan's voice crackled. "Way we're spread, take it solo. One for each side. That way we don't leave any gaps."

"Sounds good to me," J.B. agreed. "Jak? Doc?"

Doc's voice came over the airwaves. "A perfectly reasonable assumption, John Barrymore, and one which I think the good Mr. Lauren and myself would find ourselves in agreement. It only remains to be given the nod, as it were, by our immediate superiors."

Lou gave J.B. a look that was half confusion, half amusement. "Does that old crazy mean me and K.T.?"

J.B. couldn't resist a grin. "Yeah."

Lou shook his head with a throaty chuckle. "Weird old fucker."

He was about to speak into the handset when Toms's voice cut across.

"CANCEL THAT, boys," Toms said quickly, moving in front of Doc and taking the handset from him. "Go ahead with the usual plan for our people, but make none for Ryan and his people. You guys, I need to see you urgently up by my wag. As soon as the area is secured, then get yourselves up here."

He signed off and turned away from the handset, at the same time turning his back on Doc and Jak.

"What is this about?" Doc asked calmly, trying to keep the tension from his voice. He could feel Jak at his back, like a coiled spring, yet he knew that to the casual observer, the albino would seem at ease. The other crew members in the wag were exchanging puzzled looks. It was obvious that whatever agenda Toms may have, he hadn't chosen to share it with the rest of his crew. And their reactions showed that his actions were uncharacteristic.

Doc was sure that whatever was going down wasn't something that Toms was fully comfortable with.

The trader didn't answer the old man for some while—or so it seemed—before saying in a voice that was cracked with tension, "You'll soon find out. Best you know with the others."

"You tell now," Jak said. His voice was quiet, but as hard as flint. Doc could see unquiet in the eyes of the other crew members. They were scared of the wiry and impassive albino. They'd seen him in action. If he exploded as they seemed to be expecting, it could trigger a situation that couldn't easily be controlled.

"No, Jak, it is perhaps for the best that we discover what is behind this when we are with Ryan and the others," Doc said slowly. There was weight in his words, and an inference that the albino picked up on.

"Okay," he said simply.

Over the shortwave, they heard K.T. and Lou give the synchronized order, once the convoy had stopped rolling, to disembark. Giving the old man and the albino a sideways glance, the sec detail in the lead wag slipped out to cover either side.

"Well, then," he said softly after a pause, "should we be going?"

Toms turned to Jak and Doc. He looked everywhere but directly at them, nodding without being able to bring himself to utter the slightest word. He picked up a portable handset and made for the side door of the wag, Doc and Jak at his rear.

Both were poised, even if they still had—as yet—no idea what for....

RYAN AND KRYSTY climbed out of the wag, followed by K.T. Looking up and down the length of the convoy, they could see J.B. and Mildred walking toward them, the giant Lou in their wake. Between the middle and end wags, sec men were strung out in a line, backs to the wags, facing the blank wall of oily green vegetation with expressions that veered between the nervous and the confused. They had no doubt that their sec compatriots on the other side of the road looked exactly the same.

Looking toward the lead wag, they could see Trader Toms, shuffling on the pavement, holding a shortwave handset and pointedly looking away from Doc and Jak. Even at this distance, it was obvious that both men were having trouble in not betraying the tension they felt.

Ryan and Krysty stood still, intent on waiting for J.B. and Mildred to join them. It was pretty obvious that K.T. was in no hurry, either, an impression reinforced when he spoke softly as Lou came within earshot.

"Lou, what the fuck is shortass doing?"

The giant smiled amiably. "You think I can ever work out how his mind works? He knows, and we will soon enough. C'mon, let's move."

The six people began to move toward the front of the convoy, feeling the questioning glances of the sec men bore into them as they passed. The handsets that K.T. and Lou carried crackled briefly before Toms's voice sounded.

"C'mon, what are you waiting for? Hurry up."

His tone was far from happy, and Ryan couldn't help but notice the look that shot between the two sec lieutenants. They had no idea what the fat man wanted, and they were concerned at the way he sounded.

If Toms wanted a firefight, he could have it. His people obviously had little idea, if this was his intent, so despite being outnumbered, Ryan was sure his people could take out the sec force, or go down with most of them. Hopefully it wouldn't come to that.

As they drew level with the leading wag, eye contact with Doc and Jak made it clear that they should be ready to fight. The ghost of a smile crossed the albino teen's visage. When was there a time when he wasn't ready for such an eventuality?

Toms stepped back from his sec lieutenants, Ryan's people and the sec man who had stepped out of the lead wag with him. He looked over all of them, slowly. It seemed to go on forever. In the elongated and pregnant pause, it seemed to Ryan that the land around them closed in. He was aware of the humid heat as the sun rose in the sky, its rays of light barely penetrating the thick canopy of leaves even though the heat bounced off the road before reflecting back off the oily, dark leaves. They absorbed the heat and moisture before bearing it back down on the people beneath.

The entire world seemed amplified. The quiet in which they found themselves now that the wag engines had died and they waited for the silent trader to speak only served to make the undertones—otherwise hidden—seem greater.

Ryan felt like his nerve endings were stretched taut enough to break; he knew without looking that the rest of his companions felt the same.

Yet still the fat man couldn't bring himself to speak.

Finally, when he did, it wasn't at them. Rather, it was into the handset.

"Stewie, make up the jack that we owe the newbies and bring it up to me."

The tension wasn't so much broken as deflated, like a tire with a knife in it. Whatever they had been expecting—all of them—it wasn't this. K.T. and Lou looked at each other, confusion written on their faces.

"Why, pray tell, are you asking for monies owed?" Doc questioned. "You surely can't be thinking of dispensing with our services?"

Toms shrugged, but still couldn't bring himself to look at them. "Well, these things have to happen, see, and—"

"Have to happen bullshit," Ryan exploded. "What the fuck are you playing at? Paying us off out here? What do you plan to do, just take off without us?"

Even as he spoke, he could see from Toms's face that he was right. But why? It made no sense.

"Boss, we're going to a new ville that we know jackshit about, and you want to get rid of extra sec?" Lou frowned.

"That's just plain stupe. Only a complete fuckwad would do something like that," K.T. added in a more forthright manner.

"He's right," Ryan added, fighting to keep his temper. "And you know he is."

The one-eyed man's first instinct was to action—but of what kind? They weren't being threatened—if anything, the sec lieutenants did not want them to go—and yet they were about to be cast adrift outside of a ville, on a deserted road, for no reason that he could see.

"But what have we done?" Doc continued in the tone he had earlier adopted. He cast a quick glance toward where Ryan and the others were grouped, hoping that they would let him run with this. He felt that he had an affinity with the trader, or at least an affinity that the trader perceived. Perhaps he could get an answer where they would fail.

Toms shrugged. "It's not about what you've done. Shit, you've been really good the short time you've been with us. But that's kinda what this is about, I guess. How good you are at what you do."

Mildred sighed. "Man, you are making no sense at all. And you know that what you're doing is just gonna piss us off. So if you don't want things to turn nasty, then you'd sure as hell better start explaining. And make sense, this time."

Toms sighed. "Okay, okay—I will, but let's just get things settled, first." He spoke into the handset. "Stewie, for fuck's sake—"

"Just coming," a voice crackled back.

J.B. looked back as he heard a wag door, loud in the now oppressive silence of the road. A fat man—not as tall as Lou, but rounder, and without the impression of underlying muscle—jumped out and huffed his way toward them. He carried a bag that jumped and jangled in his hand. It obviously contained local currency, and a fair amount. It was heavy enough to swing out of time with the blubber on the fat man's body as he ran toward them. Red-faced and sweating, short of breath, he reached them and handed the bag to the trader.

Toms took it without acknowledgment, then spoke once more into the handset. "Okay, this is for all sec.

Our newbies are leaving us, as of now. I'm paying them off, and we leave them here. They show any resistance, chop 'em down. We look after our own first. That's an order."

Even as he spoke the words, Ryan and his people couldn't believe what they were hearing. There had been no provocation on their part, and they still had little or no idea why they were being left.

It was obvious, too, that Lou and K.T. felt the same way.

"Boss, what's this about?" Lou asked, restraining K.T. as the fiery sec lieutenant was about to speak.

Toms sighed, rubbed the back of his hand—the one in which he still grasped the crackling handset—across his forehead.

"Well, I'll tell you," he began, speaking to no one in particular, "it's like this. You don't get anything for free in this world. There's always a trade-off. Even if it's one that you might not like that much. Take Jackson Spire, for example. You think they got trade and jack all of a sudden for no reason? Course they haven't. They got it because Arcadian thinks it'd be a good idea for the villes 'round Arcady to start to grow and develop. Something to do with this idea he has about rebuilding a new society. And they got to abide by a few things he says to get that jack. In order that he'll send trade their way, by putting us onto them."

"So the asswipe gets to feel like he's got a big cock by waving at them," K.T. fumed. "What's that got to do with us? He sends us there to make them feel good, but he don't own us."

"Are you sure about that?" Krysty murmured, eyeing the trader.

Toms screwed his face up in an expression of self-disgust. "It's like I say, you don't get anything without a trade-off. They get a trader coming through, and we get first pickings…as long as I do something for Arcadian in return."

"And that something is to pay us off and leave us here?" Ryan asked, incredulous. "What does that profit him?"

Toms sucked in his breath. "You know," he said at length, "I really don't know. Not for sure. Far as I can see, you didn't do anything to piss him off while you were in Arcady. And you ain't been nothing but good for us. Fact is, I was telling him that. Mebbe he wants you to work for him."

"Bastard strange way of going about it," J.B. mused. "Why not just ask us?"

"Because we could say no," Mildred stated. "This way…"

"We have nowhere to go other than back," Doc finished.

"You don't have to do what Arcadian says," Krysty directed at Toms. "You could just drive on to Jackson Spire, then go beyond."

Toms grinned. "I could. But then I don't know if he has sec there that'll report back. Mebbe he could make it hot, start a firefight. I could certainly never come back this way again, and Arcady is good trade. It's not like I gotta have you chilled, is it?"

Jak spoke for the first time. His words were, perhaps, surprising.

"We take and go. Toms play fair—give us jack.

Supplies?" The last was a question, directed at the trader, who nodded. "Not forcing us do anything. Mebbe we go back, mebbe we move on."

Ryan shrugged. He figured that Jak was right. Toms was making it easy for them, despite the threat of retaliation if they started a firefight.

"Okay, if that's how it's got to be."

Toms's relief was palpable. "I'm pleased you see it that way. Last thing I want is to have to fight."

Because you'd be the first to get chilled, Ryan thought. But he said nothing. This wasn't the time, and Toms wasn't the enemy.

Ryan and his people stood back from the convoy while Lou and K.T. directed that their supplies be brought out and left with them. Then, as Toms ordered his sec force back into their wags, the two sec lieutenants left their former comrades. Little was said, but their unease with the resolution was plain.

The convoy started up and began to rumble down the flattop. The companions stood back and watched it disappear around a bend in the road until the last wag, and its exhaust, had cleared their view. Even the sound of the engines had become a distant rumble, fading beneath the rustling of the groves at their backs.

"Well," Doc said brightly, "do we press on for pastures new? Or do we find out what this crazed baron really wants?"

"You calling someone crazy," Mildred snorted. "Now that really isn't a good sign."

Chapter Three

If they had wondered why Toms had taken them about fifty miles out of the ville before stopping, then they had their answer soon after they opted to return. In many ways, it was a simple decision to make. Ahead, they knew, lay only Jackson Spires, over 150 miles away, on a road that was surrounded by territory that was certainly far from friendly.

Go that way, and they had no idea what lay between themselves and the next ville. And at the end of the road would be a ville that was a satellite of Arcady, along with a convoy full of wag crews who would know from their leader the possible consequences of not playing along with Baron Arcadian.

It was trouble whichever way they chose to look at it.

To go back was what the baron expected. Going against his expectation would give them some edge of advantage. But this way they knew the land, as they had recently passed it. Besides which, fifteen miles was going to leave them a lot less exhausted than 150 would. They would need to be on top of their game for whatever they faced.

"So that's why it was such a strange distance," Mildred said with a sigh as the sight hit her.

"Think he wants to test our ability?" J.B. asked with a sardonic edge.

"Play games, might get kick in balls," Jak warned.

Ryan, Doc and Krysty just stood and looked, lost in their own thoughts. It hadn't been obvious as they approached the sharp bend in the flattop, but as soon as they crested the angle of the bend, they could see that Arcadian's people had been busy in the short time since the convoy had passed this way.

The road was impassable. Linked chains of man-traps, interspersed with land mines, had been laid across the surface. Barbed-wire barricades had been erected at regular intervals between the chains and mines. Wires that threaded through the barbed strands trailed away to generators that lay at the far end of the track made by the road modifications. It was possible that the generators weren't operational. It was possible that the mines were inactive. There was little doubt about the man-traps. There was also a strong possibility that there were men waiting to take potshots at them if they slowed as they crossed the tracks, which they inevitably would.

There would also be men watching them in the groves as they went off-road. They all knew this.

"So is this is a test of our ingenuity, or does he wish to see how we cope with the mangroves?" Doc mused.

"Mangroves…yeah, guess you're right there, Doc," Mildred said. "I wonder why he's cultivated shit like this so far from where it's supposed to grow?"

"Perhaps," Doc said heavily, "if we pass his little tests, then we may be permitted to know why he deems such things necessary."

Ryan nodded. "That's about right. Guess we should get going, then. Don't want to disappoint the man. That can come later."

Indicating the direction they should take with a wave of his arm, the one-eyed man led his people off-road, moving to the right of the road as they faced Arcady.

"MOVING WEST. Quasi-military formation. The one with the glasses is taking point. The albino is at the rear. One-eye and the redhead are sandwiching the old man and the black woman. Suggests that they are considered the weak link—no, correction, not weak, but rather not as strong. There is no suggestion in their behavior that they consider any of the group to be inferior. Perhaps it is, rather, a system based on knowing the strengths and weaknesses of the group, and moving accordingly. Suggests excellent reasoning skills. We will pursue at a distance. They're moving toward Sector Five. We may be forced to drop back and lose them. Team Six should stand by."

The squat, muscular man in black dropped the small handset from his mouth and nodded to his companion. Taller, more angular and also clad in black, he acknowledged, and in silence the two men moved off.

The undergrowth was thick, and it was slow progress to move through the shrubs, tangles of bramble and vine, and twisted tree trunks. Overhanging branches with viscous leaves that seemed to suck at the men's faces as they pushed through them appeared to bar every possible path. The two watchers found it difficult going, and they were used to the territory. It came as no surprise that they made ground on their target group with relative ease. Yet it was at the same time impressive to observe the manner in which the targets under observation were making progress. The one-eyed man and the one with spectacles were using a panga and a Tekna knife—a fine piece, rarely seen in these parts, they observed—to hack their way through the thickest of the undergrowth. In so doing, they were making little noise, which in itself was testament to their ability. The others followed in their wake, careful to actually cover the trail that was being cut as soon as they had passed through. It showed an admirable caution.

As, indeed, did the fact that the albino hung back, keeping a sharp eye on their tail. Once or twice, it seemed that he knew he was being watched, necessitating that they pause. They couldn't afford to be discovered. They could, however, afford to let the observed pass on.

"The albino seems to have acute senses. I suspect we have been spotted, if not positively identified. They haven't returned for us, but rather than risk confrontation before they're truly tested, I suggest that Team Six take over…"

"FIREBLAST AND FUCK!" Ryan cursed through gritted teeth. Their progress had been slower than he would have liked, but it had been steady, and there had been nothing to impede them other than the thickness of the undergrowth itself.

But not now. Now there was this…

The random patterns of the undergrowth resolved themselves into a series of regular structures: a maze that ran for as far as they could see on either side.

"Figure it runs both sides of the road?" J.B. queried.

"Got to," Ryan replied. "Probably around the ville on all sides, leaving only the road as the one clear way in and out."

Without another word, he sent Krysty and Mildred one way, Jak and Doc the other, to try to define how far the maze stretched. They returned shortly, neither pair with anything he wanted to hear.

"Tell you what," Mildred said, "I'm betting this pro-scribes one hell of a circle. Tested it, too. I figure part of the reason for this shit—" she flicked at the creepers, vine and brambles that snaked between the trees "—is to cover this, like camou. If you feel underneath, there's stone behind the green."

Ryan grimaced. "I hate these bastards," he muttered. "Dead ends and traps. Can't even figure on it being fixed," he added, recalling the maze they had encountered surrounding the ville of Atlantis. That time, movable walls had made their task almost impossible.

"We could mark our path as best as possible," Mildred added, "but I'm telling you, we don't have much to do it with. Not without losing stuff we don't want to lose."

While they had been talking, Jak had taken a step back and was looking up into the dark canopy that lay over their heads and extended across the top of the maze. Doc noticed, and stepped back to join him.

"Sure we followed," Jak said bluntly. "Good, though. Can't be sure where are."

Doc knew that if Jak had trouble locating their tail, then they were skilled trackers. He also figured that they were keeping back for a reason.

"Jak," he said slowly, "are you perhaps studying the

top of the maze for a reason. Say, for instance, that if the trees extended over the length of the maze, then they may provide us with a route, albeit a precarious one, over the obstacles?"

Jak nodded. "Could be. Not much life here. No big predator. Not much birds. Got to be reason."

Ryan and J.B. had stopped their own conversation and, like Mildred and Krysty, were taking note of Jak and Doc. Both glanced around, then looked up.

"Why leave the top of the maze exposed?" J.B. queried. "Up and over? Too easy." He was thinking of their previous experience with a maze.

Ryan was ahead of him. "Last time it was clear across the top. This gives us some cover. Besides, with all this—" he slapped at the vine and bramble covering the stone "—who'd want to risk some nasty fucker resting up there just waiting for fresh meat? You'd take your chance on the ground, right?"

"Right," Krysty affirmed. "Except the chances are that there isn't anything up there. And if there is, we'll be ready."

"They not pick us off anyway," Jak said mildly. "Want see how we do this. Even if they do see us."

"How do you know?" J.B. queried.

"The young man affirms that we are being tailed," Doc said with a wry grin. "I see no reason to disbelieve that—after all, if this is a test…"

Ryan barked a short laugh. "Good point. Still take it triple red, though. Let's go."

"TEAM SIX IN POSITION. These guys are good. They didn't just walk in. They've scouted it, and they're not going to be hurried. Thinkers as well as doers. I figure Toms wasn't wrong, Chief."

The haggard-looking man let the handset drop. He was gaunt, lines of trauma and experience etched into his face. His slight stoop told of too long spent hunkered down on surveillance. Like the previous observers, he wore what was an approximation of old military black commando fatigues, as was the younger, more muscled man of a similar height who accompanied him. His shoulders were squared, and he was almost visibly bristling with energy.

"They're not going in. They're going to climb it?" It was half question, half exclamation. "But surely they'd suspect—"

He was stayed by a hand from his superior. "Keep it down. Yeah, they know the risk, but they've figured some odds and are taking the ones that come up best. This should be real interesting. Obs post Delta will need to take this up. We can't follow without being spotted. And the little guy knows we're here. Just can't place us."

"Probably just as well," the younger man said.

The haggard observer grinned without mirth. "Yeah? For who?" He lifted the handset. "Look, Chief, we can't take this on anymore. Delta needs to use the scopes if they're going up and over. So far, though, I'd say your judgment was bearing up well."

He let the handset fall. The younger man was giving him a dubious look.

"What?" the haggard man questioned. "Look, you know what the chief is like. A little ass-licking always goes down well with him. It's not like he doesn't realize…"

As HE SAID THAT, he was unaware that his words were being monitored. All handsets were adapted so that they transmitted at all times, no matter what the user might think.

The recipient of the observer's comments laughed softly as he heard them. It wasn't, as the haggard man suspected, anything that was new to him. But to hear it confirmed that the men of his sec force weren't stupes. That was good. Intelligence was always to be rewarded in his world.

And that was what the ville of Arcady meant to Baron Arcadian. It was his universe, and one that he intended to expand—for which he would need able assistance, in all departments of his research and expansion. When Toms had told him—boasted, in truth—of the one-eyed man and his companions, then Arcadian knew that he would have to assimilate them into his organization.

So far, things had been going according to plan. His smile broadened as he recalled how easy it had been to make the little fat man yield to his will. Pleased with the new recruits to his convoy, Toms had been less than willing to strike the bargain. But he was easily bought. His greed, like that of any trader, was transparent. Appeal to that and his vanity, and it became easy to manipulate the result required. A new territory for the convoy to plunder. A few baubles for the man's vanity— in this case, some old vids and books that were of little consequence but touched that secret desire within Toms—and he had soon acquiesced.

Arcadian stretched, yawned and stood. He had been seated in the communications room of his palace, deciding to oversee this operation himself. The radio tech had been dismissed, and the baron had taken his place. Five paces each way, and he had covered the room. Its walls were painted yellow, and although the brocaded chair was comfortable, the desk equally so, the room had no windows. Arcadian could see how the radio tech could grow dissatisfied and bored on a long shift. It was more like a cell than a place of work. He made a mental note to change the location of the room. Somewhere with more air and light.

Yet this was no altruistic urge. Arcadian believed in treating well those who worked for him not because he spared the merest thought for them as human beings; rather, he knew from long research and empirical experience that a man who was at ease in his place of work was better able to concentrate, and to do a good job.

And that level of performance was his minimum requirement.

Arcadian pushed his flowing, curly, black hair back from his forehead. He was a handsome man, well-muscled. He kept himself in shape, training hard. He was, he knew, the result of careful breeding. His forefathers chose the mothers of their children with care, to maintain the highest level of physical and mental condition in a world stripped of certainties by the nuke-caust. It was his duty to look after what he had been given. It was a gift, and one that he had to pass down to his successors, when he had selected a mother for his offspring.

Stretching cramped muscles once more, he settled down in front of the receiver and sent out a message to Observation Station Delta. Located on the edge of the

ville, positioned on a tower fashioned from two of the
tallest trees in the vicinity, the men of Delta were on a
camouflaged platform equipped with tech that had been
salvaged and maintained through the decades. Tech that
included heat-seeking scopes and infrared taken from
a military base where the founders of Arcady had once
lived and worked.

If the trial group—as he thought of them—was
taking a route over the top of the maze, then this tech
would locate them with ease.

He liked their thinking, though. He had to admit to
that.

NEGOTIATING THE CLIMB up the side of the maze wall
was the easy part. Although the leaves on the vines
were as slippery and oily as those that hung from the
trees, it was easy to get a grip on the thick stems of the
vines. Each of the companions was able to get strong
hand- and footholds, feeling the vine stem—as strong
as wood, yet more pliable—move and give way to their
weight, shifting so that it settled beneath them, actually
helping to support them as they climbed, rather than
have the rigidity of wood, forcing them to bend to positions awkward to balance.

Jak took point position, pulling his light frame up
with ease, snapping back any observations about the
way that the vine moved, and how the bramble could
be avoided. Not only painful, a thorn in the hand from
the stringy growth could also spell infection. They had
no idea if the thorns were poisonous, and no intention
of finding out the hard way.

When he had reached the top, Jak lay flat along the

edge of the maze wall. The closely intertwined growth of branch, vine and bramble made it impossible to move in anything more than a crouch. Despite the fact that he was higher than before, he found that—if anything—the light here was reduced. It was almost as though the growth had been trained to develop more densely at this point, perhaps to make the maze darker. For there was no roof to the maze other than the canopy of foliage. As he looked along, he could see dimly the shape of the maze, described by the top of each section of the wall. It seemed to stretch on to infinity, the darkness swallowing any shape into black.

Beckoning the others to follow, Jak waited until they had started to ascend—Krysty and Mildred, then Doc, with Ryan and J.B. keeping watch at the base of the wall before following on—before striking out in the gloom. Mindful of any birds or tree-dwelling reptiles that might be along the way, Jak forged a path through the overhanging branches and leaves. The dark green foliage seemed to cling to his clothes and skin as he passed. It was an unpleasant sensation, but if that was all the obstruction they would face, he would be more than satisfied.

The others followed as he picked his way across the tops of the stone walls. It was far from simple. The walls, although of thick stone, had jagged and uneven surfaces. Chunks and pebbles broke off underfoot, causing the companions to stumble and slip. As if this wasn't enough, the walls were thick with guano from the small birds that nested in the branches that brushed the tops of their heads. The gloop built up in ridges that were treacherous underfoot. Slime from the leaves and vines only added to the unsure footing.

Looking down from time to time, they could see that the maze was complex. The light was dim, but it was still discernible that within the dead ends there were traps: areas of black with glinting metal points that caught the occasional stray ray of light betrayed a number of simple man-traps; grilles and spiked traps that were released by the passing of a man were also visible, the thin wires that triggered them catching the light from above, but invisible from ground level. Most insidious were the hinged sections that could be seen: anyone passing would trigger the hinged doors that would cut off passage back, leaving the unsuspecting wayfarer trapped between the door and a dead end, either to starve to death or to be retrieved by any sec.

Jak knew that they weren't being shadowed as before. He could tell from the sounds and smells around him that they were alone up on top of the maze. Yet all the same he could feel something indefinable, yet there. Someone had an eye on them.

Someone who wasn't yet hostile, but was biding his time.

But for what?

"DELTA REPORTING. Their progress so far is good. The small albino is leading them. He seems to be the most adept at this kind of maneuver. The one-eyed man, despite being leader, is bringing up the rear of the party. He's not afraid to delegate. They appear to be scouting the maze as they go, perhaps for future note if they happen across it once more. The natural hazards seem to prevent no obstacle to them."

The team leader of the Delta post paused and turned

to where his three-man team was working. One of them was trying to make purely visual contact. It was still early afternoon, and the light was good—little cloud cover and a bright sun. However, the thick canopy of foliage that overlay the maze obstructed much direct viewing, and even with the high-powered rifle scope he was using to keep track, the sec man had to confess that he was losing sight of them more often than actually seeing them.

The other two members of the team had fared better, however. One was using an infrared scope that penetrated the gloom of the canopy. With that, he was able to see the order in which they had ascended, and also track their progress. His colleague, equipped with heat-seeking tracking equipment, was able to see in greater detail the way in which they were moving, and to detect when one of them paused to look down into the maze.

His only problem was that the image on his monitor would freeze or cut out for a few seconds, before returning as before. Like much of the equipment in Arcady that had been salvaged, maintenance was good, but age was beginning to tell. Word had it that Arcadian's research team was back-engineering this equipment to learn fully how it worked, and to see if they could synthesize components that were unavailable in a post-nukecaust world.

The only reason that this crossed his mind was that the bastard screen did it again, just at the moment when the albino reached the lip of the maze wall on the ville side. He cursed as the screen flickered and went black, muttering to himself impatiently as he waited for it to come back.

"They're clear," he announced as the screen fizzed before clicking back into color, showing the group descending the wall.

"THAT WAS MOST unpleasant," Doc said, dusting himself down with an expression of distaste at the guano he dislodged, "but if it is all we have to endure, then I think we should count ourselves lucky."

"Somehow, I think there may be something in store for us," Ryan mused.

They continued without pause. Now they were back on the ground, Ryan and J.B. took the lead, hacking a path through the undergrowth with the panga and the Tekna knife. Jak brought up the rear, and it was not long before he started to hang back.

"Jak?" Doc queried, noticing this. "Is there something we should know?"

"Not sure…something come. Too clumsy for watchers from before. Not animal."

"WHOO-HOO!" exclaimed the Delta team member with a high-powered scope as he made a sweep of the surrounding country. "They've got trouble. The usual fuckers."

"It'll be interesting to see how they handle it," the team leader said before reporting the sighting.

Chapter Four

At first they couldn't hear it. Jak knew which from which direction it originated, but all they could go on was his judgment. Sound enough, but still bewildering when you listened for something you knew had to be there, but couldn't find.

They stood, poised, feeling that they should do something—but what? Until they could scent the danger for themselves there was little they could do to effectively prepare.

And then they heard it—a deep, distant rustling. Small noises made by the small animals and birds that inhabited the dense woodlands had been identified to such an extent that the friends were no longer even conscious of them. Now there was a louder rustling that seemed to stretch over a wider expanse of ground.

"Spread out," Ryan ordered. "Stay in sight, but keep down."

There was little else to say. Blasters drawn and ready, the six companions spread out in a skirmish line, facing to the east of the maze wall.

Ryan and Jak took each end of the line. J.B. moved to the middle to act as anchor man as the friends spread out. Mildred and Krysty were nearest to him, while Doc remained between Mildred and Jak. With J.B.

acting as anchor, it was an uneven line, but as always there was the unspoken assessment that Doc was the least effective fighter in such situations. Protecting him in this way didn't go unnoticed by those who watched.

"THEY'RE CLOSING IN on each other. Our targets have taken a formation that protects the old man. The one-eye and the guy in glasses know their strengths, and have used that to get a little balance."

Arcadian's voice crackled over the air. "How many are they facing?"

The team leader looked to his men. Heat-seeking and infrared showed blobs of heat and light that fused and melded. Some of the attacking party were moving too close together to be counted accurately. He looked to the observer with the high-powered scope.

"Hard to say for sure. I count twelve at some times, fourteen at others. Think that there may be up to three others I can't pin down. I'd say they're outnumbered three to one."

The team leader whistled softly. "Don't like those odds. Should we step in and take the rebels out?" he asked the baron.

There was a pause while Arcadian considered. Finally his reply came through. "Leave them. It would be simple to deploy men and disperse them, but this way we get to test their true mettle. It may save wasting time later on. Do not—I repeat, do not—intervene."

The team leader raised an eyebrow. "Very well, sir." He shrugged at the questioning glances of his team. "It's not down to me. It's going to be a bloodbath down there."

RYAN LOOKED across the line. Jak and Doc were out of sight, though he could see Mildred's head bobbing in the undergrowth. J.B. was still upright, scoping the line. Krysty was close enough for him to see clearly. He knew that his thoughts would be echoed in the minds of all of them. As the enemy—assume that now, ask questions later—approached, the sounds of their progress began to separate so that it was possible to pick out numbers and more accurate locations.

They seemed to be moving in four groups, three or four in each. The sound of their footsteps on the undergrowth, no matter how silently they tried to move, was audible. Bramble and fallen branches littered the forest floor so thickly that it was impossible for them not to snap and break some of the dry, dead foliage. Volleys of small, sharp sounds announced the multiple numbers of each group.

Because they moved in clusters, rather than as individuals, it was impossible for them not to cause disturbance in the foliage that they used as cover. Ripples of green spread across a line, a wave of motion that would have made tracking hard if they had moved as individuals. But in a group, the epicenter of each breaking wave was easily spotted.

A bloodbath, all right—Ryan knew it would have to be if they were going to take out the superior numbers before they had a real chance to attack. To do this the companions would have to keep their positions unknown for as long as possible. The only way to gain an edge would be to stay still and hold your nerve until it was time to fire.

Ryan looked at his friends. They would know this,

but a hand signal relayed his intent to J.B. and Krysty. In turn, the Armorer passed it on down the line.

If they had just been unlucky enough to be here when an enemy stumbled on them, then it should work. If the enemy was headed this way because they had a location, then it might be different.

Whatever, there was only one thing they could do now.

Wait.

"REPORT," Arcadian's voice snapped.

The team leader looked directly into the mangroves. Their targets were in plain sight from the post now that they had traversed the maze, and the rebel force moving toward them was now in vision.

"Our targets are staying put, keeping down. They're letting the rebels come to them."

"Do the rebels know they are there?" the baron asked.

The team leader sucked in his breath. "Can't say for sure. It doesn't look like it, though. Scavengers headed for Sector Eight, at a guess."

"Very well. Keep them all in view and do not interfere. This should be instructive."

"It should be a whole lot more than that," the team leader muttered under his breath. "A whole lot more."

THEY WERE CLOSING in. Ryan sank closer to the ground, hunkered on his haunches. He could see that Krysty and J.B. were doing the same. The others were already out of sight. Now, as he rested the Steyr on his thigh, cradling it gently, he felt alone. Insects buzzed and hummed in the grass and bramble around him, swooping in and out of the tangled vines that were now at eye level.

Sweat prickled at his hairline, itching as it ran down his face, under the eye patch and into the empty socket. He moved his free hand slowly, using the back of it to wipe sweat out of his good eye.

His thighs started to ache. He shifted his weight, careful to keep his balance. The rustling ahead of him was getting louder with each beat of his heart. The waves of movement started to move the grass and vine that was only a hundred or so yards from him.

He raised the Steyr, cocked and ready to fire on sight.

No way could he blink. The warm air, moist as it was, seemed to dry out his eye, make him want to blink. He felt it begin to water.

He couldn't blink; that would be the moment they were on him.

And then the grasses and vines parted. Three people moved in a crouch. Were they armed? He couldn't see, and there wasn't time to ask.

Down the line, someone fired. The staccato chatter of J.B.'s mini-Uzi, set on 3-shot burst, was followed by a scream.

It was enough to make at least one of the group in front of him look around. Frozen for a moment, distracted, he wasn't the immediate danger. Ryan took out one of the others instead. Squeeze, ride the recoil as the Steyr exploded, then roll to the side so that any return fire would hit empty space.

The man he had aimed at—skinny limbs, paunch, in camou rags—suddenly had no face. There had only been the briefest impression of a lined face, watery eyes and a gray-flecked beard. Now there was only blood, his head snapped back on his neck by the impact.

One of the other two yelled, then raised the blaster in his fist, a remake of a revolver of some kind—long barrel, maybe a Colt Peacemaker.

The man with the revolver fired blindly in the direction from which he thought the shot had come. He would still have missed Ryan. As it was, he didn't stand a chance. The next shell from the Steyr clipped him on the shoulder, spinning him as he fell back, down but possibly not out. He was spared from a chilling by Ryan having to fire while still slightly off balance.

The third man, initially distracted, was now much more alert. He had a battered subgun, raking the area where he thought the fire had originated. Ryan went flat, his head down, tasting the bitter grass and the grit of the dirt beneath. The SMG fire flew above his head, hitting tree trunk and vine alike. Sweet sap splattered him, the smell blending oddly with the cordite from the Steyr. Chips of bark rained on him.

The fire stopped, and Ryan risked raising his head.

Both men were gone from view.

Blasterfire came from his right. He recognized, without having to think, the roar of Doc's LeMat as the old man loosed the shot charge. That accounted for some of the high-pitched, agonized screams. This close, the old blaster couldn't fail to hit home.

But let the others look out for themselves. At least for the moment. He couldn't help them until he was safe himself.

Who were these guys? They seemed to have just stumbled on the companions rather than tracked them. There was no plan of attack that Ryan could see. So if they had been tracked, as Jak thought, then that had to mean another group was out there somewhere.

But that was irrelevant. It passed through the back of his mind while his forebrain concentrated on staying alive.

One down. Two standing. One wounded, the other gone to ground. How many more? Ryan, belly to the ground, slithered across the grass and vine, ignoring the brambles that snagged his clothes and tore at his skin. They'd been careful not to be pricked before, in case the thorns were venomous. Screw that. He'd take a chance rather than be blasted to oblivion.

He moved toward where the second man had fallen. Straining his neck to see upward as he crawled, he could see the feet of the chilled man.

Branches cracked to his left. He rolled so that he was on his back, his stomach muscles straining to pull his torso up at the waist. The guy with the subgun moved out from behind a tree. Almost in slow motion, the world slowed to an agonizing degree; he could see the man's biceps pulse as he squeezed the trigger.

Ryan squeezed off a round from the Steyr, which caught the man full in the chest, above the cradle of his arms as they steadied the SMG. He pitched backward, the arc of his fire spewing upward and out as he fired while buying the farm, one arm holding the SMG while the other flew off in impact.

The one-eyed man threw himself backward, his muscles protesting at the sudden reverse in direction.

The fire roared over his head and torso. He could almost feel the hot lead as it raked the air above him.

His stomach muscles felt as if they were made of that same hot lead. He wanted to gasp, breath deeply, recover, but there was no time.

Not yet. Two down. One still out there. At least, he hoped it was just one. He was fucked if the others hadn't dealt with their opponents, or if the enemy was fluid.

There was only one way to find out.

Without pause, Ryan rolled again, his head raised as he came onto his stomach, scoping out the territory. In the maelstrom of sound that had erupted—and was still in full blast—from his left, it was almost impossible to pick out small sounds that were happening closer. But that was what he needed to do. Ryan needed some indication, some sign of where the immediate enemy was.

Cautiously, he got to one knee, lifting himself a little, using his left elbow to support himself as he moved a little farther up from the ground. Scanning the area, he could neither see nor hear the enemy.

He hadn't chilled the guy. It was only a shoulder shot. Ryan might have taken him down if he wasn't that strong, but he'd still be alive and dangerous.

But where?

Ryan looked diligently from side to side as he searched for some sign of his opponent.

It was his alertness that saved him. The dry crack of a twig, the harsh rattle of quickly drawn breath, and the held-down, almost silenced grunt of effort all added up to one thing.

The bastard had gotten behind him.

Ryan tried to twist so that he could meet the man

head-on, but it was too late for that. Muscles burned, tendons and sinews strained, but his foot stayed locked in the grip of the warm turf, and as the man landed on him, pushing him back, the one-eyed man could feel an intense burn in his calf as his twisted leg was forced into a position contrary to nature. It was so sudden that it almost took his breath away. The desire to survive made him grit his teeth and hold on.

He tried to bring the rifle around so that he could fire—the SIG-Sauer would have been better at closer range, but there was no chance he could unholster it in time—but only succeeded in getting it across his chest.

Just as well. As he fell back under the impact, his assailant driving into him, the rifle across his chest acted as a barrier. The man had a knife, and it pricked at Ryan's clothes and skin as the man slashed wildly, the rifle shaft taking the brunt of the blows. Close up, the attacker's eyes were fogged with pain, wild and despairing. He knew this was his only chance of survival.

The man reeked of fear, sweat pouring from him, making his flesh slippery, his ragged clothes damp and heavy. For a moment, the two men were frozen in position as Ryan's push upward met the resistance of his opponent's weight on the down.

With an effort that made stars of light burst behind his good eye, he heaved and pushed the man to one side. As he did so, he rolled with the momentum and came up onto his haunches, thighs straining and his calf burning like a hot knife had been thrust into the muscle.

Ryan dropped the Steyr at his feet, his hand snaking down to the scabbard on his thigh where he kept the panga. The wickedly razored blade slid from its sheath with ease, sitting comfortably in his hand like an old friend. He took a step forward.

The wounded man had landed on his back and was flailing, arms and legs pumping as he desperately tried to right himself. He still grasped the knife, but was in no position to make use of it. Tears of fear or frustration trickled down his face. Blood still seeped from the wound in his shoulder, a black patch of lost fluid staining his camou vest.

"You or me," Ryan whispered, cleaving down with the panga. It bit into flesh, jarred against bone. From the injured shoulder the panga slashed across the throat, rupturing artery and vein. Gouts of blood spurted rhythmically, growing fainter as life receded.

Ryan stood over the man for the few seconds it took him to buy the farm. He had to be sure the enemy was down permanently. It gave him no pleasure to chill a wounded man. It was necessity. All the while, he kept alert to what was going on around him.

When the blood was just a trickle, and the eyes were glassy and sightless, Ryan turned away and retrieved the Steyr. His calf ached, but already the pain was ebbing, and more bearable. It wouldn't impede him.

But what about the others? The firing was now sporadic, most identifiable as blasters used by his people. There was little other sound. Battle was almost at a close.

Cautiously, he made his way across the line they had drawn. Krysty had chilled two men and a woman. Two by clean shots, one by a gouge in the side and a broken neck that lay at an unnatural angle. Farther on, J.B.'s area was clear: four corpses, all drilled by the mini-Uzi a testament to the shooting powers of the Armorer.

By the time he reached the area where Mildred had been, he found that he was the last to join the group. Jak and Doc had joined Krysty and J.B. in moving toward the middle of the line. Krysty was pleased to see Ryan.

"We all through here?" the one-eyed man asked.

"Me and Doc get seven between us." Jak shrugged. "Mildred took three, Krysty three, J.B. four. How about you?"

"Just the three," Ryan replied, "but one of the bastards just wouldn't lie down and buy the farm."

"Always one," the Armorer muttered. "Make that twenty. Not bad odds, I guess. Headed toward the ville, too. So where did they come from?"

"Dunno," Ryan mused, "and now isn't the time to wonder. We can do that later. There might be more of them, and they'll be pissed at what we've done. Let's head toward the ville. At least we know we're expected there."

There was a general agreement, and with barely a backward glance, the group moved in the direction where they knew Arcady lay.

ARCADIAN SAT LISTENING to the observation post report on the skirmish that had taken place. When it had concluded, he sat back and thought for a moment.

"Let them pass through to Sector Eight," he finally stated. "They've shown their mettle, I think. They've also saved us the trouble of mopping up the rebels this time around. Team Four, do you copy?"

"Baron?"

"Follow them as far as Sector Eight and let them get

a look around. At the first sign of any interaction, from either side, you move in with backup and apprehend. I want them to get a flavor of that sector. It may serve them well."

He sat back, satisfied by his plan of action. If things continued in this manner, he had found some useful personnel to add to his team. And they, too, would see it that way.

Eventually.

WITH J.B. ON POINT, the group headed in the direction of Arcady. Taking a reading with the minisextant was almost an impossibility, given the canopy of mangrove that still covered them. Despite that, they had a sure enough sense of the direction to know that they would come across the edge of the ville eventually. Ryan figured they'd covered at least two-thirds of the distance, although the maze and the subsequent firefight had made it difficult to look back and make an accurate assessment.

For Ryan, it couldn't come soon enough. Allowing Mildred and Krysty to take positions ahead of him, the one-eyed man had dropped back, finding the pace punishing as his calf ached and throbbed. He could still walk, bear weight on it, so it wasn't a bad injury, but it was enough to slow him. He needed to rest the leg, and let Mildred get a good look at it.

But not now. The undergrowth was still too thick, and hacking their way through was slow. They were all exhausted but knew that this wasn't a good time to halt. The companions might have to fight others, and they were probably being followed.

It was with some relief that J.B. noted the undergrowth beginning to thin out in front of him. It became easier to make a path and suggested that they were within reach of Arcady.

The Armorer slowed, raising a hand. "Easy. Ville's coming up."

Despite tired limbs and aching eyes, the knowledge that they were within striking distance of their target added vigor to their step. It also caused them to prime blasters and resume vigilance that torpor may have blunted. After all, they had no idea whether Arcady would present as friend or foe.

The last mile was torturous, and seemed to stretch out forever. Each step, although taking them closer, seemed to be removing them. The next patch of thick vines and brambles to be cleared should reveal a distant ville, but revealed…nothing more than vines and brambles, interspersed with twisted bark.

Jak, at the rear of the party, was keeping a sharp eye for those who had been on their tail before they reached the maze. But there was no indication of anyone following in their wake. Which, in itself, was unsettling. The companions had been tailed for a reason, so why had that stopped? He said as much, in a few terse words.

"Could be that they've got ways of following us without having to get close," Ryan mused.

"If this baron is as, ah, advanced as the fat man suggested, then it could be that he has some old surveillance technology that is useable," Doc interjected.

"Could be. Could also be that they don't need to follow us now, 'cause we're right on top of them," Ryan added.

"I hope that's right," Mildred murmured, casting an eye over Ryan's leg. From the way he was walking, she knew that he needed to rest it soon.

J.B., hacking at the undergrowth, was finding it easier and easier. The vines and brambles were dwindling, leaving just the thick grass between trees that were now becoming more and more evenly spaced, as though the untamed forest had, at this point, suddenly become tamed and laid out to a plan. Moving aside a tangle of vine, the thick oily leaves sticking to him as he parted them, the Armorer saw that ahead lay a patch of sparser grassland, dotted with only a few trees.

And there, in the shadows of late afternoon, were the outlines of a few tumbledown buildings. To the rear of them lay not the outline of distant trees, but that of taller buildings, stretching back as far as could be seen.

"At last," J.B. breathed, almost to himself.

"THEY'RE IN SIGHT of Sector Eight," the observer whispered into his handset.

"Good. Keep them in full view. Wait and see what happens when they meet the natives. I want to monitor their reactions. But you must—I repeat, must—intervene if there is any chance of revelation."

"Copy," the observer whispered. "All teams, converge on Sector Eight, be ready for takedown."

THE FRIENDS MADE THEIR WAY across the open ground toward the buildings with caution. It might be easier to traverse, but by the same token it was also exposed. They would need to stay alert, as there was no place to hide.

At first sight, the buildings in front of them seemed deserted. Windows that were little more than holes cut in sheets of rusting metal, or framed by ill-cut wood that was only vaguely fitted into salvaged cinder block and brick, were black holes showing no signs of life within. It was almost as quiet here as it had been in the undergrowth. In the far distance, the indistinct sounds of movement—vehicles, masses of people, the clamor of a ville's early evening routines—could be picked out. But here, it was as though this rough pesthole had been set up for some ill-defined purpose and then deserted.

"Triple red," Ryan murmured. It was perfunctory, as they had all primed and cocked as soon as they emerged into the open. "Jak, I can't see any sign of life from here. You see or hear anything?"

The albino youth shook his head. "Hard with noise in distance. Not much here. But they behind us. Far, but there."

"Okay. We move in, recce and see if we can find shelter if it really is empty. If not, then…"

"Business as usual," Mildred murmured.

"Right," Ryan agreed.

By this time, they had reached the outermost buildings. Procedure was simple: while the majority of the group checked and covered the surrounding area, two would take the entrance to a building, one covering the other as they swept the interior.

Ryan, not trusting his leg, let J.B. and Krysty take the sweep. The first two buildings—even to call them that was an exaggeration, as they seemed to be barely standing—were empty. There were signs that people had lived here until recently, but had now departed: rotting food, soiled bedding and dirty rags that passed for clothing.

"Where did they go?" Ryan murmured, casting a searching glance at the seemingly deserted shanty ville.

"Mayhap they were frightened of us?" Doc suggested. "Or, more pertinently, afraid of those we recently fought?"

"That's a good idea," Ryan said softly. "Thing is, if they think we're those bastards, then what will they have in store for us?"

"*Caution* should most definitely be the watchword," Doc replied.

Proceeding in such a manner, they took in a number of buildings. All of them had the look of the recently deserted.

"It's like they ran scared," J.B. said with a shake of the head. "How do they manage to survive if that's what they do?"

"Perhaps that's how," Doc answered.

J.B. grimaced. "Can't run forever. Bound to catch up with you sooner or later. We all know that. Besides, if this is Arcady, then where are the sec that we heard so much about?"

"Probably on our tails," Mildred muttered wryly. "Still out there, Jak?"

"Yeah, someone," the albino teen said, looking into the clearing between the mangrove and shanty.

"But if this is Arcady," Krysty said, taking a look around, "then why is it like this? People living in shit? I thought Arcadian was a good baron, giving his people a good life. And a rich baron, who could afford it."

"That's what fat boy led us to think," Ryan mused. "And this certainly doesn't look like any part of Arcady we saw. Unless the baron likes to let outlanders see and think one thing…"

"I suspect it may not be as clear cut as that," Doc mused. Then, to answer questioning glances he added, "Come—keep watch, but please…"

He led the main body of the party into three separate huts. In each, he merely said, "Observe, please," before leading them out. Jak kept watch while Doc did that. Finally, the old man led them back to the point from which they had started.

"So what were we supposed to be looking for?" J.B. asked, puzzled.

Doc smiled, his strong white teeth giving the smile a sardonic edge. "I think Krysty hit the nail on the head, as the old saying goes. She talked of people living in shit. But they do not. Shit, piss, the kind of buildup of human ordure that we usually see in a shanty like this. Where is it? Where is the smell?"

Doc paused while they took this in: he was right. While not as sweet-smelling as it could be, there was only the smell of unwashed bodies lingering in the air. The dirt roads and paths were barely muddy.

"Fireblast!" Ryan exclaimed as it suddenly hit him. "Those huts have got latrines in them, and there's a faucet stand in the corner of each."

"Running water? Sanitation? What kind of a slum shanty has that?" Mildred posited. "That's insane. If they have that, then why do they live like this?"

"We may discover that if we unearth any of them," Doc mused. "They are supplied with water and sanitation. Moreover, those clothes may have been ragged and dirty, but they had been made that way by those who wore them. They must have plentiful clothing, otherwise why leave it behind? Have you known that before? And the food—that, too, must be plentiful, as there were many scraps. Ever known people in a seemingly poor shanty ville like this leave food lying around in such a manner?"

"But if they're not really that poor, then why live like this?" J.B. queried.

"I suspect that we may find out, if we stay around here long enough," Doc answered cryptically. "There are machinations afoot here that are hidden to us. Perhaps intentionally."

"Worry 'bout later," Jak said. "Got company."

He indicated a direction farther into the shanty ville. Ryan waved his companions back into the shelter of two huts that stood on either side of the dust road. Checking that nothing was coming up from the rear, they assumed defensive positions—Ryan, Krysty and Jak on one side, with Mildred, Doc and J.B. taking the opposite point—while waiting for whatever was headed their way.

When it came, it was somewhat of a surprise. Slowly, moving with a caution that was edged with fright, a group of raggedly clad people moved from the shadows of far-flung huts. Despite their clothing, they were far from ill-nourished. In truth, some of them were paunchy to the point of obesity. They moved almost as one amorphous mass: men, women and children, all jockeying for position. No one wanted to be in the lead, and those who found themselves thrust to the front were quick to try to fall back, pushing against those who came up behind them. It made their progress slow and shuffling.

The fear and fright was so strong coming off them that the companions could almost smell it.

The two groups of three exchanged bemused glances across the distance between them. It was difficult to know what to make of this. If these people were really that scared, then why had they come out of the shadows?

Ryan took a calculated risk. He could see no blasters among the crowd jostling slowly toward them. He stepped forward, cradling the Steyr nose down in a relaxed grip. But not so relaxed that it couldn't be brought into play easily and quickly.

As he emerged, the group of ville dwellers stopped suddenly. It was almost as though they cowered at the sight of him. Some even flinched, as though he was about to fire on them. When he stood his ground and did nothing, some of them looked up.

"You're…you're not going to take from us?" a man said haltingly.

"Why should I?" Ryan asked. "Is that what the others do?"

Mutterings shot through the crowd. He could make out some of it. They were talking about him, and not about who "the others" might be.

A woman stepped forward and pointed at him, yelling, "He only got one eye" and laughing before running back into the crowd, many of whom were now giggling.

"The others," Ryan repeated. "Who are the others?"

Many of them looked at one another, as though they found the one-eyed man beyond their comprehension. The man who had spoken first said, "Others take stuff, want to hurt us. I think they like that bit. It's not nice."

Ryan was taken aback. "You don't try to defend yourselves?"

The man shrugged. "They go soon enough. Then other others come and help, but sometimes they don't. Mebbe you know them? Mebbe you got more stuff for us?"

A satisfied murmur rippled through the crowd, and they moved forward. Ryan took a step back, not because he thought they would attack, but because for one moment it seemed that they might overwhelm him.

His people took that as their cue to step out into the open. Their presence caused the approaching mob to stop momentarily, before gasping in amazement and moving forward. Before any of Ryan's people had a chance to draw breath, the ville dwellers were milling around them, touching them and asking questions.

"You know others?"

"You have stuff?"

"Why you so white?"

"Why you so brown?"

Yet none of them waited for answers to the questions they posed before babbling on about something completely different.

Ryan looked, bewildered, over the heads of the milling throng to where he could see Krysty. She shrugged. She was as confused as he was by their behavior.

"They appear to be like sheep," Doc yelled above the babble. "Passive, and completely without any kind of—"

"What's sheep?" one of them said, tugging him on the arm.

"I—" Doc began, but was cut short by Jak's terse comment.

"They're here. Ones who follow."

Melting out of the shadows and forming into black-clad pairs holding blasters—was this where his earlier opponent had got his blaster? Ryan wondered—came six teams. Their blasters were raised in the air, but there was little doubting their intent.

"Drop your weapons and come with us," one of the black-clad men called. "You people," he added in a harsher tone, "move away from the outlanders."

The mob did as it had been told. Soon, they were standing apart, watching the proceedings. Ryan and his people were now surrounded on all sides, outnumbered two to one.

"You took out those rebels okay," the black-clad leader said, as if sensing their mood, "but we're ready for you, and better trained than that scum."

"So what do you want? You want a firefight?" Ryan asked in a hard voice, his muscles tensed as he took in the manner in which they had been surrounded. These people were good. But his, he knew, could be better.

"Don't want that any more than you do," the men said tightly. "What we want is for you to come with us. Arcadian wants to meet you."

"He's got a real strange way of going about that," Ryan replied.

"Mebbe. But he has his reasons. You might like 'em."

Ryan took another look around at the black-clad sec,

then at his companions. He could see from their expressions that they were with him.

"Okay," he said slowly, "we'll come with you. Might be interesting. But we don't surrender blasters. You got nothing to hide? It won't matter."

The sec boss grinned. "Like your style, One-eye. Wouldn't have it any other way." He lowered his blaster so that it pointed at the dirt. "Let's do it."

Chapter Five

As they fell in with the black-clad sec men, Ryan's group had a lot to ponder. It had been couched in terms that were reasonable, but they all knew that resistance would have been met with a firefight. Arcadian wanted them, for reasons as yet unknown. If he wanted them to work for him willingly, he was showing a real lack of understanding. His behavior had done nothing less than to put them on triple red, with the utmost suspicion. If he wanted to just use them, regardless of whether or not they wished to acquiesce, then he was cutting them too much slack.

For, as they were escorted on foot through the outlying districts of the ville, there was much to observe and absorb for possible future use.

The sec team that escorted them was very careful about its chosen route. Instead of traveling in what seemed a direct route to the center of the ville, they took what appeared to be meaningless detours. Straight roads would be ignored in favor of sudden sharp turns to the left or right. Obviously, that was to keep them within a sector they had already seen, and not cross some kind of line. For there wasn't a single one of them who had any doubt that Arcady was a ville of sharply differing sectors.

The Arcady they had seen when with Trader Toms was one of wealth and freedom. The center sections of the ville were filled with trade stores, craftsmen and bars providing brew and gaudys. The relative financial well-being of a ville could always be determined by the number and quality of those. The people they had met had been free to go about their business unimpeded. The sec had been present, but not overbearing—they had only stepped in when trouble flared because of arguments caused by brew or jack. The buildings had been old, for the most part obviously built by the founders of the ville or adapted from the main street and surrounding area of the old predark town that they had chosen to use as their shell, but there had been evidence of ongoing maintenance and new building that gave work to the people of the ville, and were again proof of its growing affluence.

None of which tallied with the run-down shanty ville full of tumbledown shacks that looked like their dwellers paid them no heed. For most of their winding trek through the outer reaches of the ville, this was all they had seen. Row upon row of virtually derelict shacks, but none that were empty. All showed signs of habitation, and by people very like those they had seen on their entry to the ville.

As they passed through the phalanx of sec men, they could see blank, drooling faces staring out at them. The people were fat, dirty, and even before you could see them the smell of their unwashed bodies assailed the senses. Some of them—the braver specimens—came outside their huts or stood in the doorways, watching or, if they felt particularly courageous, shouting at the newcomers in slurred, brain-numbed voices that were sometimes difficult to understand.

And yet these were people with running water and sanitation. Even the most advanced of villes that the companions had seen on their many journeys across the ravaged lands of the post-nukecaust America had been hard-pushed to have a sanitation and water system that came anywhere near aping that of the days before skydark. There had been some rich or advanced villes that had reconstructed pumping stations, and used old pipes to try to reconstruct that aspect of predark life. But never anything that had seemed to be as good as the systems they were familiar with from the many redoubts they had used during their journeys.

This was different. For a start, it had been so unobtrusive as to be almost unnoticeable...until Doc's eagle eye had drawn it to their attention. The running water and sanitation systems in this part of the ville—assuming that this entire shanty-ville sector had been treated the same, which seemed reasonable—had been recently laid. Recently as in postskydark. These buildings hadn't existed before the nukecaust, and each shanty had its own system. Someone—Arcadian or a baron before him—had laid out and engineered such a system, then allowed the shacks and tumbledown buildings to be erected around that system.

But why? Why go to all the bother of laying out such a system—a vast investment for any baron in terms of jack, resources and manpower—and then allow the people who lived above it to wallow in their own crapulence? Why feed them, as he obviously did?

It pointed toward a baron who had plans and schemes.

That wasn't unusual: they all did. To be a baron necessitated a certain degree of cunning and a lust for power. A baron without these qualities would soon fall by the wayside. But some had a more twisted psyche than others, and their schemes were more arcane and unfathomable.

To all of the companions, while passing through this sector of Arcady, it occurred that Arcadian may have a mind more labyrinthine than most. The question was simply this: how did they fit into that mind and its plans?

While those thoughts had been passing through the minds of the friends, in their differing ways, they had traversed the shanty sectors and were now about to enter the center of the ville.

They turned another corner, and the shacks and tumbledown huts suddenly fell away. A bare expanse of ground, about fifty yards in length, lay ahead of them. Beyond that was a wire fence that stretched in either direction. There were no guard posts.

The sec boss spoke for the first time since they had begun the march. He had obviously caught the way in which they had all looked at the ground, and also the glances that passed between them.

"This patch is just to make sure that the people of this sector don't stray too far. Must be obvious they ain't the brightest, but Arcadian looks after even the feeble. We don't let 'em buy the farm, not when there's enough to go around."

"Very admirable, such altruism," Doc murmured. Much as he tried, he couldn't keep the sardonic edge from his voice. The sec boss noticed.

"Listen, other villes can do things the way they want. Arcadian believes in the greater good for the greatest number. We all do. That's how we live in these parts."

And presumably those who don't think that way don't live here for long, one way or another, Doc thought. But he kept it to himself, figuring it wiser to keep his mouth shut for the moment.

In silence, the group walked along the edge of the barren ground until they reached a path that had been trodden flat. It was straight and led to a gate in the fence. Although the wire fence was about twelve feet high, the gate was only half that, and was only wide enough for two people to pass though at a time. On the other side, barely a few yards from the fence, were the backs of better constructed, better maintained buildings. Through the windows, covered in what appeared to be plastic, they could see people going about their business and sparing not a second look for the fence, the group, or the shanty ville beyond. There was something about their complete unconcern that seemed odd. They were so used to this segregation that it was invisible to them.

As they turned onto the narrow path, the sec force was very careful to herd them so that they moved three abreast—a sec man on either side of one of Ryan's group—and stayed very particularly on the beaten path. Both Ryan and J.B. spared a glance for the blank expanse of dirt on either side of them. Could the area be mined? Or was this just a piece of behavior that was ingrained? Both knew that to ask would be pointless; all the same, knowing could be important at some future point.

If either man had to lay odds, they would have put their jack on it being ingrained behavior. What happened next determined that. As they reached the gate, Ryan was astounded when the sec boss stepped up to the gate and simply pulled it open.

There was no lock. No charge running through the fence. It was simply an access cut into the wire fence that could be passed through at any time, by anyone.

They were ushered into another sector, and as they walked through the gate, each wondered about the kind of ville Arcady might be. It would appear, on first impressions, that people acted in predetermined ways simply because they had always done so, and to step outside that box would be something that would not— could not—cross their consciousness. Yet how could this tally with the thriving ville they had seen when they were with Toms? And if the sec force was as blandly rigid as it appeared to be right now, how could it act as a defense against outside forces?

Too many questions, and as of yet no indications of answers.

As they passed through the gate, all of them noticed that the sec guards seemed to loosen a little. Blasters fell from the poised to the casual; those who had been marching in step now went out of step with each other. It was hard to tell whether it was an unconscious move, now that they had crossed into another territory, or whether it was designed to make the group less conspicuous. If that was the aim, then it certainly seemed to be working. The formal procession that they had formed in the shanty ville now became a loose group. Rather than being the guarded and the guards, they seemed to be walking together. And the people who passed them on the streets didn't give them a second glance.

There was no doubt now that they had moved into a sector of the ville that they knew. This was the central area that they had stayed and worked in when passing through with Toms. It struck them all as odd that the shanty ville and the affluent sectors should be so close together. The reasons for that might become apparent, once they met with the baron and were, hopefully, made privy to his reasons for wanting them back in his ville.

For now, they could only marvel at the differences between two sectors of the same ville, so closely aligned geographically and yet so far apart in every other way.

Now, rather than people standing and staring in slack-jawed incomprehension, the companions were barely noticed as they walked the streets. In part, this was due to the way in which the black-clad sec stood slightly away from the companions, keeping their presence known yet retaining an unobtrusive air. However, part of it was also because this main section of the ville was busy—people had neither time nor inclination to stare or wonder at the group that moved among them.

As they traveled from the less-populated streets that ran near the wire fence and toward the more densely populated center of the ville, the number of people bustling in the thoroughfares became greater. Absorbed by whatever business they were going about, they had no reason to give a second glance to the group. Indeed, from the manner in which they moved, weaving their way in and out of the spaces between Ryan's people and the sec who were now merely—seemingly—accompa-

nying them, they not only hardly seemed to notice that
the companions were there, but also gave cover should
the outlanders feel the need to make a break for it.

The thought may have briefly crossed Ryan's mind,
but it was swiftly dismissed. To try to escape from the
clutches of the sec would be pointless. First, although
they could use the crowds as cover, where would they
go? The sec seemed to have the ville sewn up tighter
than the pussy of a gaudy who hadn't yet been handed
the jack. Second, if they did get past any of these obstacles, then where could they head? Jackson Spire was
the nearest ville they knew of, and that was a few days
away, as well as being an Arcady satellite. Third—and
perhaps most importantly—Arcadian had wanted them.
Ryan figured they'd better find out why before any
action was taken.

Early evening was beginning to fall, and the lamps
that lit the streets were glowing, the lamplighters whose
task it was to keep the oil and tallow lamps filled going
about their business. The interiors of stores and bars
were brightly illuminated. Some used tallow, oil or gas.
The ville seemed able to generate electricity, as well,
from the plant housed in a building that lay just a little
off the square, behind another building that Mildred
recognized from a thousand journeys, TV shows and
magazine photographs of her youth. There had been a
time when every small U.S. town had a library like the
gray stone building fronted by covered steps, the roof
supported by Doric columns. There weren't many of
them left now.

The clock set on the tower that climbed above the
building had long since ceased to operate. Not that it

mattered in this land where the chron was used for convenience rather than to be strictly adhered to. The stone had been blasted by water or sand so that it was now as clean as the day that it had been erected. Hanging from the roof of the covered steps was a banner that hung low enough to obscure the old inscription that had been carved over the building's double doors. The banner was in red, purple, yellow and green. It was a tapestry with one word—Excelsior—that was resplendent over a number of scenes that showed men and women—all smiling—performing constructive tasks in the field and in the town. It reminded Mildred of something she had seen when young. It wasn't until they were almost at the foot of the steps that she was able to recall the images it drew upon. Communist banners from the old Soviet Union under the leadership of Stalin—images of the noble worker that hid a regime of terror and poverty, half remembered from old newsreel and TV footage in history classes.

She wondered if Arcadian was aware of this, and—whether he was or not—it was somehow a clue to his character.

Meanwhile, as they crossed the square, other thoughts had been passing through the minds of her companions.

Jak had been looking for a means of escape. Like Ryan, he had considered the advantages and disadvantages of making a break, and like Ryan he could see that it was heavily weighted in favor of them staying. However, Jak was itchy as if he were infested with bugs at the idea of containment, and if for nothing other than a kind of security blanket, he looked for an escape route.

The crowded center of the ville had unattended wags, and he figured that it wouldn't be too hard for them to slip past the sec and head for one of those wags. Steal it, hope that it had enough gas to get them out of there. The problem was, how would he let the others know of his plan? How could he get them to go along with it on the spur of the moment? And how could he be sure that he would pick a wag that had enough gas? Too many questions to really do it.

Ryan was assessing a similar set of odds. Like Jak, the thought of being contained was anathema to him, and so he was looking for ways of escape. But the notion of just breaking for it had too many holes. Ryan didn't like leaving too much to chance. He didn't take the responsibility of leadership lightly. He wanted to see what the baron wanted from them first. Their skills? Their knowledge? Did Arcadian, in some way, know about their experiences with old tech? Ryan would bide his time until he met the baron and heard the terms on which he greeted them.

J.B. knew that Ryan would be weighing the odds, and he figured that it was his task as right-hand man to attend to the practicalities. Besides, that was the way his mind worked best. Already, he had scanned the square to take in the roads that led into and out of it. How wide or narrow they were. What was on the corners. From the falling sun, he worked out compass points. He knew where the wags were clustered at their most dense. He also noted what kind of wags they were—weighing up which had been on long hauls, and which had been standing awhile; from their condition, which were in-coming or ready for going out; which would have the best chance of full fuel tanks; where there were supplies of gas, spare tanks ready to be loaded.

He'd also scoped the area for sec. Not just those that were cautiously shepherding them to the baron, but the regular sec who were not so conspicuous. J.B. could spot sec at a hundred yards. He could see where they were positioned, and where they patrolled; the kind of ordnance they carried; the kind of ordnance that the ordinary citizens carried; the way they carried it, which was always an indication of how well they could use it.

All this information was at his fingertips, and could be brought to bear as soon as he knew how Ryan's plans were shaping.

All thoughts were banished when the companions mounted the steps and were shown through the heavy oak double doors, which, it didn't escape their notice, had been reinforced.

J.B. whistled slowly. "No wonder we didn't get to see this before."

How many of the citizens of Arcady had set foot through these doors? Even out of those who were obviously favored and dwelled in this section of the ville? Come to that, how many of the traders and other local barons—those within a hundred miles in these sparsely populated parts—got to see this? Toms had given the impression that he had been favored, and it wasn't hard to see how he had formed this notion.

The companions and their black-clad guard were dwarfed by the vast lobby of the building, which echoed to their footsteps as they trod the polished hardwood floor. There were other sec guards in everyday dress who were stationed throughout the lobby and at the spiral staircase. Two guards strode forward as the two parties entered. They were obviously expected, as the black-clad sec left without a backward glance after a whispered exchange, leaving the companions in the hands of the on-site sec. One of the two who had approached was obviously the sec chief. His bearing showed this, and the manner in which he spoke left any other doubts ground into dust.

"I see Rodriguez has been slack. As usual. You can drop those blasters on the floor now, and anything else you're carrying."

He snapped out the words, almost barked them, in the manner of one who was used to being instantly obeyed. The fact that he was completely ignored did nothing other than irk him.

"Drop, now!" he commanded, raising the Walther PPK he carried. A good handblaster, it had none of the power a sec chief would usually demand, but it had clean lines and was in good condition. As this sec chief had a thin, hatchet face with buzz-cut hair and clothes that were immaculate, it suited him better.

It hadn't been until his second, louder command, that his words had really registered with Ryan or his people. The reason for that was simple—for the moment, they had been completely overwhelmed by the riches that the lobby of the old building revealed to them. But not the riches of jack, furniture and fine cloth. That kind of ostentation was something they had seen from a thousand tawdry barons who sought to flaunt their wealth and station. This was more than that. Much more.

"How the hell did he get this stuff?" Mildred

murmured to herself, rather than to anyone in particular. For it was a question that, if she should find the answer, would doubtless explain much about Baron Arcadian.

The lobby of the old library was filled with display cases. Highly polished wood and glass, maintained with care, these displayed artifacts of the predark era that were beyond price. What looked to be the first telephone; Teletype machines; cumbersome early comps; pieces of machinery, isolated from their use and polished, with cards beneath revealing their uses and their innovations; book manuscripts from writers whose names, they had once believed, would live forever. The walls in the lobby and up the staircases were hung with documents, paintings and photographs, all preserved behind what appeared to be immaculately cleaned glass. Just the briefest of glances showed images and names that were familiar to Mildred and Doc, and also to Ryan and Krysty, who had acquired knowledge of the predark days. To J.B. and Jak, even though the greater significance was perhaps lost, the manner in which it had been maintained and its magnitude were telling.

So it was that the words of the sec chief were little more than background noise until the harsh tone of his second command cut through the reverie.

They each, in their own way, returned to the present to find that he or she was now flanked by guards who had moved in at all points from their stations, hands poised over armament.

Jak, not waiting for Ryan's lead on this one, was the first to react. His .357 Magnum Colt Python was in his fist before the sec chief's second command had ceased to echo. It was rock steady and would put a slug through the man's forehead before his own finger had tightened on the Walther's trigger.

Ryan had shrugged the Steyr off his shoulder and brought it to hand in one fluid motion. His companions, being of similar nature, had also responded to the command in a similar contrary manner.

It was obvious both that the sec chief was used to being blindly obeyed, and that he had little notion of how to treat intruders on his turf who posed a real threat.

Stalemate.

"There are more of us than you," the sec chief hissed. "You don't stand a chance."

"Be better if you weren't sweating like you were pegged out under the sun while you said that," Ryan replied calmly. "Thing is, your boy Rodriguez used the same argument on us when we met him. He was right. But he said it in a reasonable way, not like he was going to blast us as soon as we laid down. And he didn't take our weapons. He trusted us 'cause we trusted him. So why is it different now? And if it is, then why didn't he take them from us at the start?"

The sec chief's lip curled. "That's a lot of questions for someone staring down the barrel of a blaster."

"That's some answer for a man doing likewise," Ryan countered.

Up until this point, all the companions had kept their blasters trained on the sec men who had closed in to surround them. Now, Doc broke that pattern. He turned the LeMat so that it was directly in line with three glass cases, running between the gathered sec.

"My dear man," he said in a loud, clear and considered tone, "it may very well be that you consider your men expendable. That is the nature of the beast. However, I must tell you that this pistol—if you do not recognize it—has two distinct chambers. The first is filled with shot. Wonderful thing, shot. If I discharged the chamber from this angle, the shot would disperse over a displacement of around fifty yards. Until it reaches that point, give or take, it still has enough force to carve a man in two. Or, if you wish to look at it another way—and I think you may—enough force to gouge out that metal and glass, and to impart irreparable damage to the treasures within. I do not think your baron would appreciate that at all. Furthermore, there would still be the second chamber with which to contend. This fires a single ball. Enough, I think, for me to, ah, take out, as it were, and with a simple change of angle, any one of those priceless and—I might point out—irreplaceable artworks that line the stair wall. In light of these facts, you may care to reconsider your stance."

Doc had spoken slowly and clearly. Normally, Ryan felt that the old man's verbosity was at best an irritation, at worst a menace. But in this instance, he knew that Doc was deliberately elaborate. The longer he spoke, the longer the sec chief had time to absorb what he was saying, to consider the consequences.

From the sweat pouring down the sec chief's forehead, and the small vein throbbing in his neck, seeming to make his left eye tic, all of these possible consequences had hit home.

"No one carries blasters in the Palace of Arcady

except the appointed agents of the baron," the sec chief said slowly.

Ryan's top lip twitched in a stifled grin. "Who taught you that, and how long did it take?" he asked, keeping the Steyr steady. The sec chief might want to evade the issue, but Ryan was going to hammer it home. "You're probably thinking that you could chill Doc. That you could chill all of us. And so you could. But not without losing a few men. More important, who says we'll aim at the men? Doc's got a good point, there. Where's your precious baron going to find replacements for the things we shoot bastard big holes through? You can replace men easy enough, but I'm guessing that you can't replace any of this shit."

He waved the Steyr in an arc. Some of the sec around them were confused whether to follow the blaster or to keep their weapons trained on the man. Ryan also saw the sec chief's head twitch as he only just refrained from flinching.

"Well?" he continued, keeping the pressure on. "What are you going to do?"

"All I'm asking is that you lay down your weapons, as only sec carries them in here," the sec chief said, his voice straining and cracking under the tension.

"Now you're asking?" Ryan said softly. He wanted to press the point, but was wary of pushing the man over the edge.

"It's…a courtesy," the sec chief said hesitantly.

"Then you should have explained that from the start and not given orders. This way, we're hardly likely to trust you," Ryan countered.

Stalemate. For what seemed like an eternity, they

stood facing off. In the rooms beyond the hall activity had come to a halt.

Ryan knew that this couldn't go on indefinitely. Jak would be standing unblinking—that alone being enough to unnerve most opposition—and he could rely on the others, even the comparatively frail Doc. His people could tough it out.

No, it would be Arcadian's sec who would crack first. The only question was, would they start shooting or stand down? Right now, he'd bet on shoot first, apologize later. The only thing that could stop it would be if the baron himself stepped in. And Ryan had heard enough about Arcadian to figure that even though he was seemingly absent, he would have a very clear picture of what was occurring in his own palace.

Footsteps echoed on the stairs, coming from the third story. Slowly, they descended—just the one pair of footsteps—and the sec men didn't look up.

The footsteps ceased, and the sound of slow clapping assailed them. Ryan risked a look up at the tall, strongly built man in purple robes over richly woven cloth. He was leaning over the second-story balcony rail, looking down at them with a wry grin, and as he caught Ryan's eye he gave the briefest of nods.

"Very good. Very good, indeed. As, I think, you expected, I am here to greet you.

"I am Baron Eugene Arcadian."

Chapter Six

"Schweiz, you can drop the weapons. I don't think I have anything to fear from these people," he stated, gesturing in an offhand manner to his sec chief.

The thin man looked up and was almost relieved, it seemed, to be given the excuse to back off. With the briefest of nods, he holstered his blaster and indicated that his men could stand down. It wasn't, however, until he had also relaxed his stance and literally stepped back a pace that Jak let his Colt Python drop. Even then, the albino youth looked to Ryan for confirmation that he should do this. The one-eyed man gave the slightest of inclinations, and Jak holstered his weapon, the large blaster disappearing into the depths of his patched and glimmering camou jacket.

Following this lead, the rest of the companions likewise relaxed and holstered their armament.

"There, that's much better, isn't it?" Arcadian boomed from the balcony, his voice echoed and enlarged by the cavernous hall. His tone was supposedly friendly, but there was a note of assumption and control in it that was vaguely alarming. This was his territory, and he felt secure and completely in charge. It was an impression confirmed when Ryan looked up to see that the baron was casually leaning on the rail that circled the staircase and upper balconies, his hands clasped loosely, relaxed, and in a posture that held no hint of defense.

A quick glance around revealed that the sec men had returned to their previous posts and duties, having obeyed the word of their baron without question. The only man to still be within any distance of them, and not occupied with any other activity, was Sec Chief Schweiz. His hatchet face was impassive and gave little away. He seemed relaxed, but to the experienced eye there were signs in his posture that, although he followed orders implicitly, there was some part of him that remained on edge.

A good man to have around, then, Ryan figured. But not perhaps so good as an enemy.

"Well, are you going to stand there all day, or are you going to join me and explain what you were doing blundering into Sector Eight?"

His tone was good-natured, and there was nothing but hospitality in the way he stepped back and gestured that they should ascend to his level. Yet the choice of words betrayed an underlying attitude that rankled with the companions as, led by Ryan, they made their way up the staircase.

Doc, his previous caution submerged beneath the surprise he felt at seeing so many predark treasures, found himself warming to the idea of the baron, if not the man himself. It was rare indeed that he should see so many artifacts that made him feel so much at home.

Certainly, on closer inspection, these were genuine treasures from the predark period. They had no currency value in these times, but represented a depth of old knowledge that was rare.

At the top of the stairs, they found Arcadian waiting for them. He wore no weapons of any kind, and with a knowing grin he noted that Ryan wasn't the only one of the group to notice that.

"I carry no weapons as I am safe here. My men protect me, and they are loyal to the end. And, as you are no doubt aware," he added with a wry touch, "I usually have visitors leave their weapons at the door."

"So why not us? Why not just have your boys take them in the first place?"

Arcadian's smile broadened. "Come now, I'm aware of your intelligence, Mr. Cawdor. You must already have worked it out. Would you have come this far so easily if a kind of mutual trust—a truce, at least—hadn't been established? I think I have your curiosity. There's little point in harming me. Nothing to gain."

"But what's to stop one or all of us going loco and chilling you for the sheer hell of it?"

"Is that likely?" Arcadian inquired in a manner that suggested he thought not.

"It's always possible," Ryan replied in level tones.

"I suppose most things are," Arcadian said with a slight shrug. "The truly off-the-wall can never be predicted. But it would have to be insanity, or else you would realize that all that would happen is that my sec force would avenge me by wiping you from the face of the Earth. And who would gain from that, eh?"

While this exchange had occurred, Arcadian had led them off the balcony surrounding the lobby walls, and down a corridor that led to a number of smaller chambers. Some of these had their doors firmly closed, and their purpose was thus hidden. Others had open access, and through the doorways they were able to see that the rooms nearest to the stairway were used for the purposes of running the ville. Behind desks, some of which were laden with paper and files, men and women toiled on what were obviously administrative tasks.

To Mildred, it looked like nothing so much as municipal offices in any small town of the predark era, and it was bizarre for her to see a sight that had once been a normal part of life transposed to an era where it seemed so out of place. There were many questions she wished to ask, all of which would have betrayed her own unusual history.

"I'll tell you one thing," Mildred stated. "I can't recall ever seeing a ville run like this."

Arcadian looked back at her with an eyebrow raised. "You understand what they are doing? That's very interesting. Most who have been this way, for whatever purpose, could not grasp that." He let the matter drop, continuing in another vein. "I like to keep a close eye and a firm hand on Arcady. It's the way we have always handled matters. So what better than to keep all the administrative bodies within the one building—and one in which I can simply walk out of my own chambers and check up at any time?"

As he spoke, they passed the small chamber in which the central radio transmitter was housed. J.B.'s eye was caught by the bank of equipment, and the operator, who was listening intently to a message that was coming through.

"Rebel force now outside Sector Five. Easily containable, but some backup may be necessary. Rebel quarters identified as on a line thirty-three west, a distance of one mile and one-quarter between Five and Eight. Suggest recce party to be followed by…"

The rest was lost as they were out of earshot, and Arcadian's voice drowned the faint and tinny voice from the receiver. But one thing was for sure: J.B. knew now how they had been tracked so simply—not one tracker, but many, relaying information. The baron had a pretty strong comm setup going here, and that was worth noting for future reference.

Meanwhile, Arcadian had reached a room at the far end of the corridor.

"This," he said, standing aside and waving them through the double doors, "is where I conduct business for most of the day. It seems as good a place as any to continue our conversation."

Ryan moved into the room first, followed by Krysty, Mildred, J.B. and Jak. Doc was still at the rear, slightly behind the others, taking in the remnants of the old world that hung on the wall spaces between the doorways. Framed paintings, posters and newspaper pages, photographs of people that Doc only partially recognized: celebrities from all walks of late twentieth-century life. It was a smorgasbord of predark life.

"Quite remarkable," he murmured. "You must tell me how you came by all of this. By the Three Kennedys, this, too…" he said brokenly as he was assailed by the baron's living quarters.

The room, bizarrely, resembled nothing less than a larger, more ornate version of a 1970s suburban lounge, as Doc had seen on TV programs and videotapes during his captivity with the whitecoats of Operation Chronos. A pit had been sunk into the center of the floor, which was thickly carpeted in a white, cream and brown pattern. The pit was lined with cushions that were tasseled and covered in a variety of fabrics, mostly velvet in texture, and decorated with tapestrylike designs.

Away from this central feature, a fireplace that was presumably in use during the colder months had been inlaid with tiling of many colors, and had a mantel that was lined with ceramics and ornaments from a variety of eras.

Furnishings around the room were of battered but well-polished leather: a chesterfield, sofas and easy chairs, with footstools covered in dark, thickly padded fabric. A dining suite such as might have graced an affluent suburban home at the end of the twentieth century stood by a long window, the real glass made opaque by lace hangings, with thick, plum-velvet drapes on either side.

It was a monument to another time and place, one that was lost on most of the people assembled in the room. To them, it was just plain weird, and unlike anything they had seen before. But to Doc and Mildred, it was like stepping back into a previous life. And was, perhaps, a clue as to where the mind of Eugene Arcadian was rooted.

"It is rather nice," Arcadian said, with a pride in his tone that belied the mildness of his words. "Please, this way, be seated and I will call for refreshments." He indicated the pit, but said nothing when Ryan opted to move toward the leather furniture that was clustered close to the fireplace. A flicker of amusement passed Arcadian's lips, which caused Ryan a brief moment of irritation. He realized that the baron could see he was unwilling to lead his people into the pit, and therefore a position that had a greater vulnerability. It was as though the baron found Ryan's caution in some way funny.

Maybe it was. For the simple reason that Arcadian seemed to have nothing but the best of intentions. As the companions settled themselves into the plush leather furniture in a manner that would have seemed bizarre if they could have seen themselves, Arcadian called for a servant, and ordered food and drink. He then excused himself and exited the room.

"Think this is some kind of test?" J.B. asked softly.

"See if we take a little look around?" Krysty added.

"Could be. Better, mebbe, if we let him show his hand his way for now?"

"I'd go with that," Ryan said.

They waited in a silence that was odd and pregnant, wondering if the baron truly had business to attend to, or if he was watching them in some way.

If he had been, he showed no sign of it when he re-entered the room a short time later, followed by women bearing trays of fruits, meat and bread, which they laid on the table. Pitchers of juice, water and wine followed.

"Forgive the delay," the baron said, "I had some matters of administration to attend to."

The manner in which he said this made J.B. wonder if those matters were tied to the message he had over-heard. But now wasn't the time to bring that up. Leave it for when they were alone.

Seating himself, the baron indicated that they should take any food or drink that they wished. Then, seeing their reluctance, he rose first and went to the table, taking a small sample from every dish that was laid out, before pouring a small measure from each jug into a goblet. He tasted everything that had been brought in.

"You see?" he said with a sly grin. "Everything is fine. It would be less than subtle of me to bring you all this way and then attempt to drug you. I wouldn't insult your intelligence. Besides, there is much I want to hear from you. And there's much that I have to tell you."

He stepped back from the table, urging them to take their fill. When they had, and when they had finished eating, he asked once again how it was that they came to stumble back into his ville.

"For I know you. I didn't meet any of you, but I know that you were here recently with Trader Toms. He spoke highly of you, and I'm surprised that he let you go."

"Didn't exactly happen like that…" Ryan began.

Briefly he told Arcadian of how they had traveled out of the ville with the convoy and had then been dumped in what—to them—was the middle of nowhere. Arcady being the only ville within any distance that they knew of, they had decided to head back this way. As he detailed how they had come across the roadblocks, and of their detour over the maze, he watched the baron carefully to see if there was any flicker of recognition.

Arcadian kept up a facade of interested ignorance. There was no clue in his face that he was aware of any of this, or had engineered it. Ryan figured it had been a good call to say nothing of Toms's informing them of Arcadian's deal with him. A trader had to live on and walk the tightrope, and the fat man had played as fair with them as he could under the circumstances. No sense in getting him chilled. Besides, their knowledge of Arcadian's desire to have them here was a useful card to keep hidden, especially as the baron was playing his cards close.

When Ryan reached the part of his story where they encountered the coldhearts, Arcadian's brow clouded.

"Rebels." He spit with disdain. "We have some problems with those who wish to live outside our society, yet still take from it without contributing. I cannot—and will not—abide such unfairness taking place. If they choose to go up against my sec, then they will inevitably come off second best. But it's their choice."

Ryan held his tongue. Where had the sec been when they were attacked? If their patrols were used to this activity, then why wasn't a patrol nearby when the confrontation occurred? Simply because they had been shadowing Ryan's group and had presumably held back to assess their skills.

Letting these issues pass, he took up their story to the point where they had been picked up by the black-clad sec. While he spoke, the others stayed silent, listening to him as intently as the baron. Just how or what the one-eyed man said dictated how much the baron should know, and would inform them of how much they could give away—or not—if questioned separately at any point.

When he finished, there was a short silence while Arcadian appeared to take in the story. Finally he spoke.

"Well, it seems to me that you have been done an injustice," he said slowly. "Why Toms should do that is something that I find quite baffling. If I had people of your caliber on board, I'd want to keep you there. I suppose he has his reasons. He is, as I'm sure you're aware, a little eccentric—a little weird," he added, noting that Jak didn't appear to recognize the term. There was a chuckle in his voice that he supposed was avuncular and indulgent. To the wary companions, it was a little sinister.

"However, I have to say that his loss is most definitely my gain. I have heard of you people, Mr. Cawdor. I think there may be few barons on trade routes who have not. Even though we are relatively isolated, still the word reaches out. Traders are a garrulous species as a whole, and skills and knowledge such as yours are always at a premium. I would be glad if you would consider staying a while. If you wish, you can leave with the next convoy that passes through. Our wealth comparative to the rest of the region means that even though we're a long haul, we're worth it. You shouldn't have to wait long. But in the meantime…" He ended with a shrug.

A sly and a smart bastard, Ryan had to give him that. From what Toms had said, he was the only trader to move along this route; that was what had built his wealth. So either he had lied or Arcadian was lying— perhaps to make them feel more secure about staying?

Outside the long windows, the night was now beginning to fall, and the sounds of a prosperous ville at night began to filter through. Arcadian, in the pause that followed, turned to look toward the window. An expression crossed his face. This one seemed devoid of any hidden intent or secret humor. It was a pure expression:

love for his ville. Whatever his agenda may be, there was little doubt that the baron was a believer in Arcady.

As though he knew that this thought had flickered across their minds as one, he turned back to them and spoke again.

"You may be wondering about this place. You've seen a part of it that is very different to the parts you saw when you were with Toms. There's a reason for this, and it lies in the history of this ville. You, Dr. Tanner," he added, pointing at Doc, "seem to be fascinated by the displays of the old world that I have about this place. They are meant to be both instructive and inspirational. To remind us all of the world that was left behind, but not merely for the sake of empty nostalgia. No," he said with emphasis, slapping his fist into his palm, "it's important that we keep these memories alive to drive us on. On to building a better world than this. One that has the magnificence of the old."

"World that blew self up?" Jak scoffed.

For a moment anger blazed in the baron's eyes. Then, as if he deliberately quelled it, a calm hooded his gaze, and he continued in a mild tone.

"The old world was far from perfect. There's no denying that. But to dismiss all that it was purely because of one war? That is, perhaps, taking things a little far. No. What I propose to do is to take the best of the old and use it to forge the new."

"What if people not want?" Jak persisted, ignoring the glare that he knew would come from Ryan.

"Why wouldn't they? Who wouldn't want a better way of life than is the norm in these times?"

"You were about to tell us," Doc interjected, not

wishing Jak's belligerence to take them off track; or, more importantly, to make Arcadian hostile, "why the past is so important. About the history of Arcady?"

Arcadian looked at Doc blankly for a moment, then smiled. "Ah, yes. To know this is very much the key to understanding how we work in Arcady."

He sat back, the tension that had made him rigid now uncoiling, and began.

"Being in an isolated spot has always been a good thing for this ville. In fact, I think it's probably fair to say that we're one of the few places in this blighted land that has never seen fit to change its name. For we were Arcady before the nukecaust.

"A small town, we were made rich in the currency of the time by the old military bases that were dotted around this area. The only town in easy reach of them, we prospered off their jack. We also got to hear about what was going on in the world from the point of view of the military, and what we heard wasn't well liked. So the elders that ran this ville started to withdraw from the United States. Much as was possible, we became self-contained and prepared ourselves for what was to come. My forefathers ran this ville well, and when the nukecaust came they made a point of preserving as much as possible, and using all that they had learned to keep us, and our way of life, intact. Of course, times were hard, and it wasn't always easy to do this. Some things went by the wayside, but as soon as it was safe to emerge into the light again, we sought to rebuild ourselves, and through trade to bring in as much of the old as we could find still intact. Hence the archives that you see around you in this building. It all added to our sum of knowledge.

"Here in Arcady we're the pinnacle of civilization in these benighted lands. We know this, and we want to take it further. My forefathers took the time to rebuild the ville and make it right before thinking about spreading the word. It took a hell of a long time, and it's only in the time of my father and grandfather that this has happened.

"But now we can go further. One of the aims of the founding fathers was to breed among themselves with care, sometimes introducing new genes from female partners from afar aiming to leave each leader, each baron if we're to use the terms of today, the most intelligent of his fellows. With each generation that has been refined until we reach myself. I have been engineered to use my mind to its greatest potential, and my father—knowing this—allowed me access to the riches of our knowledge from an early age. My plans are now close to fruition. We have to crawl blinking from the caves at some point. Why not now?"

He stood and positioned himself so that he was looking down on them as they sat.

"I always welcome those who I feel are of like mind, who wish to quest for improvement in this world. I felt like that as soon as Toms told me about you. Particularly in light of the stories that have circulated about you.

"It is providence that has brought you back here to Arcady. I would like us all to take advantage of that. While you are here—until the next convoy arrives—please consider whether or not it would be better for you to join with Arcady on a more permanent basis."

He fixed them with a stare that held a manic gleam.

Ryan shifted in his seat. Sneaking a glance at the others, he could see that Krysty's posture spoke of her unease. Jak's recalcitrance had been obvious. The other three masked their feelings well, but…

"We didn't choose to come here, Baron," Ryan said slowly.

"Please, call me Eugene," he insisted. "No, perhaps not, but should you fly in the face of chance?"

That depends, Ryan thought, on how big a fist chance is aiming to throw in that face.

Chapter Seven

"So will you stay here for a while, or will you take a chance with the road?" Arcadian pressed, leaving no doubt in his tone as to which he felt would be the better option.

Ryan felt like they were being pushed and prodded into a corner that wasn't of their own choosing, but the simple fact was, the baron was right: a chance to rest and recuperate, keep an eye out for incoming, and maybe see what was going on. That was preferable to an option that he was certain would be made more difficult by the baron and his sec. Especially as Arcadian wasn't privy to the knowledge that they were aware of how he had manipulated the situation.

This ran through his mind in a moment, and it was with an almost surprising speed that he actually said, "Yeah. We'll stay. Can't see how that will do us anything but good."

If Arcadian noticed any trace of sarcasm, it didn't register on his face. Similarly, if any of Ryan's companions were surprised at the speed with which he acquiesced, then they maintained an impassive front. If anything, it was the baron's effusiveness that caused them some surprise.

"Excellent! You have no idea how pleased I am by

this decision!" he exclaimed loudly, banging his goblet on the mantel. "You won't regret it, Mr. Cawdor, nor shall your friends. Now, please, eat and drink. I'll call for rooms to be prepared. It'll take a while, as I wasn't expecting you to agree so readily."

He strode off as he said that, and the import of the last sentence wasn't lost on any of them. The baron was a man used to getting his own way, and although he hadn't taken anything for granted, he had obviously been prepared to take as long as was necessary to attain his aim.

While he left the room, the companions rose from their comfortable positions and returned to the table. Each, without saying it, welcomed the chance for a comfortable night's sleep. Certainly, if the bedrooms in this building were of a standard with the room in which they now stood, it would be the best night's sleep they'd had for some time. Now that they had relaxed physically—if not mentally—their aching limbs and lactic muscles screamed for rest.

Mildred moved to the window, looking through the hangings at the ville below. J.B. joined her.

"How does that guy reconcile this," she whispered, indicating the bustling thoroughfare below, as close to the old world as anything she had seen, "with the other part of the ville? And how many other parts are there that we haven't seen?"

J.B. shrugged. "Figure we'll find that out soon enough. The longer we're here, the closer we'll get. Arcadian's got something in mind for us."

"Yeah, that's what concerns me," she murmured.

The other four were also talking in low, hushed

tones. It was a fifty-fifty chance that the baron had the room bugged: he had the tech, that was for sure. The only question was whether or not he would bother at this point. It wasn't worth taking the chance.

"I feel comfortable here," Doc mused quietly, "but not with our host, if you see what I mean. This whole building seems to be a shrine to the past, yet when he speaks—"

"It's not a past that you recognize?" Krysty finished. When Doc nodded, she said, "I kind of know what you mean. There's something he's not telling us yet, and until I know what it is I'm going to feel uneasy."

"Just go," Jak said with as much emphasis as he could put into a whisper. "We go. Too comfortable, too soft, make us fight slow."

Ryan nodded briefly. "You're right, there. This place feels good on aching muscles, and we could all do with that. But we need to keep focused and triple red."

Krysty gave a mirthless grin. "I don't think there's much chance of anything else. Not the way this place is giving me goose bumps."

"Bad situation. Just need move now," Jak said with a shake of his head.

"I don't say you're wrong," Ryan replied, "but we could do with at least one night's rest after today. Arcadian doesn't know we're triple red. He'll be expecting us to give in to him like we seem to have done right now. Let's keep it frosty. Don't say a word, Jak. We'll move soon."

Jak fixed Ryan with piercing red eyes. "Got to. Feels wrong."

"Have no fear, lad, you are not the only one who feels

that way," Doc said, laying his hand on Jak's arm. "If I had strength, then I think I may start running and not stop until I reached China. Assuming there is anything left of China. No matter," he added, catching Jak's bemused expression. "All I say is that we all take heed of your warning, but not all of us have your physical fortitude. Recovery for tired limbs will aid flight."

A cracked smile crossed Jak's face. "Almost understand every word, Doc," he whispered.

Further conversation was stayed by the sound of the baron's heavy boots on the polished floor of the hall outside. Indicating that they would continue later, Ryan moved away from the table. So it was that the baron entered the room once more to a tableau that seemed to be so ordinary as to be bizarre in this time and place. Ryan and Krysty were sitting together on one of the leather sofas. J.B. and Mildred were still at the window, studying life below, with Jak and Doc still at the table. Doc appeared, to all intents, to be trying to explain to Jak how the artist had effected the brushstrokes that gave texture to the painting that hung on the wall nearest the table. Oddly—or so it would have been if Arcadian had been more familiar with the group—Jak appeared to be paying rapt attention.

"I must apologize for the time I have taken," the baron said as he entered. "While I was attending to your quarters, something came up that needed my immediate attention. Ah, that is such a magnificent painting," he continued, changing the subject swiftly as he approached Jak and Doc.

Not so swiftly, however, that it escaped J.B.'s notice that this was the second such sudden occurrence since their arrival. He would have laid jack on it being to do with the coldhearts they had crossed earlier.

Meanwhile, the baron had reached Jak and Tanner.

"I have always admired the way in which the seemingly random patterns leap off the canvas and assault the eye, imposing their own kind of order with their textures, which seem to regiment the unregimented and so reflect the way in which we try to bring order to the chaos of the world. A subject that, as I'm sure you've realized, is dear to my heart."

"Well, quite," Doc murmured.

Jak fixed the baron with an impassive yet unblinking stare. "Look like someone puke on cloth then put glass on," he said simply.

"Well, quite," Doc said again, this time doing his best to suppress laughter.

If the baron was nonplussed, he held his peace. Without pause, he said, "You must be weary, after such a long day. There is little more we can discuss tonight. Perhaps you would like to rest now, and I can assure you that we'll go into details tomorrow regarding the way that you can assist me while you're here."

"We'll have to discuss that," Ryan said warily. "First thing is we'll want to know what you're doing, and mebbe see a little more of the ville. Seems like a lot that we haven't seen as yet."

"In good time," Arcadian assured him.

"It's still kind of early," Mildred said, gazing out the window. "Maybe we could take a little look around now."

The simple, innocent request was met with a surprising vehemence.

"No," the baron barked in the kind of tone that suggested he brooked no argument. "That isn't possible. You've already seen this section of the ville, and there are others that we have to secure from each other at this time of night. It is for nothing but the protection of those who live there, and to visit would be impossible."

"Why, pray tell, do you find it a necessity to cordon off areas of this ville?" Doc asked mildly. "I would not have thought, from what you have said, that—"

"There have been a few problems lately. As I mentioned earlier, not everyone can see the common good when it's being served. It's a temporary measure, but nonetheless, while it's in place—" he took in a deep breath, calming himself "—then it's perhaps best if you wait until the day, when all sectors are once more open. Now, if you would follow me, I'll show you where you'll be staying while you're my guests."

In a gesture that told them any discussion was at an end, he turned on his heel and exited the room. Exchanging glances that carried on a conversation, the companions followed. Ryan's mind held questions: what was the baron's notion of common good, and who did it serve best?

They would find out soon enough. For now, they would be best to rest and take the next day as it came.

Following Arcadian, they moved along the corridor and around the balcony hugging the walls of the lobby, taking another corridor. The well of the staircase was dark and empty, the rooms on the ground floor out of commission until the morning. Shadows of sec men moved below. Almost out of habit, each of the group made note of them.

The corridor was dimly lit, and Arcadian threw open three doors, adjacent to one another. There were two beds in each room. And again, Mildred was struck by how much they had been modeled on middle-class suburban households that she had known in her previous life. It felt like she was stepping onto the set of an old sitcom. Yet how could she explain to the others how strange this was? A man of wealth who acted like a late twentieth-century suburban everyman in his tastes. Here, she felt, was the key to Arcadian.

To the others, however, the rooms were clean, comfortable and, despite their misgivings, inviting. If they had to stay under the baron's roof for one night, then let it be like this.

He guided them in pairs, very deliberately allotting rooms to Ryan and Krysty, and J.B. and Mildred, leaving Jak to room with Doc. They allowed him to take the lead: without perhaps realizing as much, he had once more given away that he had prior knowledge of their lives.

They were all, in their ways, relieved when the baron left them alone to rest.

"SHOWERS. THIS IS SO weird, lover. It's like being in a redoubt, or one of those places that has been preserved from before the nukecaust."

Krysty walked, dripping, from the ensuite bathroom toward the bed, on which Ryan already reclined. He didn't answer her for a moment as it had been a while since they had both the time and circumstances to relax like this. Her skin glistened in the gentle light cast by the overhead shade, water droplets hanging pendant from curves that swept out in sensual lines from the vertical. The red triangle between her thighs carried glittering diamonds of water, beckoning to him. He felt himself stir in a way that had been for too long it seemed, a luxury.

Ryan had already been under the shower, letting the heat of the water ease his aching muscles, playing out the strain that he had incurred earlier in the day. Krysty had seen the way in which he carried his damaged leg, and had been glad to let him take the first shower while she searched the room for hidden listening or viewing devices. If there were any, they were too well hidden for her to find. And given the searching they had all done over the years, that suggested they could speak relatively freely.

She had indicated this to him when he emerged, toweling himself down, and she had taken his place. Content to trust her judgment, he had settled himself on the bed, letting the tension that had been eased by the needle-sharp points of water seep out of him as the soft mattress yielded to his hard body.

While he listened to her singing in the shower, he let his mind wander. His fatigue was such that he couldn't focus on their situation beyond the fact that he had a beautiful woman naked in that shower, and she would soon be coming to him. No doubt she could tell that his mind had been idly wandering. A smile quirked the corner of her mouth.

"You listening to me, lover?"

"Hmm? Yeah, sure," he replied, his voice thick and heavy with imminent sleep.

"Oh, no." She laughed, the last droplets scattering from her as she took two quick strides across the room and landed herself next to him on the bed. "No, no, my man. If you can't talk about the situation we're in, then there is no way on this earth that you're going to waste comfort and space like this by just sleeping."

"But I'm tired, and we need to rest," he said, half joking in protest.

"You might be tired, but who says I need to rest," she purred huskily, her hand reaching down to stroke him. "Well," she continued in mock surprise as her fingers found him, "you're not that bastard tired, are you?"

Now it was Ryan's turn to chuckle deep in his throat. "Mebbe not…"

"Should we chill that light?" she murmured in his ear. He didn't reply for a moment as his mouth was occupied with her breasts. When he finally spoke, his attentions had caused her to forget the question.

"NOTHING," JAK SAID FLATLY.

"Come now, you are unsettled by this place. I can see that. Your instincts are much stronger than mine. If you have any idea—"

"Nothing say. Not now. Mebbe later," Jak interrupted. His red eyes flickered around the room.

"Ah…yes," Doc muttered, nodding sagely. "True, true, we cannot be assured of any privacy. Perhaps now is not… But I confess, I like this place. I know why I like it. It reminds me of, well, of home. But it should not. Not here and now. It is all wrong, in that sense. But because of that… Well, confusion is as good a word as any. I cannot tell if there is any real danger in what is happening. My sense of unease comes from a deep-seated kind of angst, you see, and—"

"Doc," Jak said sleepily, "shut up. Talk too much. Big words, no sense."

Doc allowed himself a quiet chuckle. "Perhaps you are right. Sleep well, Jak, and tomorrow we will see if we can speak with Ryan."

The old man had allowed himself some freedom in what he had said simply because both he and Jak had swept the room for any kind of bugging device as soon as the baron had closed the door on them. It had appeared to be bereft of such tech, and given that both men—like their companions—had experienced tech of all qualities during their travels, the old man had felt safe in expressing himself. His garrulous nature needed flight to enable him to clear the confusion in his own head, and although he realized that Jak was the opposite in nature, he needed the lad as a sounding board.

Yet still he was no nearer an answer. As he listened to Jak's breathing slow into the regulated, shallow rhythm of sleep, Doc lay awake, his eyes focused on the dark ceiling of the room. Heavy drapes covered the windows, and there was little noise permeating this side of the building. Both men had taken advantage of the bathroom facilities, and both were feeling cleaner, the aches washed from their limbs along with the grime. Both had welcomed the respite of the soft beds, and had switched off the lights to welcome the blanket of dark with a sense of release.

But now, while his companion slept with an ease that he found enviable, Doc was wide-awake. Through his mind raced a thousand and one questions, a thousand and two images of a world he had left behind.

He tried to sleep; he needed the rest. His body ached,

his eyes were sore and his mind raced like a galloping horse that was sweat-flecked and out of control. And that was the problem: no matter how much he wanted to switch off his mind and relax, he couldn't. All he could see were the dark outlines of faint shadow that flickered across the ceiling. Maybe the result of some light bleeding in from the corridor beyond, under the door; perhaps the odd sliver of ambient light through the drapes, from the night beyond. Or perhaps nothing more than the result of his own internal eye, flickering and reflected onto the black canvas of the ceiling.

Whatever it was, he envied Jak the rest that he found so easily. Doc felt twitchy. Every nerve ending itched. His skin crawled with fear. With curiosity…

Something here made him uneasy. If it was himself, then he could deal with that. Similarly, he reasoned as he stared at the black ceiling, if it was an external source, then he would be able to find a solution to his unease.

The key here was that he would have to know. And he couldn't wait.

Doc looked over to where Jak lay. His translucent, white skin seemed to shine in the darkness. His breathing was relaxed and steady. His eyes flickered in REM behind paper-thin lids.

"I wonder," he breathed to himself, "could I rise without disturbing you, my friend?"

"DIMMER SWITCH. Man, I haven't seen one of these since, well, since before I was here." Mildred shook her head sadly.

"This really weird for you?" J.B. asked from the

bed. His battered fedora and spectacles lay on the bedside table, and to Mildred it looked for all the world like they were ready to play out a scene in the kind of sitcom that she grew up watching. Except there hadn't been any black women in them. Not then. That would have been strange enough to her, at one time. But now…

She shook her head once more, this time more out of a sense of disbelief than anything else. She turned the dimmer up and down a few times, lost in thought, before settling for a low light and moving over to where J.B. lay, watching her.

"*Weird* is not the word. I can't explain to you what this is like. There are so many things." She got into bed and moved up close against him. "You know, even the fact that this bed is so damn soft feels weird. Time was when this was the kind of thing I'd sleep on every night without even noticing. Now, it just seems like it's taken me back."

"That a bad thing? At least for tonight?" he asked, holding her close to him. Her plaits were rough on his chest as she nestled her head, and he realized it had been a while since they had been able to relax like this.

She shook her head once again. "It's not just about me. I don't know how I can explain it to you. There are too many things that don't add up about Arcadian. Who he is. The way in which he's used his power to recreate a version of the past that just doesn't seem right."

"In what way?" the Armorer asked, genuinely puzzled. Having no real notion of what the "real" past had been, he couldn't understand her bemusement. "This is just old shit he's putting back together, right?"

"No, John, it isn't. It's old, I'll grant you, and a lot

of it is authentic in itself, but it's just that back then, his kind of man wouldn't have had somewhere that looked like this. This is just all wrong."

J.B. pondered this for a moment. "Mebbe you're seeing things that aren't there. He isn't like you. Or Doc. He hasn't seen the past like you have. He's had to piece it together like me. Or Ryan. Or Krysty. You're thinking like he was there. But he wasn't. This is mebbe just what he thinks it should have been like."

"Maybe."

There was still a nagging at the back of her mind, but it was eased out by the low light, the feeling of relief from physical discomfort that the bed brought her, and the close proximity of her partner. Just as the Armorer had a few moments before, she realized that it had been too long since they had been able to lie like this.

Any concerns were forgotten as she moved closer to him, felt his warmth and hard muscle against her. Not just muscle.

"John, really…" she murmured. It was two words too many, and two more than the Armorer would waste. He preferred to let his hands do his talking, and slowly they began to explore each other, rediscovering an intimacy that circumstance had kept too long at bay.

Chapter Eight

It didn't take Doc long to dress. All the while, he kept an eye on Jak's shallow breathing. At the slightest change, he would pause and wait to see if the albino teen awoke. But no. Doc speculated, as he dressed, that somehow Jak's senses were so attuned to danger that he could even subconsciously filter out those sounds that he could identify as being those of a friend. Perhaps that was fanciful. Even so, Doc was able to prepare without the younger man even stirring in his slumbers.

When he was ready, he stood for a moment in the center of the room. Partly to orient himself in the darkness, but partly to ponder what exactly it was that he hoped to achieve.

"To find answers," he murmured.

But what were the questions?

"That I shall only know when I find the answers," he breathed, shaking his head. He knew he shouldn't be taking a chance like this, but he also knew that he couldn't rest until he had done so.

Knowing that his actions could cause problems for those who still slept soundly, but also knowing that he couldn't resist the impulse, Doc headed for the door. He looked back briefly to check on Jak, even though he could tell from merely hearing that the albino teen hadn't responded. Then, he tried the door.

Would you, if you were a baron wishing to lull us into a false sense of security, leave these doors locked or unlocked? Doc asked himself. Locked would signal distrust and captivity. Unlocked risked exactly the kind of action he was about to take. On balance, he assured himself, unlocked—engender trust, and attend to problems further down the line.

The door gave easily and Doc grinned in the faint light from the corridor. Was it a good thing that he could second-guess the thought processes of a possibly dangerous megalomaniac? No matter. He was out, now…

The corridor was dimly lit. It gave him some cover to move in, if nothing else. At one end, there was a wall with a central window. It had large panes set in a frame that stood six feet by three, roughly. More than big enough to climb through with ease. But that would merely effect escape. Investigation was more Doc's aim. So he took the other way. He and Jak had been placed in the room farthest from the exit to a corridor. On his way back up the shadowed hall he had to pass the doors of the other two bedrooms, occupied by his companions. It was with some trepidation that he passed these two doors. Would it be his luck to walk past at the moment that Ryan or J.B. also decided to try to explore?

As he passed them, he paused and listened at the doors. Although they were of a heavy wood—not oak, he was sure, but perhaps cedar—he could hear some faint noise from within. He felt, for a moment, both embarrassed and pleased. Was it an intrusion to hear them making love? At least they had the opportunity. And, in a practical sense, it allowed him to follow his own path without fear of being followed.

It was while he was at one of the doors that he heard the approaching footsteps, distant, but echoing in the chamber adjacent to the hall. Steady and slow, allowing him time to step back into the deepest pool of shadow he could find, using a display case as cover. He hunkered down, his head level with the case.

Doc tried to sink back into the wall, so that the case and its shadow absorbed him completely. The slap of the echo now became subsumed to the thump of heavy boots on stone floor, and Doc knew that whoever approached would be level with the entrance to the corridor.

It had to be a sec patrol. One man, by the sound of it. If he passed by, then Doc was safe. If not, well, it would not take much for the man to stumble on him, and who knew what would occur by then. Doc had his sword stick with him, as always. He fingered the silver lion's head: a Toledo steel blade was a deadly thing, but not easy to unsheath in such a location. He prayed that it wouldn't be necessary to take such action at this juncture.

The footsteps ceased. He heard the growling rattle of phlegm in the sec man's throat. Then the footsteps receded, becoming once more bathed in the welcome glow of echo.

Doc rose slowly to his feet, listening for any change in the pattern of the footfalls all the while, then made his way swiftly to the head of the corridor and looked out. He was aware that he was now in light, and so checked as quickly as possible both the location of any sec, and equally the location of any pools of darkness.

He was in luck on both counts. Only selected lights were in use while the building was, ostensibly, sleeping. Points of light glimmered along the landing, and could be glimpsed on the levels beneath. Down in the central well of the building's lobby, there was a vast ocean of black. Elsewhere, the points diffused slowly into dark.

Quickly, Doc sidled along the wall until he was beyond the periphery of the pool in which he stood. Then, feeling safer in the gloom, he moved toward the stone balustrade that contained the stairways.

Ears keen for any footsteps that came within range, he became attuned to the quiet sounds of the building at night. A distant and polyrhythmic tattoo of footfalls from the heavy boots of the sec patrols became apparent. Below him, men moved slowly in and out of view. It was a regular pattern of patrol, but standing in the center of one part of that pattern wouldn't allow him the luxury of defining the whole. Even as he watched, he knew that the man he had so recently avoided was now past the farthest point of his patrol, over by the far wall, and making his way back to where Doc was standing.

Time to move. His big problem, as he saw it, would be to pass through the pools of light without being seen. Eliminating all risk from this would be impossible, yet if he were to time his runs across those spaces, then it may just be feasible for him to hunker low to the balustrade and make himself small. From below, he would be hidden to all but the keenest of eyes.

Timing his first run as much a possible to the footfalls of the sec man at his rear, Doc scampered from dark to dark, keeping low. He reached the stairs and descended carefully. This was easier, as most of the incline was bathed in darkness, and he was able to pause before he reached the next level, listening and watching for the sec patrol on that level with a lesser chance of being seen. The sec man on the second level passed in front of him and, after a pause, Doc slipped into his wake.

He continued this pattern until he reached ground level, where he was able to slip into the relative security of the dark that surrounded the displays in the old lobby. Silently, he thanked Arcadian's strange mix of vanity and curatorship for the cover it afforded him. The darkness was full of shapes with which he could meld.

Now he was down here, he wondered why he had made for the ground level and not lingered on the corridors leading to the baron's quarters and the mysterious rooms they had glimpsed on their arrival. That, surely, would be where he would find answers. Why, then, had his subconscious led him here without a thought?

As he watched the sec men move in and out of the ground-floor rooms, it came to him. From what they had been told, these were used merely for the administration of Arcady. Why, then, did they need such a heavy sec presence when compared to the levels where the baron reposed?

Two reasons sprang to mind. The first was that they were in place should any of the baron's "guests" attempt to escape or carry out reconnaissance. Considering his own position at this moment, it was a reasonable assumption. The second was that they were defending something. But what? The ground level itself held nothing that would be of significance. That was safe to assume. But what if…

This had once been a library. It would have a base-ment, in which town archives would have been stored in the days before skydark. He knew this from his brief sojourn in the twentieth century, and from the origins of such buildings in his original time frame. A substan-tial basement. One that could house any number of secrets, should a man choose. And Arcadian, Doc felt sure, was a man with secrets.

How to access this basement? That was his dilemma. The physical entrance was easy to see, once he cast around for it. Under the staircase as it began to rise was a stout, unremarkable door.

That was the easy part. However, even from his vantage point he could see problems. The door itself had a light suspended by a bracket over the frame. There only appeared to be one lock, but to pick it would re-quire standing in a telltale illumination. The sec patrols had a pattern that, he could now see, kept the door in an almost constant view.

"Problem, dear boy," Doc murmured to himself. "Lock under light, easily seen. Light goes out, work in darkness. But light goes out, guards become suspicious. Create a diversion? Possible. But then the whole build-ing comes alive."

Doc settled in a little. He could afford to wait, for the night was still young. It would be some time before dawn's early light started to seep through the windows of the old building and betray his position. His time was finite, but it should be enough to observe, and to analyze from these observations. In the world that he now lived, it was easy for Doc to forget that he had once been an academic, and although that brain was blunted by the traumas of time travel and an alien world, still it had enough of the old capacity to think.

Hunkered down by one of the display cases, he was aware of his thigh muscles cramping. He moved so that he was now on his knees, but even then he found that pins and needles warmly invading his calves were warning of being in one place for too long. He sighed. Why did his life have to be so, well, awkward?

But his discomfort and time weren't without result. He was able to watch several circuits of the sec patrols, timing them and noting the points both at which they crossed and when they were farthest from the lobby area. They worked on regular and well-drilled patterns. But now he had the chance to observe them close-up, and he could see that although the sec men had been well-drilled into their regime, they weren't necessarily the most enthusiastic footsoldiers he had ever seen. Their faces were haggard and betrayed a lack of sleep that may—if he was fortunate—be reflected in a concurrent lack of awareness. Certainly, the two who crossed over at the point where the door stood grunted or exchanged a few words each time they passed, and these words betrayed their lack of enthusiasm for their task.

Doc allowed himself a small smile as an idea came to him. It wasn't a perfect idea, and certainly it relied on these men being less than thorough in their tasks.

He rose, massaging his calves, getting the blood flowing once more. The last thing he wanted was to get halfway to his intended target and fall flat on his face. Ignominious as that might be, the danger in which it would place him was more of a spur.

There was an optimum point at which all the sec patrols—and these men in particular—would be facing away from the lobby. He would have to time his run with as much care as he possibly could, and act quickly and without fumbling. Just thinking of it made him nervous. He blanked his mind, watched and waited.

Now.

While they were at the extremity of their circuit, their footsteps distant echoes, Doc moved as smoothly as he was able. Weaving his way through the display cases, he crossed the empty space between the clustered cases and the door, unconsciously holding his breath as he entered the cone of light. He would have to move quickly, and take great care… His heart thumped in his throat as he wrapped his hand in the cuff of his shirt and reached up for the bulb that hung above the door. The thin material was no insulation for the heat, and he winced as it burned his fingertips. He wanted to pull them away, but couldn't risk dropping the bulb. For he didn't wish to extinguish it. Not yet…

It was a bayonet cap, not screw. That might make it easier to engineer. He loosened it, inhaled a sharp breath as it flickered into dark and then, as it lit up once more, stole a look in either direction.

The sec men were barely visible shadows, plodding their way through the circuit. They didn't appear to have noticed.

Good.

Retreating as swiftly as he dared, yet at the same time keeping as light on his feet as he could, Doc returned to his place of safety, crouching once more. Now he had to wait. Had to endure the burning in his calves that matched the stinging pain in the fingers of his hand. Had to hope that his calculation had been correct, and that he had just that small piece of luck that any intrepid adventurer may need.

It seemed like forever until the echo of their feet became louder and the slap of boot on concrete floor became even louder than the reverberation. Doc watched as they came into view, each from the opposite end of their orbits, and moved toward the center, where they would cross under the pool of light cast by the bulb overhanging the door. It was as though his entire universe was centered on that one point.

Success. Doc barely resisted the urge to laugh out loud as the last thing he saw before the light went out was the look of surprise on the faces of both men.

His surmise had been correct—loosen the bulb, and the vibrations caused by the heavy footfalls would be enough to set it free. It dropped, and landed with a bang as loud as a gunshot in the almost empty lobby.

The radio handsets that both sec men had hanging from their belts crackled to urgent life, buzzing angrily as they were asked what the hell was going on.

"No panic," one of them drawled into his handset. "Just one of the bastard lights gone. Fucker popped out and hit the deck. No worries."

The handset crackled back angrily. The voices were distorted and hard to understand from where Doc was crouching, but it seemed that extra sec patrols had been laid on to cover any possible attempt to escape or recce. Those pressed into service were edgy and exhausted as they had been on-shift for almost twenty-four hours without respite.

"Look, it's nothing to worry about, just a fucking bulb," the sec man gritted into his handset. "This is a bastard waste of time. Those fuckers don't want to do anything, and we're just getting more and more tired."

"You tell him, Bub," the other sec man muttered.

"Yeah, just keep it frosty, right? It's just one of the lights gone, no more. Let's just get through this shift until sunup."

There was some incoherent, angry buzzing from the handset.

"Yeah, fuck you, too," Bub barked. "Fuckers. All on the fucking edge, man."

"We all are," his fellow guard replied in flat tones. "So we gonna replace this fucker and then get back to work?"

Even though the area was now shrouded in darkness, Doc could almost see the sec man look up at the bulb.

"Hell, no. Listen, we fuck around doing that and Schweiz finds we ain't on his routes, then we get shit. It's only a fucking light, man. Ain't gonna matter if we fix it now or leave it for the maintenance guys tomorrow. All we gotta do is make sure we don't fucking walk into each other when we come back this way and shoot each other in the balls 'cause we frighten ourselves."

His companion chuckled. Even that sounded flat and weary. "Ain't much chance of that. I can barely lift this fucker, way I feel right now."

Bub wheezed a laugh. "Yeah, know what you mean. Still, gotta make it seem like we can, right? Fucking lightbulb. Bastard fucker," he finished.

"See you when I walk into you, then…"

The two men parted company, leaving Doc to count

the footfalls and wait. They had inadvertently given him a boost in confidence. Too tired to lift a blaster would also mean too tried to notice small noises or equally small movements in shadow. Good.

Doc moved out from cover and made his way across the floor until he was up against the door. Even though his eyes had adjusted to the darkness a long time back, it was still mostly by feel that he groped for the lock. He would have to move swiftly, before they returned. The darkness gave him cover, but also hampered him.

Fumbling in the pocket of his frock coat, he found a length of wire, twisted into a small loop. Using one hand to locate the keyhole, he guided the loop into the opening. He hoped that this was a simple lock and not anything complex. It seemed unlikely that the lock would have been substantially changed. Chances were that the locals either had no idea where the door led, or were sec who knew better than to pry. As long as Arcadian retained confidence in his own authority, then chances were that the original lock would remain in place.

Tumblers twisted and turned, and with a soft click Doc felt the door give. He gently tried the handle, and the door opened inward.

Once inside, on a landing of some kind, Doc closed the door and then reinserted the lock pick, this time using it to relock the door. There was no sense in tempting fate. To get this far and then be discovered for the simple expedient of an unlocked door would be absurd.

Now feeling more secure, Doc took stock of his situation. If the darkness on the other side of the door had been nearly impenetrable, then the blackness on this side of the door was complete. Tentatively poking with his toe, he could feel that the landing on which he stood stretched about three feet before stairs began.

He groped along the wall for a light switch, found it and wondered if the light leak would betray him to the passing sec patrol. Reaching up, he removed the bulb from the overhead socket and tucked it into the pocket of his frock coat. Taking a deep breath, he flicked the switch. The light cast by the three bulbs that ranged along the corridor at the bottom of the stairs wasn't bright in itself, but to a man whose eyes had become accustomed to almost total blackness, it seemed as though he were momentarily staring into the sun.

Doc blinked, red and yellow flares behind his closed eyelids burning bright for a moment before passing. He squinted, gradually widening his eyes as his sight adjusted to the light. In a few moments, he was once again able to see normally.

Silence hung like a pall over the empty air. It was stale, yet not fouled. Dust motes hung almost motionless under the direct beam of the lights. There was a stillness that suggested he was the first to set foot here for some time.

"Have I been in search of that which is not?" he murmured to himself. "How ironic—and damn inconvenient—if I have expended all this effort on a dead end."

Slowly he began to pick his way down the steps. The metal rail on one side of the stairs was covered in dust, and he avoided touching it. There was no need to leave telltale signs. The stairs underfoot, however, were cleaner than he would have expected. Likewise, the passage at the foot of the stairs, leading off into a long corridor, was also free of dust and dirt.

"Well, well," he mused to himself, "does someone just wish to make it seem as though this is not used?"

The wall on one side of the stairs was painted white, faded to a kind of dirty-cream by time. Likewise, the passage at the foot of the stairs was similarly decorated. Turning at a sharp angle, the wall closed in on both sides, curving to form an arch for the ceiling. It resembled a tunnel more than a corridor, and Doc had to shrug off the feeling of being confined and trapped that suddenly threatened to overwhelm him.

"Come now, sir, there can be no turning back," he murmured to fortify himself before physically shrugging off his fear and continuing along the passage.

At regular intervals along the passage, as it twisted and turned, were a number of locked doors. Doc tried one or two experimentally at the head of the passage, but the locks were old, and had obviously not been tampered with for many years. That caught his attention. The passage was obviously in use, from the state of the floor, yet the rooms were—so far—untampered with, and there was an attempt to hide any usage. Ergo, unless he was way off the mark, the purpose of the passage would only be revealed when he reached its terminus. One thing was for sure—this wasn't quite the layout he had expected.

As he walked along, careful to keep the noise of his feet on the flagged floor to a minimum, so as not to mask any approaching noises as much as to hide his own, he pondered on the layout he had found beneath the old library.

He had expected to find a number of storerooms. Their original use would have been to keep stock, perhaps house facilities for the maintenance of the building and its stock. Rooms that he had been expecting to have been converted into…well, what? Workshops, perhaps. Even repositories of documents, old tech, anything that would reveal to him just exactly why Arcadian was collecting so much old material. An intimation of the ends, and perhaps the means, of the baron's theories about society and the manner in which he wished to impose them on the rest of the populous.

Doc was no lover of the way in which the world had turned out. He pined for the world he had once known, and in truth tried to distance himself from that part of his mind so as to stave off the madness induced by the gap between the two. Nonetheless, he would be damned if he would let anyone tell him how to live. From Jordan Teague onward, he had seen too much of that since he had arrived in this world. Most of the coldhearts who fought tooth and claw to run a ville had the ambition, but not the brains or the means to take their ambition to the next level. Doc had the nasty suspicion, creeping like ice down his spine, that Arcadian had both.

Hence this expedition. Now that he was down here, Doc had little idea of how he could get back to the room he had left without arousing suspicion. Come to that, he had no idea of the time. He looked at his chron, suspended on a chain in his vest pocket. Stopped. Just as it had for some days.

"Oh, dear, Theophilus, it appears you have little

option but to press on and see what you find," he murmured with a sad smile. It hadn't been his most considered course of action, but if he could find out what Arcadian was doing, then that itch within him would be assuaged.

So, Tanner, what is the next question you should ask yourself? Doc thought. He stopped and looked around. The corridor had twisted in such a manner that he was now unable to see the stairs he had descended. He had also been walking for some time without pause, and so he had to be well beyond the boundaries of the library building. The stairs had been steep, and he suspected that he had descended beyond usual basement level until he was below the level of the old water and sewage system.

Why would a library basement be so deep? Come to that, why would it fan out in such a manner that it seemed to have an exit some distance away from—

Doc sighed. What had happened to the brain that had won him such academic distinction? Of course, he knew the answer.

Shelter. The ville's proximity to old military bases, as described by Arcadian when he had been droning on earlier that evening. The people of the predark ville would have been only too aware of the escalation of hostilities, and the consequences that would result. So what else would the elders do but build a shelter for themselves beneath the central focus of the ville.

So presumably this had been where they lived until the nukecaust and skydark had abated. And behind these doors, now abandoned for so long?

His curiosity piqued, Doc decided to pause to try to

seek access to one of the rooms. Choosing purely at random, he stopped and produced his lock pick. It was uncertain whether or not it would work on something that had been so long neglected, but he opted to try his luck.

As he worked the wire loop into the keyhole, feeling for the tumblers in the lock, he wondered whether the lighting would be working in the room beyond the door. So far, he had encountered not a single defective bulb in the lighting along the passage, even though they were hung at regular intervals. That bespoke of regular maintenance. Did they, he wondered, also check behind these doors?

He grunted satisfaction as the lock gave and the door grudgingly opened on hinges rusted and made stiff by dust and time. The room beyond was dimly illuminated by the light from the passage. He felt for a light switch and depressed it when found. No such luck. The room remained in half-light gloom. Pushing the door wide, Doc ventured in. His eyes adjusted to the gloom, and he could see that it had been a dormitory for five people. The beds were made, left as they had been when the occupants found it safe to venture back to the surface. The bedding was thick with dust, as were the few books and magazines that were scattered on bedside tables. Pictures still hung on the walls—some of them were posters, some were framed photographs of people long since gone.

Doc walked farther into the room, feeling as though he were violating a crypt, and picked up one of the books. A cheap paperback Western. He put it down and dusted off the front of a magazine. *Newsweek,* dated

May 1999, and carrying a picture of the last president on the cover. Doc half smiled, half sneered. He remembered reading several scandalous articles about the man. With such people in charge, it was little wonder that the endtimes had come.

Doc placed the magazine back where he had found it and looked around. There was little to tell him much about the people who had spent so long down here, waiting for skydark to fade. Yet in itself that told him much about the way in which they had obviously been well organized. There was no sudden abandonment or signs of decay here. When the all-clear was sounded, they had simply packed up and left in an orderly fashion, leaving only the least valuable of their possessions behind them.

That level of organization, carried through to the current baron and his subjects, could be very dangerous.

Thoughtful of those consequences, Doc left the room, being careful to relock the door. He moved down the corridor and picked another at random. This time, the light was still working, and he found himself in a washroom and latrine. Even though he didn't try the taps, he had little doubt that the water would still run. The shower area was clean, just dusty. They had maintained it well up until the time they had left.

Again, Doc left the room deep in thought, locking it behind him to cover any tracks he might leave. He continued along the passage, wanting now only to reach its conclusion and find what secrets lay there.

He kept walking for some minutes while the white stone walls twisted around him. The passage hadn't been cut in a straight line presumably because of the lines of rock and clay in the earth. He presumed that the rooms had been constructed hastily, albeit efficiently, and the natural geology of the Earth had partly dictated the pattern. And yet, he suspected that part of the pattern was because of wherever the passage led.

Where was he going to emerge?

He found out soon enough. As he rounded a curve, he could see that the passage ended in another staircase that led up to a small landing, like the one he had originally descended. Yet this landing didn't face onto a door. Instead, there was a ladder set into the wall, with a trapdoor in what was the ceiling of the passage.

"Curiouser and curiouser, Alice," Doc murmured, slowing as he approached. He looked back over his shoulder, even though he was certain that he was alone. Ah, well, he'd come this far…

Doc climbed the stairs, then climbed the ladder. Craning his neck, he could see that the trapdoor was locked by a wheel mechanism. Clinging to the ladder with one hand, he pulled at it experimentally. It was no great surprise that the wheel yielded easily. Obviously it was oiled for regular use.

If the rooms weren't in use, then why was this passage alone used secretly to move from one sector of the ville to another? It was puzzling. Only one way to find out, Doc decided as, with a shrug, he spun the wheel and unlocked the trap.

It was heavy, but not so much that he was unable to heave it upward. It slammed back onto an earthen floor, and Doc cautiously emerged to find himself in a darkened courtyard, surrounded on all four sides by four-story buildings, blank windows looking down on him. Distant lights within cast a glow into the otherwise black rooms, showing them to be empty while allowing him to see that the courtyard was empty, apart from the open trap and himself.

He heaved himself out, looked around and bent to close the trap.

That was when the courtyard became flooded with light and Doc found himself exposed and defenseless.

"Oh, dear. I feared this might happen."

Chapter Nine

Jak knew there was something wrong even before he was awake. Somewhere in his subconscious he had detected Doc's departure, and he had filed it away. So when his red albino eyes opened and were almost instantly attuned to the low level of light, he knew that Doc was not in the next bed.

"Stupe," he whispered. Jak didn't like Arcadian, and thought that Ryan was playing a tough game in sticking around. Doc's curiosity made the chances of the baron turning on them even greater. Okay, so they had their weapons. This meant that the baron knew of ways in which he could easily break them. No one would be stupe enough to let them keep their blasters unless they had the utmost confidence in being able to best the companions regardless.

This would play right into his hands.

Jak rose and went to the door. The situation might be redeemed if they could drag Doc back before the baron discovered his actions. As no alarm had been raised, it was doubtful he had breached the building's exits. He had to be somewhere inside. Maybe they could get him back.

The unguarded corridor didn't surprise Jak. Doc would have been easily discovered otherwise. The thing to do now would be to rouse Ryan and then decide on a course of action that could drag back the old man.

Always assuming he didn't get himself caught in the meantime.

"KEEP YOUR HANDS out in the open and move out of the tunnel slowly."

"Of course. You have the advantage on me," Doc said deliberately, placing his hands on the gravel of the courtyard and hauling himself out so that he was on his knees, before rising slowly to his feet.

"Replace the cover. Slowly."

Doc bent slowly to flip the cover back into place before spinning the wheel to lock it. He straightened, then raised a hand to shield his eyes, looking around. The courtyard was bathed in a brilliant light, illuminated from all four sides. The ground-level lights were angled up, which was presumably why he had missed them at an initial glance. He couldn't remember the last time he had seen such a brilliant white light. The source of the voice was hidden to him by their luminescence.

"You have the advantage of me," he said clearly. "I cannot see you."

"That is, of course, the point. You're the one they call Doc, aren't you?"

"A further advantage," Doc demurred. "You have the upper hand, by a long way. Would it be too much to ask that you cease blinding me?"

The voice behind the lights now took on an amused tone.

"You have an admirable grasp of the situation. If you keep your arms away from your body—I know you have weapons on your person—then I'll make the light a little more bearable."

"Of course," Doc said, complying with the wishes of the voice.

The lights blinked out, leaving a red-glow afterimage both on Doc's retina and in front of the dimmed bulbs. Everything else was momentarily black as Doc's pupils reacted to the sudden change. Within a few moments he was able to see once more, aided by the ambient light that bled from the ground floor of the buildings on one side. Presumably where the owner of the voice had emerged.

And now Doc was able to see him—a small, slight man in a long white coat, his hands clasped behind his back. He was unarmed, but any fleeting thoughts Doc may have had about his own weapons were stilled by the two thickset men in black fatigues that lurked at the slight man's rear, well-preserved submachine guns clutched in fists so large the blasters seemed like toys.

"You must excuse my caution," the slight man said, stepping forward. "We weren't expecting any of you to show such initiative at this stage. But since you're here—" he indicated that Doc follow him "—I may as well explain it to you. You have the brain to grasp it, after all."

Doc had absolutely no idea what the man was talking about, but figured that if he just kept quiet, then his captor would let it all out without needing to be questioned.

"Very well," he said simply, walking slowly toward the lit building and the two menacing sec men. After all, he seemed to have little choice.

RYAN WOKE SUDDENLY. He tried to rise, but found himself restrained by a wiry arm across his chest, a hand clamped across his mouth like an iron band. He tensed and prepared to fight.

"Ryan, me. Triple red."

Jak had spoken before Krysty had roused herself, and before Ryan had even had a chance to flex the muscles that lay under the albino youth's restraining arm. Jak removed his hand as he felt Ryan relax.

"Fireblast, Jak, what the fuck are you doing?" Ryan whispered hoarsely.

"Not have choice," Jak said tersely, before outlining to Ryan and the now awake Krysty the situation they faced. He was able to tell them the sec setup in their part of the building as he had made a brief recce after finding Doc missing and before coming to them.

"One could search, more than one be found." Jak shrugged.

Ryan nodded. He could see the albino's point. The sec could be evaded singly—Doc's continued absence proved this if little else—but the group as a whole would be too much of a risk. But he didn't want to risk another of his people going missing.

"You come here first?" he asked.

Jak nodded. "Leave J.B., Mildred till spoke to you."

"Okay..." Ryan ran the possibilities through his mind. "There's only one way we can play this." He swung himself out of bed and dressed quickly, strapping on his weapons. Krysty followed his lead, watching him all the while.

"No way we're going all out on this," she said shrewdly. "Just what have you got in mind, lover?"

"You'll see soon enough." He moved to the door. "Let's get Mildred and J.B." He tugged at the door and stepped out into the hall with no attempt to disguise his actions. Looking back, he could see the bemusement on Jak's face, although he noted that his intent was dawning on Krysty. "C'mon," he said loudly, "J.B. and Mildred need to hear this."

"OF COURSE, you know that the baron is an advocate of exploring many social systems and experiments that were performed before skydark set back the cause of civilization by several centuries, thrusting us back into a dark age," the slight man said as he ushered Doc into the building. One of the sec men had preceded them, while the other lurked at their rear. Their proximity caused Doc to do little except nod sagely at this juncture.

Inside, the building was cleaner than many Doc had seen during his time in this age. It also carried with it a smell that was alien outside a redoubt: bleaches and disinfectants, chemicals, the sterility of cleaned and recycled air…its olfactory impression was of nothing more or less than a medical clinic. Whatever happened in here, it was of a nature that made his flesh crawl. An impression that was only magnified by the white lab coat worn by the slight man.

Long corridors, lit at regular intervals, resembled nothing so much as the tunnel he had recently vacated, the blandly closed doors only reinforcing this impression. The only real difference between above- and belowground that he could see was the row of windows that peppered the corridor in both directions, facing the courtyard.

The slight man piloted him along the corridor as he spoke.

"What we do here is to try to advance some of the old theories about the enhancement of the physical. Grafting, stem-cell therapy and so forth. Of course, we're hampered by the fact that our facilities are of a poorer quality than those of our predecessors before the nukecaust. And information about their results and their methods have been—how shall I put it—patchy in some particulars. Papers were particularly susceptible to the vicissitudes of a nuclear winter. Perversely, the comp records have survived a little better. The baron has put a lot of time and effort into finding as much old equipment as possible. We've even managed to find some audiovisual documentation that has been preserved. This, as you can imagine, has been invaluable."

"Quite," Doc murmured. The man in the lab coat babbled on, and sounded more and more to Doc like the kind of whitecoat who had prodded and poked him on his arrival in the late twentieth century. He found himself seized by the insane desire to take the man and repeatedly smash his head against the wall; to push it through the nearest window and rip out his throat on the jagged edges of the glass. Insane not because he felt that the man didn't deserve it. Insane because the two sec thugs in front and behind him would riddle him with shells before his grip had even tightened on the whitecoat's throat.

Still, the whitecoat prattled on.

"You know, when I look back, I find it odd that the kind of work that we're doing now was once considered bad. And so soon after it was hailed as the salvation of humankind. It seems very odd, the manner in which opinions were subject to the moral worldview of the day, without once it being questioned as to whether those fashions in themselves were the transient option, and not the thing on which those opinions were focused being the transient thing…as it were. Am I making sense to you?"

The whitecoat turned and fixed Doc with a beady glare that was almost myopic in its intensity. Doc was quite unsure as to what would be the best way to answer him. He wanted him to reveal more, even though he felt nauseous at the direction they were headed.

As it happened, Doc needed to say nothing. The whitecoat, it would appear, welcomed the chance to exercise his garrulous nature.

"Of course I'm making sense," he affirmed. "You are an intelligent man. I know that. The intel reports from the palace are circulated to all section heads, to fully appraise them of what is going on. Your group aroused no little interest from all of us, I'll have you know. Quite the subject of debate among us," he added with a small smile. "I dare say it's chance that you ended up here first, although the connection to the palace is something only my section has directly. However, your alacrity at making a move isn't something we could have easily forecast. And on your own, too."

"I like to keep people on their toes," Doc demurred.

The whitecoat stopped and turned to him. "Ah, the ever-questing mind that seeks the same from others. I like that." He stuck out a hand.

Doc hadn't seen a gesture like that for many a day. Part of him wondered if it were some kind of test, perhaps even a trap. Certainly, the sec men loomed in a little close, their faces betraying nothing but their body language yelling alarm and alert.

Doc's eyes met those of the whitecoat. Was that sincerity he saw in those orbs? Did this man not realize that Doc wanted little more than to hit and run? Oh, well, at least he might find out more this way.

Mindful of the sec men and their possibly anxious trigger fingers, Doc extended his hand with caution. As their palms met, he suppressed a shudder at the cold, clammy flesh that pressed on his.

"You, of course, are Dr. Tanner. But allow me to introduce myself. I, too, am a doctor. No diplomas here, of course, but I grace myself with that title considering the work I do. Andower. Dr. Harold Andower at your service."

"Charmed," Doc murmured in a voice that was anything but.

MILLIE AND J.B. woke at the same moment, coming alive and apart in a tangle of limbs. They had drifted into an easy sleep after making love, a sleep that was dark, deep and dreamless.

As they pulled themselves apart and tumbled from the bed, unthinking hands grasped for weapons, and before the hammering had ceased they had their blasters to hand.

"J.B., Mildred, wake up. We need to talk."

Both were now completely awake, but were baffled by this turn of events. They looked from the door to each other, J.B. a little myopically as his spectacles were where he had left them a few hours previous.

Ryan's voice? That loud?

"Come in," J.B. said in a level voice, but without lowering his blaster. He peered across at Mildred, who nodded her understanding. Ryan wouldn't normally do this in such a situation. Coercion was a possibility.

"No, come out here," Ryan replied. "We need to talk. Krysty and Jak are with me."

Again, a look passed between them. No mention of Doc.

"Think it's just them?" J.B. asked.

"Ryan would use the code if it wasn't," Mildred replied. "He was particular about who was out there. There's something wrong, and he wants Arcadian to know about it."

"Figure you're right," J.B. said, lowering his blaster. "Guess we should get out there."

"John," Mildred said quietly as he started toward the door.

"What?" He stopped, puzzled.

She looked him up and down.

"Might be better if we put some clothes on."

KRYSTY AND JAK had looked at each other and shrugged as Ryan hammered on the door. He had made no effort at concealment, and was now making a hell of a lot of noise. As he yelled through the bedroom door, a patrolling sec man appeared at the end of the corridor, his subgun held across his chest, pointing down. But despite the passive stance, there was little doubt that he was ready to move into action if necessary. Behind him, the lights came on in darkened library as Ryan's actions were noted.

When he had finished, the one-eyed man stepped

back, taking a look at the sec man before turning his back and winking at them. It seemed this was exactly the reaction he had expected and hoped for. A glimmer of his game plan became apparent to both of them.

By the time the bedroom door opened, the building was bathed in light. Two more sec men stood behind the solitary guard who patrolled this level; footsteps and voices from beyond indicated that Ryan's actions had stirred a hornet's nest of activity.

From the quirk at the corner of his mouth, this was the reaction he had wanted.

"Ryan, what the—dark night," J.B. breathed, taking in the situation. "Arcadian's going to love you for this."

"That's the idea," Ryan said quietly, then added in a louder voice, "Doc's missing. No way he would have gone off on his own, not without telling Jak. That bastard Arcadian is behind this, and I want to know why."

The sec men at the head of the corridor broke formation and Sec Chief Schweiz strode through them. His sleekness was ruffled by being rudely awakened, and his temper was as disheveled as his usually immaculate appearance.

"You don't talk about the baron in that way," he snapped, his bark punctuated by the clicking catch of his blaster, an obvious warning. Ryan had figured he was edgy and prone to the big gesture, and this just confirmed his notion. Now to play the man.

"Listen, boy," Ryan said carefully, with just the right edge of disdain, "I don't talk to the shit carrier, I talk the man whose bucket he holds. You get the baron here, like a good little man, and mebbe we'll see what's going down."

Schweiz's eyes, no longer hooded by the shades he had worn earlier, were small and piggy in the glare of the lights. They narrowed, and the corner of his mouth quivered as he fought to control his temper.

"You push too far, son," he hissed in a voice as tight as the line of his lips. His face was drained of blood and he quivered with an impotent rage. "You're here because—"

"Because they're my guests, Schweiz, and as such you will have some common courtesy with them, no matter how misguided they may be."

Arcadian's voice boomed out from behind the sec men with an authority that made them part ranks instantly. Schweiz turned to face the baron, who strode through to stand firmly in front of the sec chief. He was dressed in a long robe and, Ryan noted, was barefoot and without any kind of weapon. Confident or stupe— a thin line, perhaps.

"Sir, these people have left their rooms, one of them has left the area and is presumably spying—"

"Has been taken by your men, you mean," Ryan interrupted in a deceptively mild tone.

Schweiz turned back to him, trembling with rage. "Don't try to cover for your activities by moving the blame onto someone else," he snarled.

Interesting, Ryan figured. He might be highly strung and barely holding his impulsiveness in check, but he was more perceptive than he seemed. He would need watching carefully.

"My dear Mr. Cawdor," Arcadian said in a smooth tone, trying to defuse the tension in the situation, "I can assure you that I hold no responsibility on the disappearance of Dr. Tanner. It seems obvious to me that his overwhelming curiosity has got the better of him, and he has wandered off to try to discover more about my collection. It was evident that he held it in great fascination. It says more about the slackness of my men—" with which he shot Schweiz an acid glance that made the sec chief tremble with an even greater rage "—than it does about any intent on his part that he has managed to wander off undetected. All quite innocent, I'm sure. Rest assured, my men will do all they can to locate him, and they will do so in a manner that won't be hostile or threatening…or could be construed as such," he added with a glare at his sec chief.

"Of course, sir," Schweiz said through teeth so gritted that Ryan could almost hear them grinding.

"Doc may spook easily if your boys go after him," Ryan said, casting a meaningful glance at the sec chief, "so mebbe it'd be better if we went looking for him ourselves."

"No, think nothing of it," Arcadian said in an easy tone that was belied by the steel in his eyes. "You don't know the building like my men. It would be easy for you to lose yourselves. Far better if you return to your rooms and get some rest. By the time dawn breaks, your man will be back with you."

"He's one of ours, and perhaps it was wrong of him to wander off like that. Least we can do is sort out our own mess, save you the bother," Ryan explained. It was worth trying, but he could see from the faint flickering of the baron's expression that it wasn't going to work.

"I assure you, Mr. Cawdor, that Dr. Tanner will be found and returned to you unharmed."

He held Ryan's gaze. Finally the one-eyed man said, "Okay, this time we'll do it your way. If Doc wandered off of his own accord, fine. If not…"

"Then I will have to answer your questions. But I can assure you there will be no need. Now…"

The baron turned away, as if dismissing them, and directed the gathered sec to form a search pattern throughout the building, and to relay this to their fellows via the handsets. Ryan noticed that he did this without going through his sec chief, who stood at his shoulder, without even noticing, in truth, that the man was there.

Looking back, Schweiz knew that Ryan was aware of that, and shot him a look of pure venom before following the baron as Arcadian strode off, directing his men as he went. It was noticeable, however, that the sec man who had previously patrolled the landing was now stationed firmly at the head of the corridor.

"He doesn't trust us that much," Krysty murmured.

"He wouldn't," Ryan agreed, "but at least he doesn't think that we were making an organized break."

"Does that matter?" Mildred asked. "You still landed Doc right in the shit."

Ryan shook his head. "No, I don't figure that. Arcadian knows Doc is a loose canon. I reckon he's the one that the baron's most interested in, truth be known. If we'd gone after him ourselves from the start, then it would have looked like we were all in it. Now, he figures Doc is curious and we want to play his game."

Mildred nodded. "Which we do until we find out what it is," she said slowly.

"Exactly."

ANDOWER HAD HIS ARM around Doc's shoulders in a manner that the old man found a little disconcerting. They were walking slowly along the corridor, the sec men eyeing them uneasily. They look very much how I feel, Doc thought. Despite that, he tried to focus on what the self-styled Dr. Andower had to say.

"I must say, when I heard you were coming back here, I was quite excited. Your brief time here only added to the intel that Arcadian had gathered."

"So your baron had an interest in us before we arrived here? How could that be?" Doc questioned.

Andower looked puzzled for a moment. Then an expression of understanding blossomed. "Ah, I see what you mean. No, you misunderstand me, Dr. Tanner. When I say that your presence added to our already existing—well, Arcadian's already existing—intel, you have to understand that this wasn't specifically focused on yourself or your fellow travelers. Although I have to say, you have been both busy and conspicuous over recent times. No, what I mean is this—Arcadian, as part of his plan to reintroduce a civilized manner to these benighted lands, makes it his business to gather information on anything that occurs that may denote a superior mindset at work. Using traders—notorious for their inability to stay silent—or any travelers as a source, along with those forays our own people make, he has built up a not inconsiderable database of information."

In other words, he gathers gossip, Doc thought, though to hear such terms as "database," these days sounded strange to his ears.

"Information about what?" Doc questioned further.

Andower shrugged. "This and that, everything and

anything. Information is the key to the future. If we know what those who surround us are doing, then we're better placed to judge our own actions. If we know of their activities, and the levels that they have reached, we're better placed to know those who may be our allies."

"And those who may be your enemies?" Doc interjected.

Andower pondered that. "Perhaps. Enemy in the sense that they may attack us? I wouldn't consider that. We do nothing at the moment to attract attention to ourselves, and when we do spread the word, then surely it'll be obvious that it's for the good of all. Why would anyone wish to go up against us?"

"Because your notions of good and bad are not the same as theirs, perhaps?" Doc said with a wry smile.

The answer was just as he expected.

"That, surely, isn't debatable. We seek to improve the life of all and to bring a civilized way of living back to the world. Who wouldn't want to partake of that?"

"Oh, you would be surprised," Doc said mildly. Then, before Andower had the chance to lunge into an abstract argument that would tell Doc nothing of any practical use, he added, "So I would assume that part of the purpose in gathering this information is to add to Arcadian's archive of the past. Technology, innovation, advances that were being made in scientific fields before skydark, that sort of thing?"

"Undoubtedly," Andower stated. "The more we find out, the more we can add to our store of human knowledge. There are gaps we can fill in ourselves, of course, and in some senses we have progressed beyond the levels that had been achieved before the nukecaust. But there are still gray areas, and even the barest scraps can sometimes bridge gaps that seemed to be beyond our reach."

"I see," Doc said slowly. "So Arcadian wishes to take the world back to where it was before the sky rained bombs." Despite his desire to know more, Doc found this arrogance starting to irritate. The bile rose in his gorge in a manner that he hadn't known for a very long time. The reason he had felt at home in the ville when they had arrived, the familiarity that was like a comfortable bed into which he could seek, all of this was the flipside to the things that had driven him to the point of madness when he had first arrived in the late twentieth century. And in spite of his wish to know more, he was finding it hard to control his anger. The words nearly choked him as he uttered them.

"He wishes to return things to how they were. To the stupidity that caused this mess in the first place. How, pray tell, can that be a constructive move?"

Andower stopped, astonished at Doc's bitter tone. His hand gripped Doc's upper arm, and although the old man wished to pull away, he was mindful of the sec men watching his every move.

"But my dear Doctor," Andower said softly, in the kind of voice people used for addressing Doc when he was first trawled by Chronos, "of course it is constructive. We aren't bringing the shit from the past. We're cauterizing those wounds, burning out the cancers. Only the useful will survive."

There was such a sincerity in Andower's tone, a kind of disingenuous innocence, that Doc was drained of his anger. By the Three Kennedys, Doc thought, this man truly believed, like the worst kind of zealot, that he was doing nothing but good. His was a type that permeated history with awful deeds that were meant for the best. Doc had read of them when young, and seen them happen in his lifetime, and the lifetime of those who should have lived after him.

His anger was useless. Andower would never see, never understand why Doc held him in such horror and contempt. As that anger flowed out of him, Doc remembered the reason he had begun this mission. It was time to get some concrete facts to take back to Ryan and the others.

"Perhaps you are right," he murmured in what he hoped was a conciliatory tone. "You must understand that in our journeys, the people I am associated with have seen some terrible things that have been perpetrated in the name of human advancement. I may, I confess, have judged hastily."

Andower smiled. It was the smile of the evangelical, believing he had another convert and could close the deal.

"My dear, dear Dr. Tanner, given the things that we know go on in the outside world, and against which we know we have to fight, then your attitude and suspicion are perfectly understandable. Please, let me show you what we are doing here, so that you may have a better grasp on one of the ways in which we hope to improve the world."

Well, Doc thought, at least that saved him having to engineer an opportunity. Ironic that all Andower wanted to do was to give him what he wanted, and his temper almost got in the way and blew away the chance. Doc knew he would have to keep himself in check.

And as that ran through his head, he said, "Nothing would give me greater pleasure. What, pray tell, do you actually do in these buildings?"

"Not just these buildings," Andower said excitedly, guiding Doc along the corridor, through swing doors that led into an adjacent block and then up a flight of stairs. "This whole sector of Arcady comes under my control."

"Ah, you did say something about the heads of different sectors becoming aware of our presence. I meant to ask—"

"But of course, Dr. Tanner, of course. You haven't had the time for Arcadian to really explain to you the full extent of how he puts his theories into action. You see, there are eight sectors within the boundaries of Arcady. Each is kept distinct, though it comes under the central administration of the whole. And each is devoted to following a particular set of sociological, psychological or biological theorems."

"Really?" Doc was a little astounded, if not surprised. That Arcadian should pursue such a course was an obvious step on from the theories that he had espoused to them the previous evening, and certainly made sense of the strange shanty settlement they had encountered on their oblique entry to the ville. But to hear a man in these times calmly use such terms with an assumption that they would be plainly understood was still something that was vaguely amusing, if a little disturbing.

"Oh, indeed," Andower said, starting to slow down.

He also became a little distracted, looking up and down the corridor in which they now stood, as though trying to make a decision. One that, on the face of it, was baffling to Doc as this corridor looked exactly as all the others they had walked through, albeit with doors on both sides, as opposed to windows. They were now well within the interior of one of the buildings. Otherwise, it was anonymous. There were no signs or numbers on the doors to differentiate them. Doc could only assume that Andower was so familiar with this complex—as was his staff—as to need no signposts, which also suggested they had few visitors. Little interference, and no one without an escort.

"And would I be right in assuming—from your attire—that your task in this sector concerns itself with matters biological?" Doc asked, taking advantage of the pause.

"Hmm? Yes, yes, of course," Andower answered, still a little distracted. It gave him the air of a whitecoat about to conduct a particularly unpleasant experiment. Doc had endured many of those, and seen many such expressions. It took an awful lot of self-control to hold himself back.

"So would I be correct in a further assumption that you conduct experiments in the control of breeding? I have noticed, on our travels, that there is a severe problem with in-breeding and the subsequent diminution of the gene pool. And perhaps dealing with mutation—that, too, is a dreadful legacy of the nukecaust," he continued, words running faster. He was beginning to babble, and he wanted to keep control. He bit off the end of the sentence, surreptitiously running an eye over the two sec men to see if they had noticed. They remained impassive.

Andower, for his part, had certainly not taken heed. He had his own concerns. He looked at Doc for a moment blankly, as though lost in thought. Then he smiled beatifically.

"Dr. Tanner, that is only the smallest part of what we do here. I was wondering where I should begin, but I think to truly grasp the extent of our work, there is only one point at which to start. Come with me," he added, beckoning with a crooked finger.

Doc had the most sickening turn of the stomach at what he felt he was about to see, but was powerless to do anything except follow.

"GUESS WE SHOULD MEBBE get some more rest. There's nothing we can do, and I figure that Doc should be pretty safe for the moment. Whatever the stupe old bastard has got himself into, there's little chance Arcadian is going to let him come to any harm yet."

"Yeah, it's the 'yet' that worries me, Ryan," Mildred countered.

Ryan grinned. It was a fair point, but right now they could only sit tight. Arcadian's men were scouring the building, and if they found the old man, there was a next to zero chance they would do anything except handle him with care. Ryan Cawdor had learned to read men pretty well, and he would have bet jack on the baron wanting to keep them sweet for now. When he felt he could put into place whatever plans he might have for them, it would be different. But not yet.

They were gathered in the room that had previously

been occupied by the Doc and Jak. It was too close to sunup to consider going back to their own allotted rooms. Ryan knew that sleep would be an impossibility. But he was keen to keep his people frosty, so that if trouble came they would be up to the task.

"Should stopped him," Jak said grimly. "Stupe fuck it up for all."

"Mebbe not," J.B. mused. "If you had to send someone off to recce, you'd send Doc in this situation."

"How so?" Jak queried, his brow furrowing.

J.B. shrugged. "Everyone can see he's crazy. If he wanders off and we claim it's got nothing to do with us, you'd believe that a whole lot more than if it was me, you, Mildred, Ryan or Krysty. Doc could do anything, face it."

"True enough," Mildred agreed. "Anyone around him for more than ten minutes can see the old buzzard's missing something up here." She tapped her temple. "But they wouldn't figure he could take in as much as we know he can. Who knows, the old bastard might come back with something useful."

Ryan nodded. "That's why I figure he'll come out of this okay. Still wish he hadn't done it yet, though."

Krysty had been listening to them while she stood at the barred and secured window, watching the first rays of the sun pierce the gloom.

"How much trouble can he get himself into?" she asked.

Chapter Ten

Doc felt as though he would vomit.

The room was brilliant white. The walls were freshly painted, as was the ceiling and floor. There was a bed and a chair, both also painted white. The bed had a thin mattress covered in white cloth. On one of the white walls was a screen, also painted white—so much so that, at first, he didn't notice that it was slightly detached from the area behind. The manner in which the two seemed to sway in and out of focus, running together then apart as his eyes tried to adjust, did little except add to his nausea.

But this wasn't the major cause of the sickness that welled up in him. On the chair, sitting upright and staring straight ahead of him, was a man. It was hard to determine his age, as his sallow skin hung in folds from his face, and his emaciated arms and legs poked out of the voluminous white gown he wore, making his body shape and condition hard to determine. He was facing the screen, sideways on to the door where Andower and Doc now stood. He didn't seem to notice their entrance.

Andower ushered Doc into the room, gesturing to the sec men that they remain outside. This would be Doc's chance to snap the neck of the man who repulsed him

so much, yet where would that get him? Still, the urge
was strong as he stared at the seated man, who had still
to notice them. Doc could see, now, that his lips were
moving rapidly in some wordless litany. His eyes were
wide and staring. At first Doc thought that the lids may
be restrained in some way, but when the man blinked
he realized that it was nothing less than the adrenaline
of fear that kept them so wide.

Andower leaned in to Doc, and spoke in a low whisper.

"Some of our work here concerns the behavior of men
and women. Children don't present so much of a problem.
They are easily diverted from any erroneous path and put
back to the right. But when men and women are older,
and have long established patterns of behavior, then—"

"What have you done to him?" Doc asked in a hoarse
whisper, trying to keep his voice neutral.

"The procedure, you mean?" Andower asked, oblivi-
ous. "Ah, now that's a most interesting thing. You'll notice the completely blank canvas upon which the man
is laid? Something that is intended to disorient him. This
way, he has no idea of time and space, and so becomes
more and more isolated and drawn in upon himself.
When there is no stimuli to speak of, then the slightest
change becomes effective. However, that would be a
very long, drawn-out process. Part of our research is to
cut down the time involved, and to make the transition
from savage to civilized that much quicker."

"And how, exactly, do you do this?" Doc's voice
trembled slightly, despite himself.

Andower smiled. It was bland, yet Doc felt it like a
physical blow.

"Like this, Dr. Tanner. Come…"

He took Doc's arm and gently guided him toward the wall at the rear of the seated man. Secreted in the white wall was a small panel, about the size of a man's head. It was so carefully fitted that the line of the panel was only visible as it started to open. Andower displaced it, and then reached in. Over his shoulder, Doc could see that there was a small projector.

"The wiring is in the wall itself," Andower whispered. "See the cones?" With his free hand he pointed to the far corners of the room. Discreet, white-painted cones melded with the white walls, invisible unless indicated.

Doc opened his mouth to speak, but was cut short by the noise that emanated from the speakers as Andower depressed a switch.

Doc immediately felt his bowels turn to water, and it was all he could do to keep control of himself as the low frequencies hit him like punch. He gasped, and then clapped his hands to his ears as the frequencies shifted up to a high, piercing wail that now assailed his eardrums like the buzzing of angry hornets; hornets with needle-sharp stings they were intent on ramming home. No sooner had he done this than the frequencies shifted again. He didn't know which part of his body to protect, although he knew his hands were useless no matter which he chose. It was just an instinct.

Andower seemed to be unaffected, although from the fixed grin on his face as he stared at Doc, it was pretty obvious that he was used to the effect, and so braced for it. Doc wondered how long they could stay in the room.

The sound had changed again. Now it was a pulsing,

insistent throb that trawled the midranges of frequencies, hypnotic and swirling, like the images that were moving on the screen. Doc had to tear his eyes away from them, as he felt his will being sapped. They were strange, shifting kaleidoscopes of color—yet what were the colors? The way that they moved seemed to bleed them one into the other until they formed some strange kind of color never seen before.

As Doc tore his eyes away, he could see that Andower was purposely looking at the doorway, averting his gaze. Had he not warned Doc because he wanted him to be hypnotized? Or merely because he wished him to see the effect and trusted in his own sense to look away?

But Doc couldn't look away completely. He kept glancing back at the man who was seated on the white chair. He was motionless, just as he had been since they had entered the room. Was he taking in anything that was happening to him? Certainly, the sonics had been affecting him. The stench from his vacated bowels, and the pool of urine that gathered at his feet bore testimony to that.

Did this treatment really change his personality? Or did it just wipe it out?

Andower reached into the cavity that housed the projector and flicked the switch. As suddenly as it had started, the noise and the images ceased.

In the sudden glare of the white room, and the almost deafening roar of the silence, where the sound of his own pounding blood filled his ears, Doc felt as though he had been thrown across the room at speed, and an unseen hand had stopped him by thrusting itself into his solar plexus. The force made him fall to his knees, retching as his stomach sought to empty itself.

He felt Andower's hand on his back.

"My apologies, Dr. Tanner. I should have warned you of the force of the treatment. Are you all right?"

Doc shrugged off Andower's hand and pulled himself to his feet, hawking up the last of the bitter taste in his mouth.

"I, sir, will be fine," Doc said shakily. He pointed at the seated man. "But what about him?"

Andower shrugged. "It's too early to say, really. Treatment hasn't been proceeding for long, and there are no conclusive results."

Doc tottered forward on legs still trembling from the sonic assault and circled the…well, what could he be called? Patient? Victim?

However he should be designated, he was still staring ahead blankly, mouthing silently to himself.

"No conclusions?" Doc queried. "Are you sure?"

The irony was lost on Andower. "Until he chooses to speak to us, it'll continue to be uncertain. Now, if you'll follow me," he continued, leading Doc to the door. And, when they were in the corridor, he murmured to one of the sec men, "Hygiene team for this room. Prompt."

The sec man nodded and left them, hurrying down the corridor in the opposite direction to that in which Andower now guided Doc.

The time traveler was still unsteady on his feet, and despite his best intentions found himself leaning on Andower for assistance.

"I should have warned you, I know," the whitecoat

said conversationally, "but I wanted you to experience the full force of our experiment. When it reaches its conclusion, then we'll have a method through which anyone who is recidivist enough not to see the benefit of our systems will soon be able to see sense."

Doc, frankly, felt that the poor man they had just left was nothing more than a vegetable. But he held his tongue.

"Now, Dr. Tanner, that has demonstrated to you the psychological side of our work in this sector. The next example you will see is a reasonable demonstration of how far we have come with the physical side of our work."

Doc felt a wave of panic rise. What foul imagining was this insane man going to show him next? Doc had long since figured Arcadian for a maniac who hid his insanity behind a mask of pseudo-intellectual reasoning. But even he would surely quail at what was happening here?

"Do the other sectors you spoke of operate in such a manner?"

Andower frowned. "I'm not sure I follow you, Doctor."

"This…" Doc waved his free hand, indicating the building around him. Words were hard as his body tried to recover swiftly from the buffeting it had taken in the previous room.

"You mean, our med facilities? No, none of them have anything like this. Only the required standard for any well-maintained ville. Or what we consider to be well maintained, at least. No, Doctor, we're unique among the sectors in that we have little to do with them.

Because of the nature of our work, it is necessary that we maintain some isolation."

"Then the others are not so…radical?"

Andower smiled. Given the nature of the work under discussion, there was something dark and unwholesome about his grin. "Radical…yes, I like that. I suppose we are. Certainly, of all the sectors, we're the ones who I feel are the most forward thinking. Perhaps I should have explained a little better. Each sector is devoted to a particular set of social ideas, theories and experiments. Arcadian has collected these, and when his father was alive he could only discuss them with those of us who were of a like mind. But we all soon realized that discussion wasn't enough. So when he became baron, he decided to divide the greater part of the ville into the eight sectors. The central section would continue as before. The other sectors would each be put under the command of a man best suited to the pursuance of the particular branch of social theory that we wished to explore. Thus, we have sectors that have vastly differing ways of exploring how people live together, and how civilization can be brought to them. We also look at selective breeding in different environments. As you suggested earlier yourself, the problem of small genetic pools and mutation are problems that will take some time and experiment to eradicate."

"How do you keep the sectors apart? And how in the name of the Three Kennedys did he get the people to agree?"

Andower's smile broadened. "Doctor, you should know yourself that people are easily bought if their comfort is assured. Food and shelter are more than many have in these lands. And if there were dissenters, they were soon reeducated. As for the separation of the sectors, why, that's the simple part. The only time they meet is when work details have to be made up of large numbers. Even then they are kept as apart as possible. Each sector is led to believe that theirs is the safest, and to mix would invite nothing but trouble."

"Each sector except this. Here, your people don't mix at all," Doc said flatly.

"No. That wouldn't be possible, given the nature of our work. But now I think we're here."

While they had been talking, and Doc had been struggling to keep up with Andower, they had traversed corridors and climbed stairs so that, by Doc's reckoning, they were on the top floor of one of the buildings. But the plain and winding corridors, with no windows to provide landmarks, were disorientating, and he had no idea if they had traveled into the heart of a complex, or merely doubled back on themselves several times.

Was this deliberate? To keep him from escape? The grim humor of the situation amused him. He was barely able to stand, let alone make any kind of bid for freedom. No, it was more likely to be nothing more than Andower knowing these corridors intimately, and assuming the same from anyone with him.

Typical arrogant whitecoat.

As if to ram home that the type didn't buy the farm with skydark, Andower clapped his hands gleefully, and said, "Now, Dr. Tanner, for the most advanced part of our experimentation. You will be impressed, oh, yes, you will be impressed."

He opened the door in front of which they now stood.

Doc winced involuntarily, expecting the brilliant white of the previous room.

Instead, he was greeted with a darkened room. Subdued, almost opaque light filtered through a heavy shade. It was akin to being in a permanent state of twilight.

"Come, Doctor. There is nothing to be afraid of," Andower said softly, taking Doc by the arm and leading him into the room. Once again, the sec man stayed outside.

The interior of the room was so gloomy that it took Doc a few moments for his eyes to adjust to the low level of light. Once they had, he was able to see that the walls, ceiling and floor of the particular room were painted in the same muted hessian color as that of the shade, keeping the room cool. There had to be some kind of air-conditioning unit in operation, as the temperature was several degrees lower than that of the corridor.

Pushed over into the corner of the room, at the farthest angle from the door, a bed was visible. In it was a huddled form. Blankets and sheeting covered it up to the neck, and these trembled slightly as the figure beneath shook.

"This is a remarkable result," Andower said, leading Doc to the bed. Doc held back, some sixth sense telling him to beware. Yet when he looked closely, the man in the bed didn't have the staring eyes and sagging jaw of the previous room's occupant. His eyes were open, it was true; but they weren't staring blankly. Rather, they flickered around, seeming to take in everything. His hair was slicked back from his forehead, and his nose twitched. He seemed to recognize Andower, and for a moment Doc saw pain and fear cloud his vision. He craned his head back slightly, and then caught sight of Doc.

To Doc's amazement, the man moved his head forward, lifting it from the bed. His mouth twitched and formed shapes: words, perhaps. His eyes glittered, were insistent. Yet all that emerged from the open mouth were strange vowel sounds, mangled and garbled.

"Why can he not speak?" Doc asked.

Andower chewed his lip thoughtfully. "We're not sure. The operation was successful, and he has been alive much longer than any others who have undergone the procedure. My personal opinion is that if he progresses as he has been, then the trauma will pass, and he will once more be able to shape words."

"Procedure…" Doc didn't want to ask—dreaded it—but knew he had to. "What kind of procedure?"

"Hmm?" Andower seemed for a moment to be lost in thought. "Well, it's part of an ongoing program into surgical transplantation. Many good people now die because of rad sickness, damaged limbs, mutations that shorten lifespan. If we can find a way to circumvent this—"

"How?" Doc demanded, his voice firmer, louder now, with an edge to it that required an answer.

"By the transplantation of the healthy parts to a new host. This man had stunted arms, one leg and a flipper, and a lung capacity that was diminished by mutated tissues. He has a brilliant mind, and to lose him for the sake of a healthy host body would have been—"

"I doubt that his mind is brilliant anymore," Doc

murmured. "I fear that you have, as you say, traumatized him to an extent that he has retreated to a place from where there is no return."

"I beg to differ. Time will tell."

"Will it, indeed? And this host that you speak of. What, in the name of all that was once holy, do you mean by that?"

Andower smiled. "Ah, there is the beauty of the process. The host has to be something willing to give up its own life, as such, or at least be unable to register that it is to lose its life. Such things—"

"Things?" Doc spit. "Do you speak of people in this way?"

Andower's smile widened. "People, Doctor?"

Doc's mind was racing. He wasn't sure what to expect. Any number of images and ideas spun through his mind as he reached out—thrusting Andower away from him—and reached for the hessian blankets, pulling them off the trembling figure.

In a sense, what he saw was mundane compared to some of his imaginings, yet the banal obscenity of seeing it in the flesh was somehow far worse than the foulest dream.

The head craned around and stared at him. Was it shame he could see in those eyes? Perhaps a plea to end the suffering? And why not? For the neck was severed at a point just below the Adam's apple, the flesh stitched crudely but well, and ran into the coarser skin and fur of the body to which it was attached. That body was lying on its side, the twitching, rippling the muscles that ran beneath the fur, the hooves jumping in involuntary spasm as the host body tried to meld with the brain that now fed it impulses. Strapping bound it to the mattress so that it couldn't fall, move or injure itself in any manner.

And perhaps to stop the poor enraged half-creature from chilling itself?

Doc would have been violently sick if there was anything left in his gut to spew. Instead, he felt the nausea make his head spin.

"A goat. That is your solution? Rather than let the poor man live out his natural span—because you feel it would be best for you and your baron—this?"

He placed the blanket back carefully, shaking his head, trembling as much as the poor, quivering creature that still stared up at him.

"I am sorry, my friend," he whispered, "I am powerless. Would that I could end your suffering."

"Really, Doctor, I'm surprised at your attitude…" Andower took Doc by the arm and pulled him away from the bed. "Think about what you're saying, the effect it might have on a traumatized patient."

Doc was astounded. Andower really couldn't see the pain in the eyes of his experiment. He truly thought that his actions were for the best. How could Doc argue with that? Mutely, he allowed himself to be led from the room and into the corridor beyond. The sec man closed the door behind them. Once in the corridor, Andower turned to face Doc.

"I'm astounded by your attitude, Dr. Tanner. I would have thought a man such as yourself would know that the road of scientific advancement is littered by signposts leading to the distasteful. Sometimes it is necessary, if we're to find the way forward to a greater future for all. The end—"

"—justifies the means," Doc concluded. "Perhaps that is what you really think. I am not so sure, Dr. Andower, but I am in no position to argue, as you well know." Doc shook his head and sighed. The anger had drained from him, replaced by a despair at what he had seen. "Tell me, Doctor, to what end is this butchery and torture? For that is how it seems to me. Tell me why it is necessary."

Andower looked at Doc as though it was the stupidest question he had ever heard. "Because all the data we build and process, all the failure and all the success, go toward the fulfillment of Arcadian's plans. It's the same with every sector. All experiments, of whatever type, are there to test the theories that have been passed down. From them, Arcadian will synthesize the great answer. The plan, the system that will incorporate the best of the past to forge the best for the future."

"Yes," Doc said, exasperated, "but what is that? What will this plan be?"

Andower answered in a tone of equal exasperation. "That, Dr. Tanner, isn't for me to question. Not for me to think about. I don't have the overall picture. The only one who has that picture, and who can build it, is Arcadian himself. It's only he who can rebuild the world with the perfect social system."

Doc shook his head. In the distance he could hear footsteps. Heavy boots. Had his absence finally been noticed? Had Andower's men notified Arcadian of his presence? Knowing time was now short, he felt compelled to ask one last question, while there was still time.

"The propositions for these experiments—not just yours, but all of them—where has Arcadian got them from? For surely he must know that the ideas of the past were also tested in many cases, and found wanting—"

"No," Andower yelled, anger rising in him, "you don't understand. The baron is a genius, the greatest brain among us, and certainly the greatest in this wasteland we have inherited. He will lead us out of the darkness and into a new age of light. That is the whole point, to take the best of the past and synthesize it into a new whole."

Doc was about to tell Andower that the idea of "best" was a mutable one, even though he knew that it would be of little use, when the doors at the far end of the corridor burst open and four sec men marched toward them. From Andower's expression, Doc could see that their arrival was as unexpected and unwelcome to the sector chief as it was to himself.

"What are you doing in this sector without permission?" Andower questioned angrily. "You know that no one from outside enters unless I have—"

"The baron's direct command," the leading sec man snapped, "countermands everything. You want to take it up with him?"

"No. I—" Andower was at a loss.

"So the baron himself requires me to be returned, eh?" Doc said mildly. "Well, I suppose I should be honored. I know the good doctor here was hoping to pick my brain. Perhaps literally."

The sec leader frowned.

"No matter," Doc said with a wave of the hand. "I

daresay I shall be back here soon enough if I am not careful. Now get me out of here before I feel compelled to vomit once again."

Chapter Eleven

Doc was glad to see the last of Andower—or at least, what he hoped would be the last—but was less than pleased when the sec patrol that had come for him took him straight to the baron. He should have figured that this would happen, but in his relief to be free of the horrors he had seen, he didn't think beyond getting out of this sector as quickly as possible.

The clean lines and tidy surrounds of the buildings took on a sinister mien when considering what went on behind those blank windows, and it was with a shudder that Doc allowed himself to be led away. The sec party surrounded him, so that he was enclosed on all sides by black-clad men armed with blasters.

The sector in which he had found himself was one that was unnaturally quiet. Distant sounds echoed across the early morning skies, but the area in which they walked was silent. "As the grave" was a phrase that popped unbidden into Doc's head as he walked. The sec men had resisted all attempts at conversation, leaving him with nothing but his thoughts. And they were poor company, returning as they did to the things he had seen. The bland facades of the buildings in this sector now resembled nothing so much as mausoleums to his troubled vision.

They reached a boundary line. Fencing, and a small patch of clear ground between the two. It wasn't long past dawn, and the regularly spaced and freestanding lamps that lit this no-man's land had now been extinguished. The low-level buildings beyond were still sleeping, with only the bare minimum of sound coming from their midst. It was too early for the day's work to have truly begun, and too late for the sounds of night. Yet the noise was still in stark contrast to the sector he left behind.

It was hard to tell which of the social models was used in this sector. The buildings gave away no secrets, and there were only a few people to be seen. They eyed Doc and his sec guard with some suspicion, only too glad to slink into shadows until he had passed.

The same was true of the next sector into which they passed, only now—as time was progressing—there was more activity. The people here seemed to move freely, and apart from the fact they were a little more poorly dressed than those in the central sector dealing with trade and ville administration, there seemed to be nothing to distinguish them.

Andower's sector was set apart by the extreme nature of the experimentation, and its clinical nature. That was fairly obvious. Yet for the life of him, Doc could see little in the way of obvious differences between the two sectors he had just traversed, and the one in which the baron lived. And how, indeed, could he reconcile this with the sector in which he and his companions had entered the ville?

Doc had hoped to get some answers with his little recce, yet all he had done was pose a number of further questions for which he was no nearer to any answers. It wasn't much to return with, for all his troubles.

The central sector was awake to the day as they reached the baron's domicile, and Doc's progress elicited some curiosity from those now going about their business. He was relived when they entered the old library. As he was escorted across the lobby of the building and bustled up the staircase, he was amused to note that the door he had used just a few hours earlier had not only had the lamp replaced, but was now secured with a stout padlock to reinforce the lock he had picked with such ease.

That route out was now closed, that was for sure.

Doc had half expected to be returned to his friends, and also to find that they had been taken to more secure quarters. Indeed, he was already preparing himself for Ryan's wrath, and to explain his actions.

So it was with some surprise that he found himself being led directly into the baron's quarters, where Arcadian was waiting for him.

The baron was seated on one of the old chesterfields, seemingly relaxed. He indicated that Doc be seated on the chesterfield opposite. A coffee service stood on a table between them. He dismissed the sec with a gesture, and bade Doc to partake of the beverage. It was only when Doc had drunk half a cup—the baron pouring a cup and taking a sip to prove to Doc that it hadn't been tampered with—that Arcadian began.

"So, Doctor, I understand that you have spoken to my old colleague Andower, and that you weren't impressed with that aspect of my research."

Doc chose his words with care. "I was surprised—

shocked, perhaps—by the nature of the experiments. But I suppose such things have to be carried out if progress is to be made."

Arcadian raised an eyebrow. "That's quite a radical change of opinion, given your comments to Andower. He was, incidentally, a little upset by your reaction, Doctor. He expected more understanding from a man like yourself."

Doc felt insulted by this, but kept his true feelings masked. With a shrug, he said, "You must understand that, during the recent past, I have seen much butchery without purpose. One either becomes hardened, or one has an instinctual reaction before intellect comes to the fore. I have had time to reflect. This is not idle butchery. It has purpose, and if Dr. Andower was in any way offended, then that is unfortunate."

The baron paused for a moment, weighing Doc's sincerity, before continuing on another tack.

"It took my men some time to work out how you effected an escape—"

"Hardly escape," Doc demurred. "I was searching for more of your artifacts from the past, that is all."

Arcadian eyed him wryly. "Searching, perhaps, but not for that alone, I think. But we won't argue about that, Doctor. What I would really like to know is how you were sure about the connection between my palace and Andower's section house. Had you some prior knowledge?"

Doc chuckled. "Were that I was that smart. If so, then I would not have been so easily found and returned. All old buildings of this type have cellars. Cellars that could have housed more from the past. I had no idea that a tunnel system existed, and if I had, then I would have taken my friends with me, and not left them here. I intended to have a look around, then return before I was even missed."

Arcadian nodded, but said nothing for some time. Absurdly, Doc felt that the baron could see right through him, and would think that he was lying. Absurd because, to all intents and purposes, Doc was being straight. He was looking for more than artifacts of the past, but not for a route out.

"Very well," the baron said finally. "You'll return to your companions. I think no real harm has been done. If anything at all, you have done little except to expedite your fate a little sooner than I would have wished."

He clicked his fingers and two sec men, accompanied by Schweiz, entered the baron's chambers. Doc realized that they had to have been waiting throughout the discussion, and when he looked at Schweiz he could see—even though the sec chief's eyes were shielded by his dark glasses—that he wasn't believed.

The sec chief gestured to Doc to move, and with a quizzical glance at the baron, the old man rose. Arcadian wasn't even looking at him. Having summarily dismissed him, he had taken up some papers that had lain at his side, and was now seemingly engrossed in them. Whether this was genuine, or merely to prove a point, it nonetheless left Doc with little choice but to follow the sec chief.

Schweiz led Doc and his two-man guard out of the baron's chambers and toward the area where the companions had been billeted the previous evening. As they approached the corridor housing the rooms, Doc noted that there was now a heavy sec presence both at the end of the corridor and dotted along its length. Two armed men stood to either side of one of the doors.

"This is what you're responsible for," Schweiz said with a heavy attempt at irony and sarcasm. "I bet your friends are real happy about this."

"Perhaps not." Doc shrugged. "But what does it say about you that it just took one old buzzard to outwit all of you?"

His tone may have been mild, but he could see that he had hit a nerve from the way that, even behind the protection of his shades, Schweiz winced. He suppressed a smile.

Without ceremony, the sec chief opened the door of the room and pushed Doc in, slamming it behind him.

"Ah, you may be wondering what I thought I was doing," Doc said without preamble as he found himself facing five people—seated or standing—who were viewing him with a mix of exasperation, relief and anger.

"That would be a good place to start," Ryan said, with what Doc considered to be admirable understatement.

And so Doc began to explain himself, starting with the desire to find out more about Arcadian, an itch that just had to be scratched. He told them about the tunnel, and what he had seen down there. Then he told them about Andower and his experiments. His tone went cold and hard as he described what he had witnessed, yet he tried to keep any kind of judgment out of his account. That could wait, for now. It was more important that he relay, while it was still clear to him, the structure of the sectors as outlined by the whitecoat, and what he had told Doc about Arcadian's motivations. He finished by telling them of his capture, and of his recent audience with Arcadian, including his view of the experiments as relayed to the baron.

"So he thinks that you approve of the way in which he runs things?" Ryan questioned.

Doc smiled and shrugged. "I can only hope that my limited thespian skills were enough to fool him. I felt like he could see through me, but he gave no indication. I feel that may be irrelevant, though. He already had plans for us. All my actions have achieved is the accelerated precipitation of those plans."

"That can't be helped," Ryan said. "It was a stupe bastard thing to do, Doc, and I don't know what you were thinking. But at least we've got a bit more background on what goes on here. And face it, if Arcadian was going to do this shit, better we face it now than later."

"You do not think I have made matters worse?" Doc asked.

Ryan shook his head. "No. I don't think they could get worse as such. All that could happen was that we could suddenly be made aware of just how bastard bad they were. What Arcadian wants to do with us is the trade-off that Toms talked about. He wanted us back here for a reason. Whatever he wants from us, he was going to take it sooner or later. Better sooner. At least we'll know what we're facing."

"We already do, thanks to Doc," Mildred said softly. "And it makes my blood run cold."

"Doc," Krysty said in an equally quiet voice, "you

told us what you said to Arcadian about his lovely little ville, but what do you really think? You're the only one who's seen enough of it to judge."

Doc sighed, rubbed his eyes and looked at them. "I think that, without doubt, Arcadian and his little acolytes have the potential to be the greatest threat to this land since the nukes hit home. I have seen barons who are more bloodthirsty and more prone to meaningless violence. Victims of their own stupidity and emotion. He is not like that, and that in turn is the very thing that makes him all the more dangerous. He is driven not by personal ambition centered on greed, but rather by ideology. True, his ego demands that he think he can achieve this, and he wishes to be feted for it. But that is not what drives him. The chance to build an empire that will bring the world in line with his vision, and to run that world in a way that is *best*—" he spit this latter word with venom "—is the end in itself."

"Then surely such a man can be reasoned with," Krysty reflected.

Doc's laugh was hollow and sad. "Reason is only in the eye of the beholder. To him, anyone who does not agree or see things his way is wrong, and there is no counter to such a belief. He is the worst kind of butcher—at least the other butchers we have seen are powered by nothing more than their animal lusts. They delight in their sport, but have not the sensibility to see that what they are doing is anything other natural. Arcadian, on the contrary, wants to master nature, and brings the intellect of ideas to bear on bending it to his will. Those vile experiments are disgusting, and he knows it. Yet he ignores it in the belief that the end justifies the means. Such a belief is a relentless juggernaut. The sector headed by the whitecoat Andower is the grossest kind of concentration camp."

Mildred caught the bewildered glances of the others, who were unfamiliar with the term and explained.

"Jails and camps where those who were considered inferior—by whatever criteria the madmen controlling them set—were herded together then worked till they bought the farm, were used for medical experiments or were just chilled. To make a better world," she added with sneering irony.

"Succinctly put, my dear Doctor," Doc affirmed. "And I fear that this is what Arcadian has in mind for us. I have little doubt from what Andower said to me that he has some vague ideas—if nothing fully formed—that we have differences to those others who have passed through here. Tales are passed around, of course, but although he probably has no real indications as to the unusual histories of both Dr. Wyeth and myself, still he knows that we have experiences and knowledge that passes beyond the norm. The question is, how will he choose to extract these things?"

Silence fell over the group. They were still seated in the same room in which Doc had been returned to them, but somehow it seemed a different place. The guards outside seemed more ominous. One room, one exit: an army of sec between themselves and the outside world. An outside world that was contained in the center of a ville that they now knew to be surrounded and sectioned off by rings of defenses.

Whichever way it was looked at, this wasn't a situation from which an easy solution presented itself.

It was Ryan who eventually broke the silence.

"This coldheart revels in his little world, and I figure his trade-off with Toms to make us part of it is because he has definite roles in mind for us," he said coldly. "So we need to find out what they are. No way he wants us to buy the farm yet. Wouldn't even chill us if we tried to break out, not unless it was necessary."

"I am not so sure about his chief boy, Schweiz," Doc interjected.

Ryan grinned. "I figure he'd love it, but he's far too scared of Arcadian. We can't break now, so we'll have to bide our time, watch our backs, and wait for the chance."

"If gives one," Jak muttered sullenly.

"He will," Ryan stated. "He wants something from us, even if he's not sure what it is just yet. He's got to give us some rope to find that out. We've just got to make sure we wrap it around his neck, not our own."

J.B. scratched his head, took off his glasses and polished them in a gesture that always denoted he was deep in thought.

"Guess you're right," he said slowly, "though it isn't like the bastard is giving us any choice."

"Won't be the first time we've had to just follow the stream and hope we can pull ourselves out," Ryan concluded. "Best thing we can do now is try to get some rest, so we're ready when it starts."

Easier said than done. Each of them retreated into his or her own private worlds and tried rest in preparation for what was to come. But the not knowing, both in terms of time scale and event, was unsettling. They could face any fight if they knew who or what they were fighting.

But the unknown? How could you prepare for that?

THEY DIDN'T HAVE to wait long. It seemed like days, but was only a matter of a few hours before they heard the door to the room being unlocked. Schweiz appeared in the doorway, flanked by a phalanx of heavily armed men.

"Okay, time for you to move," he snapped. Then a grin split his weasel-thin, unpleasant features. "Arcadian's got plans for you that he wants to talk about. He still ain't had your blasters off you, as a show of faith, but you must know that any attempt to go for them will get you blasted out of the building. And don't think I wouldn't welcome the excuse."

"My dear boy, I would expect nothing less from you. Although I notice you only have the temerity to say it when your lord and master is not within earshot."

Schweiz was fuming as he and his men parted to allow them through, and Ryan shot Doc a warning glance. Arcadian may not want anything to happen to them yet, but Ryan didn't trust the sec chief's temper to hold.

The short walk from the room in which they had been held to the baron's quarters was conducted in an uneasy silence. Schweiz ushered them into Arcadian's presence, then stepped back, flanked by four of his men, so that they maintained a presence that was a respectful distance from their leader, but close enough to act swiftly if any of the companions looked as though they were about to act.

Arcadian was sitting as they entered, leafing through a sheaf of papers. He beckoned them to sit, almost without looking up, then finished what he was doing before lifting his head to survey them in silence. It may have been genuine, but to Doc it seemed like an act designed to unnerve them, to soften them up for what he was about to say.

"So," Arcadian said finally, "I have little doubt that Dr. Tanner has told you what goes on in Arcady. Or, at least, a part of what goes on. He doesn't know the whole of it, as he hasn't seen all of our experiments at work. But he does have some notion of what we're aiming for. I won't bandy words with you, nor seek to be untruthful. I wanted you here, and I'm glad you are here. Your reputations precede you, and give me cause to believe that your skills and capabilities can do little but enhance the progress of my ville as we work toward the perfect society. I want you to work with me, not against me. And I want you to work of your own free will."

"Do we really have a choice?" Ryan asked. "We're here. Surrounded by your sec," he added, indicating the men at their rear.

Arcadian considered this. "You may have a point. Certainly, if you made a break for freedom, it would be simple to stop you. The fact that we found Dr. Tanner proves we can sweep this ville with relative ease. But if you choose to run, then a firefight would only take out some of my men and lead to your demise. After all, we outnumber you too heavily for such an option to be viable."

The manner in which he considered their fate was grimly amusing, but Ryan pressed on.

"So if we say no?"

"Then you'll be held until you see sense. And you will."

Ryan looked the baron in the eye. There was a steel

and ice there that betrayed a will that wouldn't be refused.

"What do you have in mind for us?"

All were curious to hear what Arcadian had to say. With little option other than to go along with him, they would need to make their own plans as soon as possible.

But what they did hear was surprising. With the ville broken up into sectors, the baron proposed to split up the group, so that they would be sent to those sectors in which their attributes would best serve the whole. Jak was to be sent to Sector Three, which specialized in the study of instinctual behavior, and how this may be modified to fit a structured social order. Jak's face didn't change, but a warning sounded in his head. Modification sounded suspiciously like something that would try to force him against his own will and better instinct. Triple red for that.

Doc and Mildred were to be billeted together in the sector dealing with psychological and behavioral experimentation. Doc's momentary relief at not being sent back to Andower and his whitecoat hell was tempered by the notion of brainwashing that went along with the notion of psychological experimentation. He looked across to Mildred, whose own expression was shielded from the baron by her plaits as she inclined her head. Only Doc could see that she was also uncertain. But as their eyes locked for a second, he knew that they were in a better position than Jak, as at least they had each other should the need for backup arise.

Ryan and Krysty were to be sent to that sector of the ville that dealt with selective breeding programs.

"I do this not just because of the superb physical condition that both of you share," Arcadian emphasized. "Some of the people in this sector are muties, like yourself," he directed toward Krysty, "and we're very interested in harnessing certain genetic traits. Also, I feel that your physical prowess can useful in the training of adolescent specimens that need coaching to the pitch of perfection."

It didn't sound the kind of thing that either of them felt comfortable with; it did, however, betoken a certain amount of physical freedom that could be turned to their advantage.

Which only left J.B. After expressing how difficult it had been to place him according to his talents, the baron merely stated that he would be positioned where it was the most appropriate. His failure to be more explicit was noted by all of them. J.B. fought hard not to let his concern show, but feared he may be getting the rawest deal in terms of immediate danger.

"Now, as you agree to my terms, Schweiz and his men will allot you to your new quarters. I hope our work together will be productive," Arcadian said before dismissing them by dint of returning to his papers.

As they followed the sec out of the room, all thought the same thing—no matter which sector they were in, their first move would be to find a way of keeping in contact with the others.

Question was, how hard would that prove to be?

Chapter Twelve

They were given no chance to communicate before they were separated. The sec that flanked the companions were joined by Schweiz as they moved down the staircase and into the lobby of the old building, guided through the display cases by the sec chief as he indicated that more of the heavy guard swarming the building be added to the group. Any attempt to speak was silenced by the barking of the sec chief, who was obviously relishing the power given to him by the baron. They had to endure the stares of those who worked on the ground floor of the building. It was a small thing, but to be viewed like caged animals rankled all the more because they could do nothing about it.

It was only when they were at the open space in front of the huge double doors that Schweiz stopped them. Quickly and efficiently, eyeing all the while their weaponry and their stance, he separated the group into its constituent parts of two duos and two singles, allotting to each a small sec party.

"This is where you get to say your goodbyes," he said to the still assembled group. "If I was sector leader, I'd take those bastard weapons off you as soon as you arrive. They have the authority. While you're still in this sector, then Arcadian has the final say. I'd give you no chances. He might take your compliance at face value, but I don't. So this is where you part company, and we take you to your sectors." Then, as he could see that the friends were about to communicate, he held up his hand and added, "Hey, guess what, people? I changed my mind. Take them out."

Before they had a chance to actually speak, the sec guards assigned to them muscled them apart. Jak bridled visibly, but a subtle gesture from Ryan stayed him. Time for that later. Right now, they were outnumbered. They would have to allow it.

Schweiz followed onto the steps of the building while the four groups of outlanders and sec parted company.

"You have a nice time, you hear? Don't forget to write. Nah, mebbe just don't bother."

The sec chief was enjoying his moment of power. Each of the companions filed it away for the future. For when they had a chance to gain revenge. Right now, it was more important to look ahead to where they were each headed.

The ville was in the middle of a usual morning— trading and business as on any day. But the sight of four sec parties separating and leading—what, prisoners? Guests?—through the center of the ville brought it to a standstill, just as the previous day, when the group had been led in en masse. The center of the ville came to a momentary standstill while the citizens viewed the strange sight. They were the lucky ones. In this central sector, whether by luck, selection or a combination of both, they were subject to less in the way of experimentation and subjugation. Perhaps there wouldn't be that luxury in the sectors that the separated companions were headed.

From the center of the ville, the four groups parted, each headed in a different direction out of the main square. With just the barest of glances back, all that was allowed to them by their sec escorts, they headed off to their respective fates, hoping that the chance to establish lines of communication would arise, and that escape could be planned.

If not, then what?

JAK COULD BARELY CONTROL his temper. It was as if his skin itched with the frustration that boiled in his veins. His natural instincts—the ones that he was aware were about to be tested in some way—told him to make a break. His rational mind told him that that would be stupe. But the thought of being constrained and experimented on rankled. Never the most garrulous of people, Jak now kept a silence that wouldn't be broken.

Not that the sec men leading him through the center of the ville showed any sign of wanting to strike up a conversation. They barely looked at him, except to check that he wasn't readying himself for an escape attempt. It gave Jak a chance to concentrate on the route they took. He had already worked out that the roads in this part of the ville ran on straight lines, intersecting at right angles. It was a very neat, very old piece of construction, and the change in buildings from the three-story center of the ville through the two- and single-story buildings that radiated out gave him plenty in the way of landmarks. The people milling the streets thinned out, and those who did pass by weren't inclined to stare.

In a short while they reached a gated fence, with a strip of empty land separating it from another fence. The buildings on the far side differed little.

"Sector Three," the lead sec man intoned, looking at Jak for the first time. "Your new home, boy. Better settle in. It'll be easier for you."

There was note in his voice that intrigued the albino youth, almost as if he felt uncomfortable with the situation. Were there many that harbored that feeling? It wasn't important now; it may well be in the near future.

They passed through the gate, using the well-trodden path. Once again Jak wondered if the fence was booby-trapped in some way, or if the land that lay on either side of the path was mined. Could it be, as they had all wondered earlier, that the barriers between the sectors were as much psychological as physical? If so, then it was the strength of the sec force in each sector that could determine the difficulty of escape.

As this passed through Jak's mind, they marched through the sector. Although the buildings were similar to those on the other side of the wire, it was much quieter. There were far fewer people on the streets, and those who were seemed subdued, pointedly not looking at the sec party as it passed, as though punishment would follow if any dared.

A people cowed and frightened didn't say much for any of the baron's experiments if Jak was any judge. But he would find out soon enough. They wheeled right, and Jak found himself standing in front of a building that looked much like the ones that surrounded it on either side: brick built, scarred by the rigors of skydark, but rebuilt much like those around it. With one difference, perhaps: this building had opaque glass windows, behind which—Jak guessed as he couldn't see—were bars or guards of some kind. It was bland, and apart from the opacity said nothing about what may occur within. But a cold prickling on his scalp told him that it wasn't a good place. It had a smell about it that differed from the buildings on either side. He couldn't identify the precise elements of that smell, but knew that they added up to nothing that was good.

As they came to a halt, the doors of the building opened and three men walked out. One was a black-clad sec man, with a Lee Enfield .303 longblaster slung over his shoulder. The other two were dressed normally, but carried with them an air of authority. The smaller of the two, a slight and balding man of greater age, peered at Jak short-sightedly, his head craning forward as he halted at the top of the three steps that led to the entrance.

"Hmm, I think he's everything that we've been led to believe, Pulaski," he said in a voice as cracked and desiccated as his skin.

The taller, heavier-set man who had gray-streaked hair brushed back from his forehead and a thick beard that obscured the bottom half of his face, grunted.

"You say so, Foxx. I say we test him first, get some accurate readings, before we start any procedures."

"Well, okay. Though I don't think you'll find it necessary. Still, if you must be a stickler."

Jak didn't care much for the way that they spoke about him as though he wasn't there. Even when they turned away and walked into the building, they gave no indication that he should follow. It was only when the sec man beckoned to him with the barrel of his rifle, and his guard stepped back, that he realized what they wanted from him.

"Good luck," the lead sec man muttered under his breath in a tone that was sardonic and tinged with sorrow. Jak frowned, and briefly glanced at him. The sec man's face was impassive, but the voice had been unmistakable.

Without looking back, Jak walked up the steps and in front of the sec man from the sector building, who held the door back for him to enter. He realized that the building was soundproofed when the door shut with a hiss, sealing out the world beyond.

Inside, the corridor ahead was lit in a fluorescent glare. There were no windows along this passage, only a succession of doors. The sec guard prodded Jak without a word. As the two men who had greeted him were some distance ahead, passing through the double doors at the end of the corridor, his meaning was clear. Jak quickened his pace. There was little he could do at the moment except follow and discover their intentions.

Through the double doors and a sharp right brought him to an open set of double doors, inset with glass. Pulaski and Foxx were already busy, preparing a series of wires and cables that were linked to an old, blue-gray metal console. Speakers were positioned around the room, at different angles and heights. The console was at one end of the room, and at the other stood a screen, currently blank. As Jak entered, the smaller, older man looked up.

"Ah, here he is." He beckoned Jak to the chair, moving over to it with a bundle of wires and pad terminals in his free hand. "Come, my friend, there's nothing for you to worry about. I wouldn't bother with this process myself, but Pulaski is a stickler for precision from the very start. This won't take long, and it won't hurt."

Jak kept his usual impassive visage, but some involuntary twitch of a muscle had to have betrayed him.

Foxx smiled and said over his shoulder. "You see, Pulaski? He doesn't trust us. This will surely affect your precious readings. Reflexes and instincts, time distorted by fear and mistrust. Only a practical situation gives a true reading. Only when we get this young man out there on the ranges will we have a true idea. But still, if you must have your precious data."

Jak figured from what the old man said that this part would be simple, and wouldn't threaten him in any way. Fine. Submit to that and let them think he was compliant, at least for now.

But he didn't like the sound of the thing—whatever it may be—that they called "the range."

As THEY CROSSED the wire and found themselves at their intended destination, the first thing to strike Ryan and Krysty was the manner in which the people of this sector were working. Lots between the old and rebuilt dwellings had been flattened, and were being used as areas for grain and vegetable cultivation. Scattered around the lots, either bent over the earth or almost hidden by the height of the crop, were a number of people. Men and women alike, all looked as though they were in good health, and at the peak of physical condition. Toned and muscled, with no flab in sight. All were fairly tall—the variation in height was noticeable by its absence.

However Arcadian put his theories about selective breeding into operation, at first glance it appeared to be bearing fruit. By comparison, their sec guard seemed to be misshapen and mismatched.

As they were marched toward the center of the sector, the people milling around on the streets were also of a uniform height, musculature and fitness. Sure, some of them were dark and some blond; some were black, some of Native American descent and some Caucasian; some were broader than others, who tended toward a more wiry build. But within this range of types, the common features suggested not just breeding programs, but regimes of training that were designed to aid nature to maximum effect.

The passersby eyed Krysty and Ryan speculatively. It was unsettling, as there was no hostility or even curiosity in their glare. It was more a kind of assessment that made Krysty wonder just what was in store for them. The way in which they were coolly studied made Ryan aware of his scar and missing eye. These people were perfect physical specimens in every way, or so it seemed. As was Krysty. As was Ryan himself, except in that particular area. He wondered if that would mark him for trouble when they were let loose in this sector. It wasn't a genetic fault, but rather one made by man. Nonetheless, it set him apart from the others, even Krysty.

However, no one spared them much beyond an initial glance. They seemed too busy to spare the time. What their activities may be, beyond those they had already witnessed, they could only wonder.

When they reached the center of the sector, they found themselves in front of a three-story building that stood out from those around it. A vacant lot on either side was left barren, which was unusual in comparison to all else they had seen. The reasons why would no doubt become clear in time. Through the windows of the building, as they looked up, they could see that there were whitecoats walking around, engaged in unknown tasks. There were also men and women stripped to the waist or in very little, some of whom seemed to be running on the spot. Others flashed back and forth in front of the windows, engaged in some kind of unspeci-fied and, from this remove, unfathomable activity.

They were expected. A tall, sun-bronzed man stood alone in front of the building. His hair was lustrous and wavy, brushed back from his forehead. He wore a short-sleeved shirt that emphasized his well-developed biceps and pecs, and his pants were pulled in tight at the waist by a belt, as if to emphasise the development of his upper body as opposed to the slimness of his lower. It was only as they got closer that part of the reason for such obvious vanity became apparent. His sun-bleached hair was heavily streaked with gray, and his face was lined, the skin wrinkled at his eyes and neck. He may have had the physique of a young man, but his face betrayed that his real age was much greater.

"Took your time getting here," he said in a loud, hearty voice, stepping forward to greet them. "You boys can fuck off now, we don't need you here," he said dis-missively to the sec escort.

Ryan noted that they complied without rising to either the explicit or implied insult, turning and leaving without a word. The man had an absolute authority. He clapped the one-eyed man on the shoulder.

"Good to have you here," he said in the same exuberant tones. "I'm guessing that you mebbe weren't a hundred percent convinced of this move—I know it's hard to adjust to what we're doing here, as it's unique, right?—but you'll soon see that we're onto something." He extended his other arm so that it encompassed Krysty's shoulders before continuing. "Listen, you need to freshen up, see where you're going to be billeted, then I'll take you on the grand tour and fill you in on where I see you fitting in. One thing—I'd rather you lose those," he added, inclining his head to indicate their blasters. "We don't carry weapons in this sector, and we don't have a sec team like the others. We look after ourselves here, and if we have a problem we use our bare hands to sort it out. That okay with you? Hell, sure it is."

With which, and without bothering to wait for an answer, he swept them toward the building. Once they were inside, he stopped at a door on the left. Kicking it open, he ushered them through the doorway, only taking his arms away from them when it became impossible for them all to pass through together.

"Tod," he boomed in the same tone. It was as though, Krysty thought, he had only the one setting. "Hey, Tod," he boomed again when the man with his back to them didn't immediately answer.

"Alex, I'm actually busy." The man sighed, turning to face them. He scanned them quickly, but Krysty caught more than curiosity in the way he looked at her. "These the new ones sent to us by the baron?"

It was a rhetorical question, and Alex treated it as such. He continued as though Tod hadn't spoken.

"Get those weapons off and give them to Tod, here. He'll make sure they're safely filed away."

"That's me, the original keeper of the keys," Tod added humorously, though both Ryan and Krysty were at a loss to the joke.

Figuring that they knew where their weapons would be if they needed to retrieve them, and that they wouldn't be at a disadvantage if everyone in the ville was unarmed, they handed over their weaponry. For Ryan, he felt almost naked without the Steyr, the SIG-Sauer and the panga. But he kept his scarf, hoping that neither Alex nor Tod would notice how the ends seemed weighted. Krysty unholstered her blaster and handed it over. Alex made to take it from her, but Tod was quicker. His hand brushed against hers as he took possession of the Smith & Wesson, and she could feel the energy coming from him.

Selective breeding programs, Arcadian had called them. She had no wish to be part of any such thing, but she could see that perhaps Tod had other ideas.

While the younger man made a note of the weaponry in a ledger, then filed it away in a cabinet that he locked with a key that came from the top left-hand desk drawer, Alex extended his arms again, as if to gather them in before sweeping them from the room.

"Now then, Tod here is busy, like he said. This sector doesn't run itself, and I don't know what I'd do without him—"

"Exactly what you did before I started, Alex. Rely on someone else," Tod said with that humorous tone again; except this time, Krysty was sure she detected an edge of malice. She did some filing herself. It could be a useful piece of information.

If the older man had noted that, he made no indication as he led them out into the corridor.

"Now then, let's not waste time on settling you in. What we do here is develop a population that aims at a peak of physical fitness and development. You've traveled, and you know that the major problem with a lot of the land that lies beyond our ville is that it's physically suspect. Mutations, deformities, weakness, an inability to develop what has been given and make it better. A weakened body leads to a weakened mind, and then the two start to feed off each other, eating into each other so that you're left with nothing but decay, moral, physical and mental. I'm betting that could sum up what you've seen out there. Am I right?"

"I guess you could put it that way," Ryan answered, weighing his words with care.

"Damn right I'm right," Alex snapped. "If people are born with weakness in the body, then they can't help that. But they can be taught that it can be improved upon with mental effort. At the same time, if you get people to that peak, and you take people that have attained that naturally, and you put them together, then you start to develop a strain of humanity that doesn't have the weakness inherent. That's what we're doing here, in essence. Putting together people like that, and also keeping them to their peak, so that the attitude becomes in-bred in them."

In-bred is right, Krysty thought. Especially if you have a small gene pool to begin with. But seeing as she suspected that their presence was partly to help prevent that, she held her peace for the moment.

"Now then," Alex continued in a manner that was beginning to rankle, "let's show you what we do."

He took the stairs two or three at a time, seemingly effortlessly, and intended in part to demonstrate his fitness and test theirs. Determined not to be bested, they followed at his pace. He flung open a door and gestured that they look in. Five people—two men, three women—were running on treadmills while a man and a woman in lab coats monitored their speed and distance on dials fitted to the mills, noting the results on clipboards.

"Endurance. Lung capacity. Muscle strength. Now follow me," he said, before closing the door and running down the corridor and up another flight of stairs.

Krysty and Ryan were at his heels when he stopped and opened another door. Inside, the room was padded on the walls and floor. Four men and two women were engaged in hand-to-hand combat, with seemingly no quarter. Once again, to the side, were a man and a woman in lab coats, making notes on clipboards.

"Reactions, aggression, the desire to win. Speed and efficiency. Survival of the fittest isn't just brute strength, my friends. Cunning and the ability to think with the lightning speed of your reflexes is also important. But from what I hear, I don't need to tell you that."

He slammed the door and was off again, sprinting ahead and up to the top story, Ryan and Krysty close on his heels. Another corridor, another door. But this one truly stopped them in their tracks.

Observed by two men with the obligatory clipboard,

two couples were mating. There was no other word for it. They were coupled with no passion or tenderness, like livestock brought together for the sole purpose of reproduction, watched dispassionately as though by herdsmen. Two hard beds housed the couples. The men were on top, both pumping to a regular rhythm, while the women lay underneath. Occasionally, the right physical connection would cause a gasp or groan, but this wasn't reflected in the serious and almost bored mien of the women.

One of the men gasped as he reached the point of no return, then waited for a moment before climbing off his partner. The woman made to move, but was stayed by one of the lab-coated men, who put down his clipboard and indicated that she tilt her pelvis, so that she was raised up. He timed her on a stopwatch, then nodded his consent that she lie flat once more. While this had occurred, the other man had also climaxed. His departure was followed by a similar procedure from the other lab-coated observer.

"Every step is taken to ensure a successful coupling," Alex barked. "A good result is paramount, as you will find out."

Krysty thought of the expression on Tod's face and gave an involuntary shudder. They would have to move fast. She had no intention of having to find out.

For Doc and Mildred, there wasn't even the chance to see the sector headquarters, as they were interrupted in their passage by two women and a man who approached them from a side street.

"Wait," commanded one of the women, in a voice

that was shrill yet contained a note of authority. The sec guard immediately brought the party to a halt and stood silently while the woman approached and circled. She sniffed the air around them, then stepped back and said over her shoulder, "An interesting proposition? Yes, I think so."

She beckoned her two companions forward. While she was dressed in black-and-white-check squares that resembled nothing so much as a chess board, her fellow female was in a spiral white on black—or it may have been the other way around—that drew the eyes in and disoriented if looked at for too long. Especially as it rippled when she moved. Doc, for one, found this to be the case, and he had to look away before nausea welled up in his throat.

The two women walked around, sniffing the air, craning their heads between the bodies of the sec party, so that with bizarre pecking motions they appeared to be almost attacking Doc and Mildred, who were trapped in the middle. They said nothing. Mildred glanced at Doc, one eyebrow raised quizzically. He smiled briefly, gave an even briefer shake of the head. Whatever was going on, they had to keep their nerve and their peace for the moment.

The women were an odd sight, in their monochrome-patterned clothes, the checkered woman short and thin, the spiral woman tall and fat. Even their flowing hair conformed, as the fat woman was jet-black, whereas her companion was gray almost to the point of being white.

Then the man, who had been lurking at the threshold of their orbit, stepped in. In contrast to the stark monochrome of his companions, the strawberry-blond man was dressed in clothes that had been tie-dyed in a variety of clashing colors.

"Fuzebow. Darlang. Kitta-kitta. Bwoow. Nit-nit-nit. Darlap? Darlang."

"This where they keep the crazies, then?" Mildred asked mildly. "Or is this some kind of test? 'Cause I'm telling you, people, if it is, then it's kind of tedious."

"Especially the phonetic poetry. I always thought that was terrible idea, although I must confess I know little about it," Doc added.

The three bizarrely dressed interlopers stepped back.

"They're good," the fat woman said grudgingly. "Whether they can keep it up, it's for real, or they're just bluffing is another matter."

"Even if they're just using bluff, it still shows a re-markable composure. Did you note the complete lack of surprise when we appeared? I would have expected a flicker of shock," the man mused. "It is, after all, a usual response. Perhaps, then, we can say that they aren't good, in the sense that they don't fit the usual range of responses."

"There was a look between them," the thin woman said, addressing the man, but still looking squarely at Doc and Mildred. "So I'd say that they were actually surprised by our appearance—both literally, and in its suddenness—but they have learned to control reac-tions."

"To meld the instinct and the rational," the man said with an inclination of the head. "Have they been sent to the right place, then?"

"We'll have to see," the fat woman said with a more decisive tone. She addressed the sec guard, who had remained impassive throughout. "You can leave us. We'll take it from here." Then, as they turned and marched away, she held up a hand to forestall the question that she could see forming on Mildred's lips. "I know. They didn't react, so why should your reaction, which was a little different, be remarkable compared to theirs. Simple—the same sec personnel are always deputed to escort newcomers to this sector. They are trained for the purpose, so that they don't affect the reactions of such as yourself with their own. You see?"

Mildred shrugged. "That answers that, I guess. But it's far from the only question I have."

"I'm sure it is," the thin woman said. "All will become clear to you in time, if you have the wherewithal to comprehend. But that, of course, is part of the reason you are here."

"Is it?" Mildred said slowly.

"Oh, yes. This sector may resemble almost all the others in the outward appearance of the buildings, but what goes on behind those doors—and indeed, out in the open in some cases—is far from similar."

"I'm sure," Mildred said flatly.

Doc, meanwhile, had been studying the terrain around them. Like most of the ville, there were a collection of buildings either intact, repaired or rebuilt in the style of the days before skydark. The sidewalks and roads were empty. No traffic. No people except themselves.

"Do you, perhaps, have some kind of personnel deficiency in this sector?" he asked mildly. "Perhaps a drought of people who may live up to your expectation and needs?"

"Ah," the fat woman said, nodding, "sarcasm as a defense mechanism. Interesting."

"Sarcasm? Yes." Doc shrugged. "Defense? No, I would not say so myself. More a reaction against boredom. Games never much interested me, and you seem to be keen on them. I'd rather know what we are here for. And, of course, why the streets are so empty."

The blond man stepped across and put an arm around Doc's shoulders. He ignored the old man's attempt to shrug it off.

"To take matters in reverse order. The streets are empty as the people who live in this sector are all engaged, either inside or in the play area. As for your first point… Well, Dr. Tanner, I'm afraid you'll have to get use to games. One of the first things man did was learn to play. Play expresses all the desires and fears of man within safe confines. It allows us all to express ideas and work out dilemmas without harm to one another. It is how we learn, and how we can change."

Was it Doc's imagination, or was there something about the intonation of that last word that caused him alarm? He decided to keep his peace for the moment, and to keep his face poker-straight.

"Now, come with us," the man said more briskly, "and you will see something of what we do here."

"You will be allocated quarters shortly," the fat woman added in her shrill tones. "But first, it would be useful for you to see something of our work, and the work to which you are expected to contribute."

"Useful for who?" Mildred asked.

No answer was forthcoming. Instead the three bizarrely dressed people moved off, leaving Doc and

Mildred standing. Figuring that part of the process—whatever that may prove to be—was about working out what was expected from them and adjusting accordingly, they followed without a word.

The trio set them a brisk pace, and it was only a short while before they had navigated the maze of side streets that led to an open space that extended over a vacant lot the size of one block. Around the edges sat a number of men and women of varying age and race, paired on benches across from each other, a table between each of them. The center of each table was carved in dark and light woods, forming a permanent board. The pairs were poring over carved pieces that were laid out on the squares. Although Doc and Mildred could see, as they passed, that the carvings varied from primitive to ornate, indicating that they had been cobbled together or made however was possible. But there was no mistaking what they were.

"Chess?" Mildred couldn't help but express her surprise. "It's been a long time since I saw a chess set, let alone see people play like this."

She realized as soon as she spoke that she had said too much. Doc shook his head, brow furrowed, but it was too late. Their guides to this sector were too sharp.

"You have seen such things? Where? Where else do they play like this? We believed it was only in predark times that people gathered in this way to play chess." The fat woman was shrill and insistent.

Mildred shrugged. "It was a while ago—shit, where was that? We've traveled so much, that—"

"Why do you value chess, of all games, so highly?" Doc interrupted, trying to pull her out of the hole.

"Because of its logical progression. The mental exercise in assessing possibility and chance. The way in which it encourages you to assess the psychology of your opponent, to think in lateral ways as well as logical. It is the perfect mental training." The thin woman took responsibility for answering, but it was apparent from the way that she was looking at Mildred as she spoke that she was as intrigued as her colleague.

"That's very interesting," Doc replied mildly. He doubted, for himself, that a game could fulfill those functions. But their belief was perhaps very telling.

"Don't think you have distracted us," the man said softly, "but it can wait. First, we want you to see this." He beckoned them to quicken their pace and follow.

Threading between the tables and the players, who seemed barely to register their presence, so intent were they on their games, they made their way through to the middle of the open space. While all around was sparse grassland, this center section was made of concrete. It was set out in a series of squares, intersected with zigzag lines. Circles lined the outside of the board-marked ground, and were dotted across the squares and zigzag lines at intervals that seemed at first glance irregular, but were in fact based upon a 2-1-3 dispersal pattern. The lines were painted red and blue, the squares black and white, and the circles were yellow.

The board was square, and at opposing ends were four chairs, raised up to six feet above the ground, reached by ladders. Each chair was inhabited: two men and two women, each with a megaphone. There were sixteen people acting as living pieces, moving on the board at the command of the seated players. The sixteen people were all dressed in orange, and if they were divided into teams, it was hard to see how they could be differentiated.

"How do they know which belongs to who?" Mildred asked.

"Perhaps they are divided by whether or not they move on the lines, the circles, or the squares," Doc pondered. He glanced at their guides, who were watching intently. "I suspect our ability to work this out will tell them much," he added in an undertone.

"Great," Mildred muttered sardonically, "'cause that guy's just moved from circle to line, so it's not that."

"But what is the aim?" Doc wondered, stroking his chin. "Are they attempting to move the 'pieces' from one side to the other?"

"You mean, the players are competing to control the pieces, and that's determined by the number of places they move before collision?" Mildred pondered as two players appeared to collide. But then one of the seated players directed them to move apart.

"And why do they keep saying that?" Doc wondered.

Mildred hadn't been listening closely to what the players had been yelling through the megaphones, as it had mostly been distorted instructions. But as she listened closer, she realized that they kept repeating one phrase.

"Have you got it yet?" she whispered. "No, I haven't. And you know what?"

"Neither have they," Doc answered with a chuckle. "There are no rules as such, just a set of fluid motions based around the parameters of the board. Each time one of them seems to guess what the other is doing, then that person changes the rules in order to outfox the others."

"So it could go on forever," Mildred said with a shake of the head.

"Certainly until they run out of invention, or the ability to outguess the others," he said.

"Splendid," the fat woman shrilled, clapping her hands. "You've worked that one out a whole lot quicker than is usual. Now, I think, you should see where you are staying. Please, follow us."

As their guides led them away from the board, where the orange pieces still moved haphazardly at the behest of the players, Mildred muttered from the side of her mouth, "Ever hear that old saying about the lunatics taking over the asylum?"

"Indeed," Doc muttered in return, "though in such a case I should feel well and truly at home."

"No, Doc, you're just crazy. These bastards are completely mad…and that's what I'm worried about."

J.B. FELT HIS HEART SINK and a blackness descend on him. The unwillingness of the baron to detail the sector in which he would be placed had made him expect something that wouldn't be an easy ride. Considering the overall situation, that was an understatement. And now his worst fear had been confirmed.

As the sec guard marched him through the center of the ville, he recognized the route only too well. They crossed one boundary line into another sector, and for a moment he wondered if his worst fears weren't to be confirmed, and he would perhaps be billeted in this sector. The hope was soon shattered as the sec continued at the same pace. He watched the sector pass him by, and as they reached a second boundary line, he knew where he was headed.

They crossed the line into the sector where J.B. and his companions had first entered the ville.

The shanty ville seemed even more bizarre and sorrowful now that he knew that it was part of an experiment. At least that finally explained the mix of squalor and cleanliness that had been so confusing. The shambling idiocy of the people they had met was emphasized for J.B. by the way that some of them stared, open-mouthed, while others asked one another in loud voices and simple words if he was the man they had seen yesterday, and where were those who had been with him. They were disingenuous in a way that was both alarming and frightening.

Why the hell had he been brought here? What was in store for him?

The sec guard took him through the ville, scouting the area where he and the others had been captured previously. They were headed for another part of the sprawling and ramshackle sector. As they progressed, J.B. looked over his shoulder and saw that a group of dwellers followed in their wake. Like the last time he had met them, they were keeping back, a mix of curiosity and fear driving them on.

They came to a shack that was a little better constructed than the others. It was also better maintained. Where the others looked as though they could be demolished with ease, this one had a more sturdy air. J.B. knew that this had to be where the sector leader was billeted, a feeling confirmed by the way in which the group at their rear fell back, as if in awe. The sec guard halted, and one of them stepped forward, disappearing into the black maw of the shack's open doorway.

After a wait in which J.B. wondered what was occurring, he came out. Even though he was trying to keep his visage unreadable, still a faint wrinkling of disgust could be detected. It was even more apparent in the cracking of his voice as he said, "You go in now."

J.B. looked around. The sec guard had parted to allow him to pass through. Hesitantly, he took a few steps that took him past the sec man who had been inside.

"You be careful," the sec man whispered.

The Armorer paused, looking at him with something approaching bewilderment and amazement.

"You'll see," the sec man added in the same undertone. With which he moved back toward the rest of the guard. They turned and walked away, scattering the sector dwellers in front of them.

J.B. watched them, chewing his lip thoughtfully, then turned to the open doorway. Under the bright midday sun, the doorway lurked like a pitch-black shadow. A ripple of apprehension fluttered in his stomach, and he could feel the adrenaline begin to flow. Purposeful, he stepped into the black.

The heat of the day outside gave way to a more humid kind of heat. The air was thick and sticky with moisture and the smell of burning spices. They were obviously intended to mask the smell of sweat and decay that permeated the atmosphere. They failed. J.B.'s gut lurched, but he bit down hard on the metallic taste that sprung from his throat. He could hear breathing: one, two…at least three people, maybe four. A woman's voice giggled, high and nervous. His eyes began to adjust to the gloom, and he could make out shapes, but little more.

"You can't see. Your eyes are dimmed by more than the lack of light."

The voice was dull, flat, and yet carried within it an almost mocking undertone. It was coming from the center of the room, and as J.B. squinted through his glasses he could make out the shape of a man, his torso flowing into an amorphous shape. Another high-pitched giggle revealed the reason—a woman was draped against him on one side, for sure; perhaps another, to judge from the symmetrical flow of shadow.

The air was growing heavier, not just from the tension, but also from the musk that was growing stronger the longer that he stood in the shack.

"Give the man some help," the voice said in the same flat tone. As an almost immediate response, a light flickered on the left-hand periphery of J.B.'s vision and the glow spread across the room. He turned his head and could see that there was a fourth person in the room— an emaciated woman who was far from the first flush of youth. She was kneeling, naked except for a cloth that was wrapped around her waist. Her breasts were empty dugs that hung pendulously as she leaned over the hurricane lamp, flopping against her rib cage with a hollow smack as she sat back on her calves. She looked at J.B. with a hollow stare, then smiled toothlessly. She reached down beside her and picked up a scrawny dog that she clutched to her.

J.B. looked away as he heard movement. The man

had shifted from his position on the ground, rising and leaving the two women who had been draped over him. They were both naked. One was fat, with greasy blond hair that cascaded over her large breasts, but didn't cover the rolls of fat on her stomach and hanging over her bare pubis. She looked up at the man as he rose, and giggled again. Her expression was as vacant as the sound she made. The other woman was smaller, but was still chubby. She had dark hair, chopped short, and she was looking directly at J.B. with an expression that could have been curiosity, but was possibly lust.

The man was tall and well-muscled. He had a narrow face, cavernous cheekbones and deep-set eyes sinister in the heavy shadow. His eyes bore into J.B. He was naked apart from a brief pair of ragged shorts, his chest tattooed in unfathomable patterns. He was still standing on the rush mat that covered the dirt floor. Behind him, at the rear of the hut and barely visible, was a filing cabinet that seemed out of place in the dirt shack. More in tune, yet unnerving, was the pile of animal skulls that lay against one of the shack walls. Hangings of primitive paintings depicting hunting of animals and men lined the walls.

The man stepped forward so that he was directly in front of the Armorer. He inclined his face downward, being half a head taller, so that he was bearing down, his breath hot on J.B.'s cheek.

"You're the one they sent me," he murmured. "Heard a lot about you. About all your people. Don't know what you can do for me, though."

"Then why was I sent here?" J.B. asked, trying to keep his own tones as level as those of the man facing him down.

"Well, it could be for any number of reasons. I get to run this sector pretty much how I like, but having said that our glorious leader tends to send me people for whom I have neither need nor desire." He shrugged. "What can you do?"

"You seem to enjoy yourself," J.B. answered in a laconic tone, indicating the two women who were still recumbent on the rush matting.

The man smiled slowly. "Time goes by slow here."

"So I see," J.B. murmured. "What part of the big experiment do you cover here? I can't see anything but dimmies and cowards."

The man chuckled. "They're slow, sure. We make 'em and keep 'em that way. The cripples, the dimmies, the fat and ugly. The rejects. Those with something wrong. See, ideally they wouldn't exist. But they do. So we have to work out how to get the best of 'em, which is why we set up a primitive society and see how they work it out for themselves."

"Doesn't sound much of an experiment to me."

"Oh, it is. See, those who do well can mebbe be moved to other sectors, and they also add to our data about how the individual can develop within a constricted society when given autonomy."

J.B. barked a sardonic laugh. "Big words. Just let 'em do what they want and see what works out for you, right?"

The man shrugged. "Fair assessment."

"What about the others? The ones who don't improve?"

"Well, it's like this. Dr. Andower runs a sector for biological experimentation—"

"Yeah, I know about that butcher," J.B. interrupted.

The man smiled. This time it was cold, sharklike. "Well, then, you know what he does. Thing is, that kind of work demands subjects. And they have to come from somewhere."

J.B.'s blood ran cold. "Then why," he said slowly, "am I in this sector?"

The man inhaled, then shook his head. "You're no stupe. I didn't ask for you, but Arcadian has ideas of his own. You can bring a lot to the people here, if they're receptive. But consider this—you have a defect. Without these—" he flicked a finger at J.B.'s glasses, causing the Armorer to pull back "—you're at a disadvantage. Andower likes to try to put right nature's imperfections, and where better to find them than here."

J.B. looked past the sector leader. The dark-haired woman was rubbing enthusiastically at herself while she looked back at them. The blonde was staring at the dark-haired woman in fascination, her mouth hanging open and drooling. To one side, the older woman was muttering to herself, petting the dog. His gaze came back to the sector leader. The man grinned mirthlessly.

"Yeah. I think you get it, now."

Chapter Thirteen

The companions knew that Arcadian had aims for them that centered around their absorption into the life of the ville, and their subsuming to his ideals—something that all of them knew was never going to happen. Which left the separated companions with the knowledge that they had to effect escape routes and a means of communication between one another. More than that, they needed to find allies within their sector who could aid them. They didn't have the time to build trust slowly; they would have to go by instinct.

It was a huge risk, but perhaps not as much as they thought. For it had never really occurred to them that not everyone in the ville fell in with the aims and methods of the baron. Maybe, as much as they were looking for allies, there were those who were looking for them.

AFTER CURTIS, the sector leader who had revealed his name almost as an afterthought, had dismissed J.B. and returned to the two women who had been occupying his time, the old woman with the dog had led him out of the hut.

"This way, show you where you live," she said blankly, not even looking at him as she walked past, the mangy dog hobbling in her wake. Yet, despite the air of seedy disgust that she carried with her, she didn't smell as J.B. thought she might. The Armorer had been prepared to get downwind of her, then found it wasn't necessary. Though the way in which she walked, almost naked and unconcerned, through the dirt tracks of the sector was a little disconcerting.

Especially as he could see huddles of people gathering, staring, some following at a distance. Then it hit him. They weren't looking at the woman. Given the way that some of them looked, that shouldn't have been surprising. No, they were looking at him, muttering about him. Recognized from the group's initial arrival, and conspicuous by the way in which he had been delivered this time, he was also a newcomer. And he should have realized that communities like this were wary of outsiders.

It took nearly half an hour to arrive at the tumbledown shack where the woman and her canine halted. J.B. thought he recognized the area vaguely as the one on which they had first stumbled. There were sparse woodlands as the huts petered out, and perhaps the maze—tempting right now—just beyond. But then he figured that the whole of this sector was ringed by sparse forest, and without his minisextant he was unable to take an accurate reading. Curtis had relieved him of his weapons and the bag in which he kept the sextant—"You won't need them here." Looking back, J.B. wondered just why he had given them up so easily to a man who was himself unarmed. Perhaps there was something in the fact that he thought of the man's voice as hypnotic? Maybe that was how he ran this sector?

The old woman walked away, leaving J.B. to his thoughts and the shack itself. The windows were nothing more than gaps in the metal sheeting that covered the timber frame, and although there was the running water and facilities that had so bemused them before, there was nothing else other than dust and dirt. How was he supposed to eat? How was food supplied, clothes other than those in which he stood? All these were questions that would, perhaps, only be answered in time. J.B. went into the shack and looked around. Not that there was much to see: a simple two rooms, with no traces of whoever had lived there prior to his allocation.

What was he supposed to do? He felt at a complete loose end. Usually, there was always something on his mind, some task that needed attention. But here? Why was he here? What was expected of him? What was going to happen, and what could he do to prepare for it? It was all nebulous and beyond his grasp.

One thing for sure: there was an atmosphere that he didn't feel at all comfortable with. As he looked out of one of the raggedly hacked holes that passed for a window, he could see little sign of life. The shacks around seemed empty. It had been like that when he had first arrived, with Ryan and the others, as though these people lived shadow lives. That time it had been because they were keeping out of the way of intruders. This time, there was a more sinister feel in the air.

J.B. moved so that he was standing in the doorway. As if by the act of standing there he had invoked their presence, a crowd of the shambling misfits that populated the sector began to cluster in the paths that led between the empty shacks. They were three or four deep, and there were four groups of them, two or three abreast. Men, women and children of all ages. There was low muttering that passed between them as they moved slowly forward, converging on the space in front of J.B.'s shack.

The Armorer counted them quickly. About thirty to forty. They weren't strong, neither were they brave. Not all of them would have the balls to fight. Most, he figured, would be wanting to watch someone else do the fighting. But even so, there could be a dozen or more who would be willing to get physical. That could be a real problem. The Armorer knew that he was stronger than any of them, and that he knew how to fight. It was unlikely that any of them had those skills.

But did he want to fight them? The sheer weight of numbers could defeat him, particularly if he lost his feet. Moreover, he had to live with these people. To inflict damage on them would only draw attention to himself, making it harder to find an escape route.

He walked over the threshold. "Well?" he asked simply. His voice was loud and clear when compared to those that answered him.

"Seen you before—"

"You're one of them—"

"What you want with us? Why not leave us alone?"

"Curtis don't put you here for no reason."

"You not going to be the boss of us—"

Fear. The reek of it clung to his nostrils and made him feel a mixture of revulsion and pity. They were coming for him because they thought he was coming for them. And this was the only way they felt safe.

The Armorer made a decision that he was sure he

was going to regret in the short term. In the long term, though…

The bravest of them began to run toward him, hoping to hit home before he had a chance to launch a counterattack. He just had time to remove his glasses and put them in his pants' pocket before they reached him. Although it meant that he could see little but a blur, he would be damned if he was going to let his glasses get broken in a scuffle where he was overwhelmed by sheer weight of numbers.

A blur of shadow and color on each side, delineated only by the sweat stench of fear—that was all he could register as the first few reached him. Their blows were poorly and inexpertly aimed, their strength nowhere near enough to hurt him, even if they hit home. He was able to duck and weave, avoiding all but the most glancing of blows. They were little more than a distraction. The real problem that his decision not to fight back, but only to offer resistance such that he wouldn't be hurt, was taken as a sign of weakness by the crowd, and encouraged them to move forward.

Blows began to rain on him from behind, where those who had led the charge were now wheeling around on their own momentum to come back at him from the rear. Those he wasn't so prepared for, and although there was no one in the crowd who had any real power against such a combat-hardened veteran as the Armorer, still their surprise and cumulative effect was enough to make him stumble forward.

Buoyed by their seeming success, the group began to swarm around him, all of them trying to get in kicks and punches of their own. This worked in his favor, in as much as the sheer mass of humanity got in one another's way, many of the blows missing their intended target and falling on others in the crowd. But as they closed and jostled around him, he found himself hemmed in by them, the weight of their numbers pushing him so that, in the dust and confusion, he began to stumble. He had been able to deflect many of the blows, but as the crowd became tight around him, he found that he no longer had the reach. His space had become restricted, and more of the blows were hitting home. They were still weak and ineffective for the most part, but the cumulative effect concerned him.

He began to think that he'd made a poor call. He'd counted on their cowardice, whereas his passive resistance had done nothing but encourage them. He felt even worse—in many ways—when a lucky blow glanced at the back of his ear, stunning him and pitching him forward just enough to stumble over the feet that milled around.

For a moment he thought that he might have shuffled enough to recover his balance, but another leg in his path caught him below the knee, and then he was down. Their voices around and above him crowed in triumph as they milled around, each seeking to get in a blow or kick of his or her own.

Being down and prone was the thing that he had feared. Now he was truly vulnerable, as even if he wanted to fight back, he couldn't. The blows and kicks began to hurt. His ribs and spine felt bruised and battered. It was still nothing compared to what he had taken in the past, but it was far from an easy ride. In truth, it wasn't the kicks and punches that could have done the real damage, but rather that he was now in a position to be trampled into the ground.

And then, as he curled himself into a fetal ball for as much protection as possible, preparing himself for the pain that was to come, it was over. He stayed where he was, tucked in tight, unwilling to expose himself to any blows, in case this was little more than a lull. But as he lay there, he could hear the muttering of voices as the mob dispersed.

Soon, all was quiet, and he carefully uncurled himself. Even through the blur of his unaided vision, he could see that the spaces in front of the hut and the dirt tracks were now empty.

Apart, that was, from the old woman and her dog. She walked up to him, and while the dog sniffed and licked experimentally at J.B.'s arm and face, she took hold of him and helped him to his feet before aiding him back into the tumbledown shack that was now his home.

Then, while the dog curled up and slept, she got water from the faucet and helped him bathe the dust and blood from those few areas that had been cut rather than bruised.

"They'll leave you now," she said. "Who you are scares them. They need to make sure you're not going to be like Curtis, telling them what to do all the time. You did the right thing."

J.B. took his glasses out of his pants' pocket. They were intact. He put them on.

"You knew what I was doing?" he asked, suddenly unsure if his judgment of her had been correct. The twinkle he now saw in her eyes made him sure.

"It's what we do to hide," she said with the ghost of

a smile. "Doesn't always pay to be who you are around here. Got me?"

J.B.'s smile was broader. "Yeah. Got you."

KRYSTY MANAGED to avoid Tod for three days. There had been something about the way he touched her, spoke to her, brushed against her, that had set her senses on alert. It was a simple enough animal thing: he wanted her. Naturally, she didn't feel that way. She loved and wanted only Ryan. And she didn't need any distraction at this point: their joint objective was to find a way of communicating with their companions, then getting the hell out of the ville.

It wasn't going to be easy; that was obvious from the outset. Alex ran a tight sector, and he was completely focused on the objectives of his experiments, which meant that everyone else in the sector was expected to feel and act the same way. Mating, fitness, the pursuit of physical excellence—it was a hard regime that left little time for anything else.

The first two days had been further periods of orientation, with the notion of settling in being little more than a cursory breath taken in their new quarters before they were launched on the programs that ran like a well-oiled machine in this state-within-a-state.

They had been billeted together, a room in a building that housed six other couples. The pairing of male and female was arbitrary. Although each couple shared a room, they weren't linked in any other way. Sex wasn't encouraged in the "home" environment, although to describe the sterile dwelling conditions as such was possibly stretching a definition. The rooms in the

building were tidy and empty of anything that had
personal connotations. The people of this sector were
encouraged to think of themselves as part of a collec-
tive, working as a whole for the greater good. As such,
there were only the occasional flashes of individual
personality that shone through the uniform monotony
of work. Even though it was only a few days, and they
had seen their new companions at mealtimes and in the
morning, it would be fair to say that neither Ryan nor
Krysty had been able to tell if they had run across them
in the course of the day's orientations. Names, too, were
still a blur.

It had the advantage of them being able to keep
some distance and assess the situation, yet at the same
time made it hard to find out if there were any potential allies. Everyone they encountered in the sector
seemed, on the surface, to be as dedicated to the
program as their leader. Any who dissented kept it so
well hidden that it would take time to dig it out. Time
they didn't have.

It was intensive: medical examinations from the
whitecoats were the first thing on the agenda. Some of
it was intrusive, probes and samples from parts of the
anatomy that either of them would have committed
violence to avoid under other circumstances. Krysty
was overly sensitive due to a past experience, but they
bore it by focusing on what they could learn from the
process. Alex's whitecoats might have felt they were the
ones gathering data, but in truth it was a two-way
process. Their fitness was assessed in a series of similarly grueling—albeit in a different manner—tests,
overseen by the sector leader himself. Assault courses

and unarmed combat left them sore and tired at the end of the second day.

The unarmed combat had also confirmed what Ryan had suspected: the men of the sector viewed him with some disdain and contempt because of his eye. The defect, albeit one from combat rather than congenital, was viewed as a weakness. He had viewed unarmed combat exercises, and had seen the level of ferocity. When it came to his turn, the men went for him with a greater intent, as though willing one another to purge him from their perfect community. He had to fight harder than he would have liked, rendering opponents unconscious to negate their threat. The whitecoats were more than happy, seeing him as a way to push their programs further. All he could see was the resentment his actions would add to the hostility.

Krysty, on the other hand, was welcomed. Her physical perfection seeming to make her fit perfectly. Nothing was said to the people around her of her mutation. The whitecoats kept it quiet for reasons of their own. That suited her for the moment, as it put her in a position where she was more able than Ryan to wander freely. When it came out, as she was sure it had to eventually, then that would be another matter. For now, she was keen to take any advantage given to them.

Thus it was that she was able to wander the streets of the sector after the third day of training and orientation. She had been shown images and old vid clips to determine her sexual orientation and preferences. Ryan had been through a similar process, and she had been appalled by his description of how a whitecoat had prodded his prostrate to produce a sperm sample for fertility analysis. It made her own experiences of the day seem mild. Yet she knew that this had just been the foretaste for what was to come. It wouldn't be long before they were sent to the coupling chambers. And they'd seen that on their arrival: there was no way she wanted that.

So it was that she made her way from their billet, headed toward the building where she knew their weapons were stored. Her aim wasn't to take them back, but rather to recce the location to see how easy it would be. To take them now would be to risk discovery. Preparation was everything.

Ryan stayed behind. It was a mutual decision made in light of their respective profiles in the sector. Krysty could move pretty freely, already assumed to be one of the group. Ryan stood out and attracted attention. Krysty could be entering the building for any number of reasons to do with the program; Ryan would always be suspected of something. As a basic insight into the unchanging nature of the human psyche, Krysty would have been too pleased to ironically draw it to the attention of sector chief, Alex, if not for the fact that it would screw their plans completely.

The entrance to the building was, as ever, unguarded. She found it hard to accept that the people of the ville were so well indoctrinated that any form of dissent was unthinkable. There had to be someone, somewhere. Still, it served her well, now. There were few people around as twilight began to fall on the sector, and she was able to enter without notice. Inside, the main corridor was unlighted. There was evidently no timer system on the lights, and only the distant well of light around the stairs to upper levels bespoke of any habitation. The ground level had the silence of emptiness. Distant sounds, echoing the ghostly nature of the light, betrayed activity on the upper levels. Down here, though, all was quiet.

The door to the room in which she had seen their weapons stored was locked. She allowed herself a little smile. No sec, but they didn't trust the people that much. It was a fairly flimsy wooden door, inset with frosted glass. Breaking it would be no problem, but would be too conspicuous. The lock was a simple one. There was space between the door itself and the lintel, so if she could just...

Krysty thought about it for a moment, then tried the door to the room opposite. It was unlocked. Obviously nothing of note in there. But it was used for administration, like the room opposite, and in the unlocked drawers of the cabinets containing files and documents from the whitecoats, she found what she wanted. The runners of the drawers housed folders containing the files, each tagged with a numbered card in a yellowed plastic holder. Thanking Gaia for the fact that not all of the predark materials had perished, she slipped the plastic off the folder, carefully unpicked it and split a piece off, leaving the face of the card covered, then replaced it. No one would notice, and if they did would probably think nothing of it.

Crossing back to the locked door and closing the other behind her, she checked that all was still quiet before slipping the plastic into the gap between door and lintel. Carefully rocking the door, she pushed the plastic. It seemed to take forever, but finally she felt it give under the pressure, slipping around the lock itself and into the bed, pushing the bolt back. She felt the door give with a soft click.

Another quick look around and she slipped into the room, closing the door behind her. She knew where she had seen the weapons stashed, so she started to head for the cabinet.

It was only then that, with a sinking feeling, she realized that she wasn't alone. She stopped, then turned slowly.

Tod was sitting with his feet up on a desk, silent and unmoving. He remained as still as he said softly, "I wondered how many nights I'd have to wait here. I knew you'd come, though."

Krysty felt her heart sink.

"So what are you going to do about it?" she said, trying to keep her voice level.

"There are a lot of things I could do about it," he replied. "Depends on how far you're prepared to go."

"Meaning?"

He shrugged. She could see that, but not his face in the gloom of the shuttered room. His tone, however, told her all she needed to know.

"Alex runs this place, but he's got tunnel vision so bad that he can't see what happens right next to him. He's not going to check those weapons. You could take them now, and as long as you could keep them concealed in your room, then no one need ever know."

"Only you."

"Only me. As you say."

Krysty considered that. "Everything comes at a price. What's yours?"

"Mine?" He paused. It seemed to her that he was weighing every syllable carefully. "I think you know. Alex sticks to the program and makes sure we all do. Coupling and mating are done to a strict rota. Not because we want to, not when we want to, and not with who we want to. Sometimes you yearn for something a little different."

"I thought as much," she said coldly. "I could break your neck if you try anything. Before you even had a chance to yell. I've watched you. Not like you've watched me," she added meaningly, "but I have. And you're soft. Not like a lot of the others here."

He smiled, although she couldn't see it, only hear it in his voice.

"Soft? Yeah, that's probably about right. In the way you mean, too. But not just that. There's more to human experience than just the mechanics. That's what we do here. Some of us don't like it, but we just have to go along with it. You're right. I would. But not try to make you. What would be the point? No, a world where there's the choice, and mebbe someone like you."

Krysty frowned. He was rambling like a man on jolt, but unless she was badly mistaken...

"You know about the way this ville is made?"

"I know that the strips between the sectors aren't defended. We only think they are. All you have to do is avoid the sec, and you can link up with your friends. I can help you to do that. I can make the weapons available to you."

"And you want what from me in return?"

The air was heavy with her expectation, still and tense. Finally he spoke. "You know what I'd like. But

I've seen you look at Ryan like I look at you, and I know it wouldn't happen unless under duress. And that's not what I want. Duress is every day here. I'm not alone. You help me and those like me, and I'll help you and Ryan. All we have to do is be a little… Krysty, do you know what circumspect is?"

She laughed, the relief obvious in her voice. "I should do. We've just spent the last ten minutes acting it out."

FOR MILDRED AND DOC, it was also a matter of three days before the reality of the situation began to bite. In their case, given the mind games that were an integral part of the sector in which they had been housed, the unreality of a situation was very much the norm.

For two days they had been shown the way in which the sector worked—group experiments in psychodynamics and the modification of behavior through group therapy and one-on-one experimentation. For Doc, who had been brought up and then trawled before Freud had come to prominence, and to whom psychobabble was a tongue heard from whitecoats and distrusted for that very reason, it had been merely bizarre to see the way in which those leading the sector conducted their business. But to Mildred, part of whose medical schooling had taken in psychiatric medicine, it was recognizable as a strange parody of what she had learned, as though the information had been partially preserved through the nukecaust and then interpreted in a way that seemed to turn it inside out and examine it from an obtuse angle.

When she had remarked to Doc that the lunatics had

taken over the asylum, she had been joking. Yet now she wasn't sure that she hadn't inadvertently hit upon the truth. The people who were, presumably, the white-coats and leaders of the sector lived and worked side-by-side with those who were the subjects. Who was there to perform Arcadian's wishes, and who were the performers dancing to the tune they played, was a matter of conjecture. It was only during a musical game, which brought the analogy to her mind, that Mildred realized from their behavior that the fat woman who had been in the party meeting them wasn't, as she had assumed, one of the sector leaders, but was a subject who was being allowed to act in that role as a way of making her see her own behavior as being disruptive, and thus brought into line. The thin woman and the man were definitely whitecoats, but who was senior was a mystery to her.

The scenario had made her think of a therapist whose theories had grabbed her at medical school, partly because he was an outsider in the field whose work was being hotly disputed. From a conventional early career, she recalled, he had evolved his theories about there being no psychological disorders as such, merely breakdowns in the way that people communi-cated and interacted. To that end, he had set up a house where the "doctors" and "patients" lived on equal terms. Of course, with boundaries blurred and no con-ventional structure in place, results weren't easily defined, and hotly disputed. The music class, where a variety of predark and homemade instruments wailed a cacophony that gradually evolved into a pattern that was certainly not harmonious, but perhaps signaled a level of behavior modification through cooperation that could be extended beyond the room and into the rest of life, made her realize that this was, at least in part, how they evolved. The way in which the fat woman lost her way, became frustrated, then broke down and cried before being comforted by the others made her see the distinctions.

It was certainly contrary to the way that life was lived outside of the ville. How it would fit with some of the villes they had fought their way out of was something that was hard to contemplate. Unless it was just that this was in isolation, and when applied to other practices in the ville it would gain teeth. She discussed this with Doc.

"Your therapist was certainly taking chances," Doc mused. "A lunatic may be a lost soul, but is still a loose canon for all that. And I should know. This cannot be all there is."

"It's all they're showing us." Mildred shrugged. "Maybe they just deal with this tiny detail."

Doc grinned crookedly. "I sincerely doubt that anyone is that benign these days. Would it not be a working hypothesis to state that, as much as we are observing them, they are using this to observe us? To see how we react, how much we take at face value? Perhaps to assess how much, ah, adjustment we may need?"

"Or to see how open we may be to those practices of theirs that aren't so harmless?"

Doc nodded. "I am no judge of their judgment, my dear Dr. Wyeth, but I do know myself. And, I pride myself, I know you well enough to make a guess that they will see you are more likely to respond…if not positively, then perhaps without such vehemence to procedures that may not be so palatable. I think you should beware. I also think we will be separated soon. We must maintain contact when this happens."

Mildred nodded. "We need to look out for each other as much as for a way out. Don't worry, Doc, when it comes, we'll be ready."

So it was that when the time came upon them during the following morning, both were prepared. The fat woman, now restored in temperament after the breakdown they had witnessed the previous day, came to their quarters with a man Doc didn't recognize. Lugubrious in a manner that seemed absurd on his short, squat frame he requested that Doc accompany him to take part in a chess tournament. It was time for him to stop spectating and start participating. Mildred started to join him, but was stopped by the fat woman.

"No. It's perhaps better if you take part in another of our activities." There was an undertone in her voice that mixed fear with aggression, as though she expected an argument. Thus, she was a little bemused if pleased when Mildred agreed with alacrity. If she and the lugubrious man noticed the brief glance that passed between Doc and Mildred as they parted, then they showed no sign.

Doc and the lugubrious man—who didn't reveal his name—made small talk as they progressed to the grassed area where the chess tables were gathered. Doc, unsure as to whether he was a whitecoat, was unwilling to talk too much and too deeply in case he give something away. It struck him that it was going to be a tricky situation for Mildred and himself to extract themselves. Who could they trust, and who could they build alliances with when they were unsure of sides?

Any further such thoughts were expunged as they arrived to find that a draw was being made. The tournament would be a timed elimination, with two groups of players being pitched against each other to find a final pairing that would contest for the grand prize: a passage back into the first sector of Arcady. Freedom by any other name.

Freedom of sorts, Doc thought. Freedom on Arcadian's terms. But he let that pass, observing instead the buzz of excitement it caused. He was expected to join in, no doubt, and he attempted to make a display of such. Whether he was successful he very much doubted. He was, however, taken by a similarly false display that came from a woman standing a hundred yards from him. Even through the milling throng, he could see the cynicism and ennui in her eyes. He hoped he would be drawn to play against her. The chance to talk as privately as was possible, across a table while others were engaged in their own matches, was intriguing.

Of course, it wasn't that simple. They drew other opponents. All Doc could do was to set out to win his matches and hope that she was a good chess player. He doubted she was that bothered about winning, but trusted to a fate that would decree the least willing could snatch the prize.

While Doc set about his task, in another part of the sector, Mildred was coming face-to-face with a practice she thought long gone. A practice that was all the more shocking in its barbarism for being so opposed to what she had seen so far.

The dark side of the sector revealed itself to her as she was taken by the fat woman into a building that was located between two vacant lots. The windows, she noticed, were of opaque glass, all of them closed. And, unlike the other buildings she had passed in the past two days, there was no feeling of life within. Even given the strange air of quiet that pervaded the sector as a whole, there was always the sense—perhaps the faint, almost inaudible sounds of movement within—of life behind the brick.

Not here. The building felt empty. As she approached with the fat woman, who remained silent, Mildred felt an anxiety creep over her. There was no reason she would be taken to an empty building, though sense and the practices of this sector might sometimes seem only distantly related. No, it wasn't lack of life that her gut sensed; rather, it was the negation of life.

As soon as they crossed the threshold of the building, and the doors closed with a hiss behind them, she realized that the reason for the silence on the outside was that the building was soundproofed. Inside, there was a cacophony of noise, the sudden burst of which made her wince with pain and, perhaps, a quiver of fear. For here were voices raised in screams of agony that went beyond the physical, souls who were truly in torment.

"This is what we want you to see," the fat woman said, raising her voice and gesturing expansively toward the corridor in front of her. "There are some who do not respond to the behavioral modification we advocate through mutual learning. They are, sadly, beyond the rational. The only way to try to bring them back to that path is by a neurological adjustment."

"Such as?" Mildred asked slowly, not sure if she wanted to know, but certain that she was about to find out.

"Let us see," the fat woman intoned, moving off and gesturing for Mildred to follow her. They paused at a number of rooms on the ground and second stories. Each was like a padded cell. From some of these the howling had emanated. Looking through the sliding observation panels, she could see that some of these people were pacing, screaming. Some were scraping at the padding with nails bloodied and to the bone, their faces etched with lines of pain that went deeper than the flesh. Some sat motionless, mouths agape in a long scream. But by far the most terrifying were those who just sat, blank of expression and eye, motionless and silent as though waiting patiently for eternity to claim them.

None of these modifications had been successful. Whatever they were doing in this building, it seemed as pointless and barbarous as the activities of Andower that Doc had spoken of. Mildred was glad that Doc couldn't see this.

Even more so when she saw how the people in the building had gotten this way. On the top story there were three rooms, doors flung wide, cacophonous to the point of white noise. Static bursts and the loud, low frequency hum of electric generators mixed with screams and laughter. People were strapped to tables in the center of each room, giggling, drooling fools administering electric shock treatment. By the look of the burns on their own heads, the victims and subjects here were also the same. The principle followed through to an illogical conclusion. The fat woman was mouthing something at her that she couldn't hear.

She felt herself gagging on the vomit that rose in her gorge, turned away and was glad Doc couldn't see this.

TANNER WAS DOING just fine. He had beaten his opponents by sheer determination and an application of logic he had thought no longer within him. He had noted that the woman had done the same. If they had met in what was, in effect, the semifinal of the tournament, then all eyes would be upon them, and the audience he craved would be an impossibility.

Fortune smiled upon him. They met in the relatively early stages, with most still occupied in their own matches, or those of their friends.

Seemingly in a bubble of their own silence, they sat opposite each other, the first moves proceeding smoothly. Doc made his move, then sat back and waited until she had made hers, each time studying her intently. She was of medium height, dressed in a loose-fitting tunic and pants of olive-green and black. Her hair was iron-gray, and had a wave that caused her to push it back behind her ear each time she leaned over the board, her bangs sweeping forward over her steel-framed spectacles. Her face was lined, grooves etched into her forehead as she studied the board. These eased off as she sat back after each move. She had once been a handsome woman, but time and the vicissitudes of this sector had taken their toll. The constant psychic strain of not knowing keeper or kept had impressed itself on her; of that he was sure.

Although he gave no sign, Doc knew that she watched

him carefully as he made his moves. She was sizing him up, as much as he was doing the same to her. Who would be the first to crack, and make a move outside the board? Aware that he didn't wish to waste time unnecessarily, Doc took the plunge as she prepared to move her queen.

"An interesting move," he began.

"Only if it achieves its aim," she countered. "That's the problem. Chance and probability dictate that you have a certain number of options. Somewhere down the line, I have to have judged you enough to have eliminated all but the most likely."

"Yet you have not had the time to get to know my game, and define how my mind works," he said with no little deliberation.

"Indeed." She paused, queen in midair, and looked up. He was aware of a fierce intelligence glittering in those eyes, an intelligence that had been used to masking itself.

"Perhaps some indicators to my personality would be of assistance," he said softly. "I have always been one to play for the little victory, believing that incremental victories can win a war. I have caution for those pieces I value. And I most admire their ability to move with freedom and impunity."

"I like the way you play," she said in a level tone. "I suspected as much. There are some of us who also like this method, but find ourselves constrained by the rules, and by the methods of others. We yearn for a new kind of game, but we perhaps need a thinker outside the board. Someone who can open up possibilities."

"I pride myself that has always been my forte," Doc

said. She laid down the queen, and Doc picked up a pawn. He used it as a piece in checkers, claiming three of her pieces and taking them from the board before holding them out to her in the palm of his hand. She took them from him and replaced them on the board.

"There have been those who try to invent new rules for the game," she said in a discursive tone that did little to hide her meaning. "They make new boards, new areas for playing. But in doing so they cut themselves off from the rest of us. And it's hard to play the game when you are denied pieces. They can try to borrow, but there are those who like to keep the pieces firmly in the box."

"I think I have seem such maverick game players," Doc said carefully, remembering the coldhearts who had attacked them when they crossed the maze. Perhaps not such coldhearts, after all. An—how should he call it?—understandable mistake. Not to be repeated. And it would perhaps be politic not to mention it right now.

"They are few," she continued, "but there are some fundamentals about the game that they have bequeathed to us. Take the board, for example." She used her hands, palms out, to proscribe the edges of the marked table. "The edges have nothing to keep the pieces on the board. The invisible wall that we automatically assume doesn't exist. What really prevents us from stepping off are the watchers who hover over the board, and over adjoining boards. The game could proceed off the board, if only it was when the watchers had their eyes averted."

"So perhaps what you really need for a different game to be forged is for the watchers to have their attention taken?" Doc suggested.

"It would certainly allow for new rules to be tried," she stated. "At present, all we have are the promises of being transferred from one board to another. Which is all very well, but we still play by the same rules."

Their eyes met across the board. Despite her caution, there was a yearning in her eyes. One chance was all they asked, and all they might need.

"Madam, there are those of us who find the attentions of one game a trifle tedious. We like to try a variety, and if possible we like to cause distraction and move the parameters. It is not beyond the bounds of possibility that we may tire of these restrictions and seek a fresh game in a very short while."

"I was hoping that this spirit of quest would be forthcoming," she murmured guardedly. "In the meantime, games already under way need to come to conclusions. The watchers like to see a definite result, otherwise they become a little restive."

"Very well, then. Shall we say that I will be forthcoming, and you should await further speculation on rule changes?"

"That sounds good," she replied simply.

Aware that too long spent without movement on the board could attract attention, they proceeded. The woman allowed Doc to take the game within a few moves, to cover for lost time, and as he carried on to the next opponent, he could see as he looked around between moves that the woman was surreptitiously moving among the growing crowd of those eliminated, pausing occasionally to impart a few words to others. Potential allies? he wondered.

Knowing that it was unlikely that he would be

moved back to the central sector merely because of a chess game, and yet unwilling to seem too keen to lose, he forced himself to concentrate for another two matches, winning them both, before being relieved that he found himself opposite a better—and seemingly more driven—player. He eased up on his game gracefully, allowing the man to win and move forward to his goal. All the while, Doc pondered on what he would tell Mildred, little realizing the horror she had to reveal.

It was only at this point that he was astonished to realize that he didn't even know the name of their new ally.

IT TOOK JAK a short time to work out what was happening in his sector. People who were considered to work on an instinctual level, and so followed a gut reaction rather than a considered course of action, were seen as somewhere between animals and man. They were put through a series of assault courses that were designed to test specific sets of reactions.

The first one he had been on was a walled-off part of the sector that housed several buildings pockmarked by blasterfire. A number of mannequins were visible, and he knew that there were others hidden from view. He was given an air blaster with marked darts.

"The purpose of this course—" a whitecoat began slowly, as though talking to a child.

"Shoot ones with blasters, not without, as come to life," Jak finished tersely.

"Very good," the whitecoat said, looking down his nose in a manner so patronizing it made Jak want to forget about the mannequins and empty the blaster in the man's ass.

"Get on with it," Jak snapped.

The whitecoat was less than pleased by Jak's attitude, but he disappeared into an adjacent building without a backward glance, leaving Jak at the beginning of the course.

It was straightforward. Three streets, with eighteen visible and hidden mannequins. Some had blasters that fired balls of dye. Some had nothing. Jak had to run hell-for-leather through the course as fast as possible, and make it to the other end free of dye, while shooting those mannequins that were aiming for him and leaving the others.

The upside was that they couldn't harm him. The downside, perversely, was that without this imminent danger, his instincts were blunted. Yet it was simple for the albino teen. Time slowed for him as the adrenaline pumped, and he saw each mannequin almost in the moment before it turned to him, or slid in front of a window or doorway. His aim was unerring, landing a dart in each mannequin with a blaster while rolling and tumbling to avoid the balls of dye they fired. Some shadow or weight in the way they moved told him which were armed.

His perfect score at the end of the course seemed to almost annoy the whitecoat, which only added to Jak's pleasure.

Other courses weren't as easy. Under sec escort, Jak was taken with three other men into a densely wooded area that lay somewhere to the north of the ville. A fenced-in area, barbed wire standing three yards high with cameras along the length of each side, was their destination. Within this, starving dogs and bizarre mutie creatures who were mammal, but unlike anything Jak had ever seen, prowled hungrily. It crossed his mind that Doc's erstwhile friend Andower had been experimenting on more than humans.

The four men were herded into the expansive pen and then told that they would have to survive forty-eight hours, finding their own food and water in the dense enclosure, while avoiding the predators. Their weapons had been taken from them.

The purpose of the exercise was immediately obvious. The sheer density of the enclosure and the proliferation of ravening beasts meant that the men would have to overcome their first instinct to go solo, and work together. As a way of observing both instinctual behavior and the modification of such under extreme duress, it struck Jak as both effective and dangerous.

Especially as the three men he was with showed little initial sign of a willingness to cooperate. One of them cursed heavily, told them he was better off on his own, and at the first sight of a dog pack deserted them. The wisdom of his move was belied by the anguished screams that sounded from within the dense growth.

"Better stick together than buy farm," Jak told the others. Unwillingly, they agreed.

Although each of them could hunt and had excellent instincts for danger, to merely avoid being chilled wasn't enough. They had to establish a safe place where they could take turns at watch during the dark, and protect whatever food and water they could find.

It was while one of them slept, and Jak was on watch,

that he was approached by the third man. He sat side-by-side with Jak at the fire they had built, and said nothing for some time. Finally, in an undertone, he said, "You want to get out?"

"Trap?" Jak asked simply.

The man shrugged. "You could see it that way. But I'll make you do nothing. Just make a suggestion."

Jak nodded, and the man spit into the fire before continuing.

"Vid's all around here to see how we do. Vid everywhere. But no sec. Not enough, see. Baron likes us to think so, but you keep your eyes open and you'll see there ain't that many. So if you find the vid blindspots, then you can move. Nothing between sectors but empty dirt. Good vid, though."

"How you know?"

The man grinned. "Got me some pussy in another sector. Separated 'bout a year back, but she's too sweet to lose. So I worked out the angles. You look at them vid cams, you can do that. Try it, dude. That's if we get out of here."

"How I know you not with sec?"

"You don't. But you're smart. Even if it is a trap, then you can beat it, boy."

Jak said nothing. The man stared at him for a while, as if trying to work him out.

Finally he said, "Your choice. Leave it at that."

Chapter Fourteen

Jak wasted little time. He and his two erstwhile companions made it through the forty-eight hours with little threat. The beasts in the enclosure were hungry and vicious for sure, but they were kept too hungry. It gave them an edge of desperation that made them clumsy. Jak could have heard them coming from a mile away. Being ready for them and avoiding having to fight them was easy under such circumstances. Their carelessness also meant that they were easily trapped for food.

Jak was almost contemptuous when he and the others were freed. The three men were rushed to the center of the sector, where they were put into individual rooms and questioned on their responses and what they felt was good and bad about their actions. The whitecoat who questioned him had Jak watch a vid of the forty-eight hours. Jak was sure he glimpsed the moment when he had been told about the cameras and their blind-spots. He kept his face blank, and the moment passed. If the whitecoat had been hoping for a reaction, he was unlucky. If he wasn't, then good.

Jak was impatient for the interrogation to end, and glad when they were led back to their respective quarters. He sat on his bunk, staring out the window, waiting for night to fall.

So he had experienced the ranges, and they hadn't been the frightening things that had been suggested by the words of Pulaski and Foxx. He suspected that they talked a better bunch of experiments than they actually ran. A lot of the ville seemed to be based on words that those using them barely understood. Not that he understood them, either. Point was, he didn't claim to. They were fooling themselves. That would be fine, if not for the fact that they were harming a lot of people along the way. More important, they were likely to harm his friends and himself if things didn't change. Jak didn't want that to happen.

So it was that, when darkness fell, Jak stayed in his room and waited for the sounds of the night to settle outside his window. When background noises had reached a level where he could identify every little sound, he nodded to himself and moved.

The two madmen who ran this sector believed in heavy sec when they were conducting experiments, and around their own building. But Pulaski and Foxx were plain stupe when it came to the rest of the sector. They relied solely on the ingrained behavior of their subjects and the vid cameras. Jak didn't have the one, and knew the failings of the other.

Jak exited the room and moved swiftly to the stairwell. He was down it in a matter of seconds and onto the ground floor. There was little sign of life. Most of the other inhabitants of the building were either taking part in experiments, or sleeping off the effects of those from which they had recently returned. There was little light here, and pools of shadow where he could pause and take stock.

The entrance would be a bad place to exit, as there was a camera roving the sidewalk outside, just as there was one at the back. But the side of the building looked out onto a narrow alley. It was easy to find an empty room and slip out of the window.

Now that he was outside, he would wait. He had all night.

There was one sec patrol. Two men. They passed him after a half hour, not even looking down the alley. He listened intently. It was so quiet that he could hear their footsteps as they echoed away, turned a corner, walked on, then turned again. By the time they were out of his sight, he had a good idea of their route. He settled on his haunches, hunched against the chill night air, and waited.

It was an hour before they passed by again. It had been a tedious hour, but he had made use of it by running over the layout of the sectors, as much as he knew of them, in his head. By the time he had heard the sec patrol pass by and round two corners, he had a plan. He set out and shadowed them as far as the point where the barren stretches of land delineated the marker points between sectors. Where the sec patrol took the middle of the road, Jak used alleys to cut out exposed stretches of sidewalk, pausing to wait while the cameras turned on their podiums before slipping past on the blindside. For those that were fixed, he simply slipped up to them while the moving cameras were away from him, then passed beneath the body of the vid.

It was only when he reached the empty stretch of land that he had a problem. There were cameras along the wire. Sec patrols also passed at regular intervals on his side. On the other, he noticed, there was none. He would have to find a dark spot and wait it out, working out the patterns of the cameras and the patrols before light came to ruin his plans.

One patrol made its circuit, and came in contact with the deserted land in such a way that Jak would be seen if caught out.

He cursed to himself as he timed them. They came exactly halfway along the patrol circuit he had followed. And they chose a time when most of the cameras were turned away from him—his optimum moment to cross the barren area. Very well, then, he would have to take a chance. The strait became a blind spot in only one location that gave him enough time to cross, and that would mean risking coming within the purview of one camera in this sector. The window of opportunity when he could hit the barbed wire and tumble over into the barren area would be just over ten seconds. And just under a hundred yards. Jak was fast, but it was asking a lot.

He looked up at the moon as sparse cloud scudded across its face. If he was to get over, find Doc and Mildred and get back, he would have to move. He was sure they would be in this sector. Arcadian may have assumed he was dumb because he didn't say much, but the baron had underestimated him.

Jak's thoughts blanked as instinct came to the fore: now was the time. Heart pounding, he shot from the shadows and made for the wire, one eye on the camera as it just pivoted beyond the path he was taking. He took the wire at a running leap, grabbing at the knotted metal between the barbs and using his own momentum to lift him up and over the top. He felt the wire catch and rip at his clothes, and the sharp needle pain of scored flesh on his hands. He ignored it as he landed on the balls of his feet. A quick look to see that he had left no telltale remnants of cloth and he was across the barren area in a few strides. Looking back, he could see in the moonlight that the earth was packed too hard for footprints to register. That had been a gamble won. Now for the next. He took the wire on the far side with more caution, having had less chance to build up a head of steam. He winced as he felt the wire bite into those parts of his hands that had been scored. Blanking the pain, he was over and into the shadows once more. A look back showed him cameras that were still turned away.

Now he was in a sector that he didn't know. The instincts and senses that the coldheart whitecoats wanted to test and analyze would be their downfall in a way they couldn't understand. He moved around the streets, past the open area where the chess tables and the giant ground board were located. Their absurdity didn't register with him. He had more pressing business.

Scent and sound were his raw materials: areas and buildings where the people of this sector were sleeping at this hour. Areas where they were awake to be treated with particular caution. There was no indication of any sec. It should have puzzled him, but in his current mood he just took it as a bonus.

Jak moved quickly. He knew the particular scents that attached themselves to Doc and Mildred. As with everyone, there was something unique about them. He also knew that if they were awake, Doc would be talking. He allowed himself a smile at that. Even more so when he caught Doc's voice, no more than a whisper on the still air. Enough for him to find the building. His smile broadened as he heard Doc's discourse on how they needed to break the bounds of the sector. He accessed the building via an alleyway and an open window. From there, finding Doc and Mildred's room was simple. He could hear Doc as he reached for the handle of the door, then his voice cease as they watched the handle drop.

"Need stop talking and start acting, Doc," he said with a vulpine grin as he pushed the door open and stepped back.

They were framed in the doorway, both in the act of reaching for their sidearms. The look of astonishment on their faces alone was almost worth his efforts.

"LOOK, I KNOW YOU don't want to trust me, but just give me this chance, okay?"

Ryan Cawdor stared at Tod with his one good eye, the burning blue orb trying to penetrate into his very being. No, he didn't want to trust him. Truth was, he didn't like him at all. Even before Krysty had told him about their little discussion when she tried to retrieve the weapons, the one-eyed man had picked up something in the way that Tod looked at Krysty. No, what he really wanted to do was to put his fist right through the slightly smug and condescending face in front of him. He didn't doubt Tod's sincerity—the man had put a lot on the line leveling with Krysty, and by all accounts had played more than fair—but the gnawing canker of jealousy still ate at him.

An interesting feeling for Ryan. It had been a long time since he and Krysty had been in a situation where he had come face-to-face with someone who wanted his woman so openly. If he had put it to her like that, likely as not the Titian-haired beauty would have put her own fist into his eye. His judgment was being impaired, and he knew that it wasn't a good time for that to happen.

"Suppose I do trust you. What guarantee have I got that you won't screw me over?"

"Not just you. Both of you," Tod countered slowly, staring from one to the other. "I'm not just taking you, Ryan. I'm taking Krysty, too."

He was aware of Ryan's feelings. Including Krysty made it clear that it wasn't merely a move to get the one-eyed man out of the way. Ryan appreciated that, but there was more than just that personal itch to be scratched.

"What if it's both of us you want out of the way?"

Tod snorted, exasperated. His manner was almost certain to rub Ryan the wrong way, but maybe it wasn't deliberate? Ryan let him speak, considering this as he listened.

"What," Tod snapped, "so I'm going to lead you both into a trap because she spurned me? Fuck it, you think this is all about you? Or even all about me? This is more than that. You think I want revenge? Think again. Listen, there's nothing wrong with wanting to make a better world—you've seen more of this land than I have, and you can't tell me that it isn't a pesthole. But the way Arcadian goes about it? No, that's all wrong. You don't make a better world by treating your own people like animals just so you can experiment on them. You work with them. Now mebbe if things change we can start making this ville better as a start. Mebbe it'll all go to shit. But at least it'll be our shit."

He stopped, breathing hard, glaring at Ryan. It was obvious that he'd stopped before completely losing his temper. The one-eyed man returned the glare, then extended his hand.

"That's a hell of a lot of words, friend, but I reckon you mean 'em. And they sound about right to me. I won't pretend we'll be best buddies, but we can be allies."

Tod nodded curtly and took Ryan's hand. "Okay, then let's get going before it's too late."

They were in the office where Krysty had spoken to Tod the previous evening. The rendezvous had been arranged, and Ryan had reluctantly agreed. Now they had their weapons back and he was, if not exactly happy with the situation, then at least prepared to go along with it. The plan was to lead them across two sectors and to the edge of the wooded areas surrounding the ville, where they would rendezvous with a rebel faction that was barely keeping its head above water.

As they left the building by a side window and took a circuitous route that led them past vid posts and patrolling sec, across the barren areas dividing the sectors, and out into the wooded areas, Ryan gave thought to what he and Krysty had been told.

In each sector there were small groups of people who didn't like the way the sectors were being run. Consensus among these people was that Arcadian and his cronies had long since lost whatever strategy for the future they had once had, and were lost in the morass of their own theories. Most of the population was either

beaten down by the way in which they had to live or was
too scared to organize and fight. The only ones without
these burdens were those in the central sector, and they
were too busy clinging to their semifreedom, scared of
slipping back into one of the other sectors. Which left
those few who tried to find a way of fighting back in
their own sectors, or those who couldn't take it any
more and made a desperate bid to escape, banding
together outside of the ville to try to survive by stealing
supplies and avoiding the sec patrols until such time as
they were sufficient in number to mount a revolution.

Meanwhile, those who stayed in the ville had found
ways to maintain irregular lines of communication by
working out how to avoid the patrols and vids. Arcadian
was too used to his people being kept in line, apart from
a small majority, and so if they kept their profiles low
and moved only singly or in pairs, they could go from
sector to sector and back again overnight. It was something, but they lacked the combat instinct or know-how
to move the game up a notch.

Which was where the newcomers came in: Arcadian
might have his own ideas of their use, but those who
maintained an underground—of dissent if not resistance—had other notions, figuring that the newcomers
wouldn't want to stick around if an alternative presented itself.

They were, of course, right. But Ryan was well
aware that the largest cell of rebellion was also the one
from which his people had taken out several members.
Who was the coldheart in this equation, and how would
that affect their first meeting?

He would soon find out.

They were across the first empty strip of land within minutes, Ryan and Krysty allowing Tod to dictate pace and action as he knew the land. They moved through another sector at an equally fast pace, neither of them realizing at that moment that they passed the building where Jak was talking to Mildred and Doc. It wouldn't have mattered. There was no time to waste. Once they passed another barren area they were into the sector where J.B. was billeted. As they went, Tod told them in a hushed whisper that this sector ringed the whole of the ville. The people here were the most malleable, and so the least likely to cause disruption or run. There were some exceptions, he added, without clarifying.

Here, it was quieter still, and easier than anywhere else to hear the sec patrols. Avoiding them was relatively simple. Progress was swift, and they were soon into the undergrowth that surrounded the ville, moving from the sparse woodland into thickets that were mangrovelike in their density. It was familiar territory to Ryan and Krysty.

"Arcadian has cultivated this with plant life that he has that bastard Andower work on in his labs. There were rumors of man-plant mutie hybrids they were working on there, to patrol here with greater stealth. Nothing came of it that we've seen, but it wouldn't surprise me if the coldheart gets it right one day," Tod whispered with a shudder. "Wait here," he added, gesturing them to stay.

Ryan and Krysty obeyed, but not without a glance of caution passing between them. Tod disappeared into the undergrowth, and they heard a soft cawing in imitation of a nightjar. It was answered from a direction to the east of his position. Minutes passed in which they waited silently, straining for telltale sounds. There was only the softest of rustlings that broke the quiet of night, and that when it was almost on top of them. Ryan had the panga to hand, figuring a blade for better use in the silence, when he relaxed as Tod appeared through the leaves, followed by two men in ragged clothing. They looked as gaunt and worn as the men the companions had encountered a few days before.

"This is them, then," one of the men rasped without ceremony. "Good men you chilled the other day, you know that?"

Ryan nodded. "Them or us. No time to ask questions. No apology, but not something we did willingly," he answered in a steel-edged tone.

"Mebbe too quick," the man returned. He was tall and wasted-thin, his shirt hanging from him. The other had stronger musculature, and was perhaps not so strung-out from hiding so long. He stepped in, coming between the gaunt-eyed rebel and Ryan.

"Us or them, them or us, what's the difference?" he snapped. "We didn't know them any more than they knew us. Makes them more impressive and useful, in my mind. So let's cut the shit and talk about what we need."

His tone bespoke of leadership, and the gaunt-eyed man reluctantly deferred. In tones that were kept low, with one ear kept permanently on alert for movement in the otherwise still and silent mangroves, they spoke rapidly. Ryan and Krysty quickly learned that the rebel force was small—and was having trouble keeping itself together as a unit. Constantly on the move to avoid being tracked down by the sec patrols, and unable to forage much from the mangrove because much of the foliage was poisonous from genetic modification and natural mutation, they had to snatch food from the ring sector, and take water where they could find it.

"We're not fighters by nature or experience," the rebel leader explained, "that's not the way the baron likes us to live under his munificence. So we have to pick it up as we go, and pray the sec—who do get that kind of training—can't pick us off before we've learned. We need help from experienced fighters, both to train us and to unite the rebels on the inside."

"You know how much time that could take?" Ryan asked him. "And you know how much time we'll have?"

"You're not going anywhere," the rebel replied.

"Mebbe not," Ryan countered, "but there's more attention focused on us than mebbe anyone else. Keeping clear of that and doing what you ask—it won't be long before someone catches on. Arcadian may be a lot of things, but stupe he isn't."

"Yeah, but he's an arrogant fucker. He doesn't think we've got the balls or the skills to do anything. Well, he's right about the last one, but you can give us those. Fuck, we got the first. 'Sides which, you think you'd really take this shit for long before wanting to hit back?"

Ryan considered what the rebel said. "Mebbe you're right. Guess we wouldn't want to be around here too long. And mebbe working with you gives us a better chance, just like it does you."

"Exactly," the rebel agreed. "We might as well work together. It more than doubles what we could do alone."

Ryan nodded. "You've got a deal. Now let's plan our next moves."

They spoke hurriedly as time was running short before it was necessary to return. A training session was set for two nights from then, with the time in between spent making contact between the other companions. The rebels would also use their communication lines to spread word of what was to occur. Perhaps, if those not ready to run with the rebels could see what was coming, they might be persuaded to become more active.

By this time, the horizon began to grow lighter as sunrise approached, and with hurried farewells and affirmations of intent, the rebel duo returned to hiding while Tod led Ryan and Krysty back the route they had come.

It would be a hard day, getting by in Alex's sector with no sleep, but the adrenaline of knowing that action was near might just keep them together.

"SIMPLE PAVLOVIAN experimentation. Crude, nasty, potentially dangerous. A splendid way to spend your day," Doc grumbled under his breath as he and Mildred stood in the center of the warehouse block that had been hollowed out and painted a brilliant white. At least, it had once been brilliant white. The walls and floor were now smeared with dirt and grime, with stains that could have been dried blood ineffectively wiped and blotted into the stone floor and walls.

Perhaps not as ineffective as it seemed. Mildred looked at the others huddled in the early-morning chill, and could see that some of them were eyeing the stains with barely disguised foreboding. These marks held meaning for them. Was it part of the experiment?

Come to that, what was the experiment in which they were unwilling participants? Roused from their beds before dawn—glad that Jak had departed—Doc and Mildred had been shepherded through the streets, where others had been corralled to join them. Their collectors kept up a nonstop stream of constant and nonsensical chatter. The point of it at first escaped Mildred. It was Doc, with the lateral thinking of the borderline mad, who tumbled to its purpose.

"The noise stops us thinking of anything other than what it may mean, or will they please shut the fuck up and give us peace," he had murmured to her. "Also gives us no chance or space in which to ask questions. Simple but effective, is it not?"

And so they had been herded into the building. It seemed from the outside like any other on this sector building. The inside was different. The space and white made it seem larger on the inside than out, which was immediately disorienting. The group of twelve was split into six pairs who were placed in different sections of the floor space. It seemed to make little sense to Mildred until she looked down, and could see that there were lines on the floor—faint, and in a different shade of white made even more indistinct by time—that formed irregular boxes.

Then it had started. The chill: colder than outside, she was sure, and maybe from an old air conditioner unit? It came in bursts. As did the sudden, blaring noise from speakers that she could see up in the shadowed ceiling. Then the commands, barking at random: one pair ordered to move, then another. A bell interspersed between some of the commands. And some of the pairs that moved were hit with high-pressure hoses, the likes of which Mildred hadn't seen for some time. It was a testament to the levels of tech Arcadian fostered, if not his charity. The water sluiced the floor, forming runnels around the feet of those who hadn't been targets, leaving those who had been knocked from their feet, bruised and chattering as the cold bit through their damp clothes. The fear and confusion as to who would be next spread across the floor like the water.

Then Doc had spoken, and Mildred fell in with him, the fug of confusion and disorientation falling from her.

"The bell," she murmured. "Simple. And no imagination. Straight from…not even the book, just some vague summary someone once heard of and then passed on half-remembered," she continued with a heavy humor that she was far from feeling.

"Why this is necessary escapes me," Doc returned, "but when in Rome it may be more politic to play along and get out quick."

They stood in the oppressive and tense silence that followed each burst, waiting for instruction. As yet they hadn't been ordered to move. In truth, they had been the only pair who hadn't. Was it because they were here to observe, even though they had no assurance of that? Or was it that they were being tested more than the others for their ability to stand up to the stresses of waiting and wondering?

The pauses between the bursts of action were irregular, and in this nerve-shredding elongated silence, Doc looked around. In the far corner, he could see the woman he had spoken to the previous day. She was wet and miserable and seemed ill at ease. No real surprise. He kept looking at her, willing her to turn to see him before the next burst of instruction.

Force of will or act of chance he neither knew nor cared, but she did turn and saw him standing in the distance. Their eyes locked across the divide, and he raised one hand slightly, making the gesture of ringing a bell, hoping she would be able to understand. Or that her vision wasn't poor at distance. She seemed—with his own eyes it was hard to tell—to nod shortly.

It was gesture that was unnecessary in light of what happened next. A burst of white noise, followed by barked orders for three pairs, one of which was Doc and Mildred. Theirs was the only one preceded by a bell. They obeyed and moved. The other two pairs vacillated. One man tried to move, restrained by the hand of his companion, but that still wasn't enough to save them from the high-pressure water jets. The other pair moved in confusion, and were likewise knocked back. Doc cast a look over his shoulder, and could see his unnamed friend watch them carefully, whispering to her companion.

The experiment—to call it thus was almost a euphemism for the torture, or so it seemed to Doc—continued for some time after that. Gradually, all the pairs seemed to get the point, and it was only when they had all completed the maneuvers successfully that the experiment ceased. The doors opened and beckoned by their shepherds, waiting outside, the pairs gratefully exited. Bedraggled and exhausted, but glad of the respite.

Outside, the pairs once again came together in a group as they were herded back toward their respective quarters. The purpose in treating them as animals was obvious: the disorientation of the experiment added to this pack treatment to test their self-esteem. Nasty, Doc thought, but understandable from the point of the view of the sector leaders. Also a big mistake, as they couldn't have realized that this would give Doc and Mildred the chance they needed to make contact.

"I see why you would wish to play to different rules," Doc murmured, edging close to the woman in the midst of the pack.

She looked around carefully before answering. "Indeed. Your grasp of the rule changes this morning was good, and gratefully received."

"My pleasure," Doc said softly. "Perhaps a discussion on drawing up a new game could proceed?"

"Later. We know where you are. Wait for us tonight."

"Very good," Doc agreed before putting distance between them, murmuring a few words to others in the group that were of no consequence but would put any observer off the scent, before relaying the message to Mildred.

"Another sleepless night," she said wryly. "Time was that I'd say it'd tell on me. Those were the days."

"Weren't they just," Doc replied.

They passed the rest of the day in expectation of what was to come. It was hard not to let their impatience show, but as it was impossible in that sector to determine the shepherds from the sheep, it was imperative to go about their business with no sign of anticipation. For Mildred, a series of psychological tests with colors and shapes was rendered more dull than she could have imagined. The only thing keeping her attention focused was to wonder if any of the other eight people undertaking the experiment with her were likely to be on their side come the night.

Doc, on the other hand, was happy to let his mind wander as he had to take part in a bizarre experiment involving the dissection of a chilled frog, followed by an identical dissection on one that was living. Until he heard the piercing and weirdly human scream of the agonized amphibian, he had no idea that frogs could vocalize in such a manner. Beyond sadism, he couldn't see how the experiment could prove anything. Testing the reactions of those involved was surely rendered false by the fact that those present wouldn't wish to show signs of weakness under such a situation and would so maintain a front, no matter how artificial. The double-think of this sector could, if he considered it too much, drive him to despair and a permanent craziness.

But no: to focus on the night, and the creation of an escape route, was more than enough to distract him.

Both Mildred and Doc, therefore, were relieved when they were able to return to their quarters for the night. Nonetheless, the wait for their contact's arrival was seemingly endless.

Eventually, in the dark watches, when all was silent, they could hear the faint scrabbling of someone climbing the wall. Mildred opened the window to allow entry to whoever was outside. The gray-haired woman climbed through, followed by a portly man with a growing bald patch around a fringe of black hair, and ripped pants. He was blowing heavily.

"We can't go on meeting like this," he panted by way of greeting.

"This is the first time," Doc said, bemused.

"Joke," the man puffed, leaning on his flexed knees and taking a deep breath before extending a hand. "Hamilton Dupree, at your service. Cloris here told me that you wanted to see us."

Doc looked at the gray-haired woman, glad he now knew her name as he would never have guessed it given all the time in the world.

Mildred liked the man's attitude. She was sick of wasting time. She didn't realize that would soon change. "Guess you know who we are," she began, "so let's cut the crap and get to it."

While they listened, she told them about Jak's visit, and the knowledge they now had about travel between sectors. "If we can make arrangements with our friends in other sectors, then we can get the hell out. But we could do it a lot better if you were with us."

"On the other hand, if you did it alone then we wouldn't get in the shit if you failed," Cloris pointed out.

"So what do you gain by that?" Mildred asked, puzzled.

"Nothing. And I'm not saying that we don't wish to gain. But we've been here all along," Cloris said with a shrug.

"You have to take into account a few things," Hamilton added ruefully. "In the first place, I could make an argument that we've been in this sector so long that we've become used to the way things are, and our will and desire has been sapped. And there might be something in that. But the truth, I fear, is that we're more than a little cowardly. We're not fighters. No one here is. We have no weapons."

"There is no sec here, and no one is armed," Mildred said flatly. "What's the problem?"

"There are men with blasters in the other sectors," Hamilton replied. "That's what worries us. Cowards, you see. Afraid of pain."

"What about the pain of today, and the pain of being in constant bondage?" Doc said mildly. "Is that not as bad?"

"While you know you can still stay alive, you can mebbe put up with a little pain," Cloris answered. "Putting it plainly, those of us who find support and comfort in banding together and mebbe pretending we're rebels by breaking bounds need reassurance that we're not going to go the whole way and end up with nothing but the farm to show for it."

"There are no definites. I could lie to you, but I won't," Mildred replied. "But I'll tell you something. If we do this, then the whole ville is going to explode whether you like it or not. Jak's ready, and he's contacting the others. It'll happen, as simple as that. Question is, do we do it alone, or do we have support?"

There was a silence. Finally, Hamilton said, "It doesn't look like there'll be much choice. The onslaught of the inevitable, so to speak." He looked at Cloris and shrugged. "And mebbe that's just what we need."

Chapter Fifteen

Jak spent the next night traversing the sectors. He moved swiftly, and took proscribed routes. It was simple to work out the best way to avoid the vid cams as they were usually mounted in much the same way, no matter where they were positioned in the ville. The sec patrols also planned and executed their routes in much the same way. Schweiz was a lazy sec chief. From the beginning, the albino teen had scented that he was a man who liked posturing more than actually doing any work. The ease with which he was able to slip past the man's personnel proved this. The paths they took were well-worn. Why those in each sector who dissented hadn't been able to rise up was another factor that Jak couldn't figure.

If these thoughts had been running through the mind of Mildred or Doc, they would have reasoned that an oppressed people used to be commanded with an iron fist would lack the necessary steel to make that first move. But this was Jak. If you told him such a thing, his pragmatic hunter's nature would tell him simply that you can only go on so long before rising for freedom.

As he scouted the sectors, he didn't stop to make contact with Ryan, Krysty and J.B. That could come later. For now, he wanted to get a feel for the ville as a whole.

What he found—something that would be useful in the near future, he thought—was that there was a greater traffic between sectors than either Schweiz or Arcadian would have thought possible. Keeping to the shadows, there were men and women moving between sectors for reasons that were possibly as personal as those of the man who had first described this route to him. Jak figured that if you could just get these people to carry messages and perhaps weapons…

It was a nice idea, but one that he knew was doomed. Those who traveled between the wires considered this revolt enough. Maybe—just maybe—that was what the baron wanted. While they had this, which they considered rebellion enough, then they wouldn't go further. The real rebels, those who truly wanted to fight, would make for the outside. Perhaps they were the only hope? Jak didn't share Ryan and Krysty's knowledge of the rebels, but he could make the leap between the group they had initially encountered and a rebel force.

Which, in his reckoning, meant that it was down to himself and his friends. No one else could be trusted. No matter what Doc or Mildred might think.

All this went through his mind as he mechanically made his way through the day, completing an assault course that was followed by a bout of aversion therapy. All those on the course were led from the completion point to a small, one-story building where they were strapped into a series of chairs, under the watchful eye of an armed sec. Jak noted that most of the men with him were unarmed. But he still had the Colt Python and his knives. The temptation to fight back when they took him and secured the straps was strong. The psychology was basic: he was outnumbered, and resistance would only result in his chilling. To what end? Maybe that was how the ville as a whole was kept down.

This was what he had to fight. And the knowledge of this kept him stoic as the aversion therapy began. Vid images of the course they had just traversed were flashed on a screen in front of them. Their reactions were just as they had been as they avoided the mines, blasters and mannequins that had been flung in their path. Even though they were seated, they still tried to move in automatic response. Except that now their natural reactions were greeted with a jolting charge of electricity that shot white-hot pain through limbs and paralyzed the brain. Responses were therefore muted the further along the course the vid images played. But still nature dictated that they try to respond. Still the jolting charge shot through them, causing muscles to spasm and control of bladder and bowels to be lost.

Jak felt his vision cloud with explosions of violent color as his neurons were shorted out. Yet still he clung to the thoughts in his head, that he had to keep himself fit and alert enough for that night's incursion into the outer sector. While those around him yelled and screamed in pain, subsiding to low moans as the course progressed, Jak bit on his tongue until he could taste blood, using this as a focus.

Then, almost with an anticlimax, the vid stopped. they had reached the end of the course. The aftershock of the pain still coursed through him as he tried to look at the men around him. His vision was fogged by pain, and it swam in and out of focus. He felt, rather than saw, the sec men move among them, taking off the electrodes and replacing them with pads of some other kind. And then, before he had a chance to work it out, the vid began again. This time, at each juncture where a shock had been delivered—and he gave an involuntary start— there was nothing. It took several such junctures before he realized that the replacement pads were registering his new reactions for the benefit of the coldheart white-coats Pulaski and Foxx.

Eventually, after what seemed like an eternity, they were released from the experiment. The sun above showed him that it was now late afternoon. As the sec escorted the pained and exhausted men back to their quarters, Jak could only hope that he would be fit enough for his necessary after-dark excursion. Rest came as a blissful relief. He thankfully sank into the embrace of black oblivion, the raw skin and blistering nerve endings no opposition to the fatigue that over-whelmed him.

He awoke with a start, sitting bolt upright and shaking the fogged sleep from his brain. He was still sore from the electric shock therapy, but it hadn't man-aged to impair his mental functions. He didn't know much about electricity on the brain, but he had seen the condition of some of those who had sat with him, and he considered himself lucky.

Maybe now was the time to capitalize on that luck. He rose and went to the window, staring out over the night. In the distance he could see the lights of the central sector. As the only part of the ville that func-tioned in any way like a regular ville, it was still lit up.

Distant sounds of people at play came to him across the dark emptiness, and he wondered for a moment if anyone else here had ever heard them and felt so isolated from real life.

But there was no time for that, now. If he and his companions were to get anything approaching real life back for themselves, then he had to move. The outer sector was his goal. He needed to find J.B., Ryan and Krysty. And he needed to contact any others like those they had fought on the way in. A hell of a task for one night, but time was at a premium.

Jak left the building and skirted the vid and sec in a way that was fast becoming routine to him. Still, despite that he stayed triple red, wary that the experiments of the daytime may affect his nighttime judgment.

He made swift progress to the outer sector. But once there, he was unsure of how to proceed. Encircling the ville as it did, it presented a vast area to cover. He would have to be content with as much as possible for now, then carry on his search on subsequent nights, should it prove fruitless.

Like many other sectors of Arcady, this one rose and set with the sun. It was quiet, but far from silent. As Jake wove his way through the shanties and huts, he could hear breathing, muttering, and the sounds of some indulging in carnal activity. But there was nothing he recognized as the Armorer. They had spent so long on the road that he could even determine J.B.'s breathing pattern when he was asleep.

However, something did catch his ear. The murmured undertone of a man's voice, coming from one of the larger huts. It was accompanied by giggling that rose

and fell under and above his voice, making words hard
to determine. There was something about his tone,
though…

Jak ventured closer, and as he drew near he could
hear the man telling the giggling women what he
wanted them to do. His voice held power, and the confidence of one who was used to wielding such power.
A light showed slit-clear under the doorway and from
the edges of the covered windows. The smell of wood
ash, mingled with sweat and lust, carried on the night
breeze.

Jak crept up on the building. Stealth was hardly necessary. From the sounds within, you could have let off
a gren next to the hut and they wouldn't have noticed.
There was just enough space for Jak to put an eye to the
gap and be able to make out what was happening within.
The smoky atmosphere drifting through the gap made
his eye smart; he had to keep looking away, blinking.

Inside, there was a man sitting on a rush chair, naked
and idly fingering a massive erection. He was ordering
two chubby women to perform sex acts on each other,
playing with himself while he watched. Their giggles
increased with the stimulation they gave each other, but
were sometimes stifled when breast or thigh was thrust
into a mouth. Jak took no erotic pleasure from this, but
concluded from the display of power that the man was
probably the sector leader, or a close ally. His vision
strayed to the rest of the room: cabinets and a desk that
seemed out of place with the animal skulls piled in on
corner only reinforced this view.

But most of all his attention was taken by the old
woman who sat naked against a wall, cross-legged with

a hairless dog sleeping across her knees. She, too, seemed to giggle stupidly, particularly when the man looked over to her. Yet when he turned away, her face changed: unmistakably, contempt swept over her.

Part of the reason for this became clear when the man called her over. With a reluctance that he had to have been either arrogant or a stupe to miss, she got to her feet and walked across, kneeling in front of him, following his instructions.

He sat back, no longer interested in the two fat woman. He sighed, pushing the old woman away from him with his foot so that she slumped backward.

"You can go now, and take that mangy hound with you," he said in a weary voice. Without a word, she picked herself up and clicked her fingers, the dog trotting to her. She made for the door with what Jak could see was an undue haste. He was about to pull back into the shadows when the man's next words made him stop suddenly.

"Tell Dix I want to see him tomorrow."

"Why ask me?" the woman questioned, barely keeping the edge of contempt in her voice under control.

The man smiled, but there was no humor in it. Just malice.

"I know you're thick with him. Nothing escapes me here. Just tell him. There are plans for him."

The woman nodded and left without a word, the dog at her heels. Jak kept back in the shadows, but started to follow her. His mind raced: the Armorer. It was the stroke of fortune he needed. The look on her face as she pulled the door shut, before the darkness swallowed her up, told Jak that the man's arrogance was misplaced.

It was a look that told the albino teen that there was plenty that went on without the sector leader's knowledge.

But the mention of plans for the Armorer held a warning note. Jak might have found him just in time.

He set off in pursuit of the old woman. Maybe she wasn't as old as she looked. She was fast, now, and just maybe the hard weight of experience had aged her prematurely. Jak thought of Doc, and how young he was compared to how he looked. She moved like Doc, and the expression on her face had reminded him of the old man: there was an intelligence that chose to hide behind the veneer of madness or simplicity. He only hoped that her cunning worked as much to his favor as it did with Doc.

She kept looking over her shoulder. It was as though she could sense that he was behind her, but couldn't locate him, no matter how hard she tried. Jak was good. To even sense he was there showed how sharp she could be. And her attempts to shake him were annoying. He felt like he was winding around every part of the sector, doubling back on himself, and wasting precious time. He was on the verge on throwing all caution and revealing himself, hoping she would trust him, when such a decision was suddenly unnecessary. She arrived at a shanty where she stopped, looking around carefully before knocking on the wooden door that hung loosely in the ill-fitting frame. The dog sniffed idly at her heels, unheeding of the quick glances she darted around. Jak hung back in shadow, still and silent, barely breathing.

The door of the shanty opened. The inside was shrouded in darkness, and as the woman muttered something so low that it was inaudible even to Jak, it seemed that there was a patch of dark that moved, beckoning her in. A last lingering look around, and she went in, the dog at her heels and the door closing softly.

This had to be J.B. Jak came out of shadows and made the ground swiftly, coming up to the shuttered window opening. There was a low, muttered conversation within, and as he came within earshot he could make out two voices. One of which was more than familiar to him. A grin spread across the impassive white visage, despite the words he could make out.

"Curtis must have some idea of what it is," a man's voice said, unmistakably that of the Armorer.

"—not saying, at least not to me. But if another sector wants you—"

"Then it's a way out of here, mebbe to a place where I can find the others."

"You shouldn't be thinking that way. There's something you have to consider. This sector is full of the infirm, the old, the misfit and the misbegotten. There's a reason for that."

"I know," he said after a pause. "But if that's what it's to be, then I'll just have to deal with it."

Jak had been listening at the shuttered window space. There was a faint light from within that had only been illuminated once the woman was inside. It was now casting a glow around the ragged edges of the shutter. There wasn't enough of a gap for him to put his eye to it and see in; regardless, he had a spatial awareness of what was going on inside from the way that the sound moved.

His grin widened, and he stepped back. While J.B.

had been speaking, the position of his voice had changed, and there was the slightest of sounds that was almost hidden by the words, but bespoke of a movement that was all too familiar.

So it was that he wasn't taken by surprise when the shutter was flung outward, and by the illumination of a shaded lamp within he found himself staring into the face of both the Armorer and the mini-Uzi, its snubbed nose leveled on his forehead. The expression on J.B.'s face was something the albino youth could privately treasure, just as he had those of Mildred and Doc.

"Don't waste ammo," Jak said before staring at J.B.'s battered face and adding, "What happen you? Looks like lost fight with armored wag."

For a fraction of a second, J.B. was openmouthed. Then, without a word, he moved to the door and ushered Jak inside. Words tumbled over themselves as he asked how and why; Jak told him quickly of everything he had seen and learned over the past few nights, before returning the question. J.B. told him of the beating he had taken.

"Lucky the people here have no idea of how to fight. For me, not them. The numbers did this to me. Any normal ville, and I'd have bought the farm. Martha patched me up, and has turned a few of the people here around." He indicated the old woman, who nodded a greeting to Jak.

"You're a pretty sharp boy," she said, eyeing him shrewdly. "I knew there was someone there, but damned if I could find you. Say so myself, but I'm sharp enough—hell, compared to most here that ain't saying much—still couldn't place you, though."

"Survival," Jak said flatly. "Do anything for that. Right?" His gaze met hers. She knew then that he had seen her earlier. He could read the relief on her face when he continued without saying anything more. "Need move quick. Find Ryan and Krysty, then get out."

J.B. shook his head. "Can't. No matter what happens to me in the next twenty-four. Sun will be up in the next few hours, and no way we can get Mildred and Doc from where you say, find Ryan and Krysty and then get to cover in that time. Best thing you can do is use the next couple of nights to round them up and track where I am."

"What if end up in Andower's labs?" Jak questioned, barely able to keep his contempt under control as he uttered the whitecoat's name.

J.B. drew a deep breath. "Well, just a chance I'll have to take. Better that most of us get out in one piece than we all go down."

"Ryan not agree," Jak returned. "Or Mildred. Or me. Or—"

"Okay, I get the point," J.B. interrupted, "but I can't call it any other way."

Martha had been listening carefully. "There might be another way," she said slowly. Then, when they were both looking at her questioningly she added, "The rebel group you were talking about. I know where they are."

"Why didn't you say this before?" J.B. questioned.

She looked away, unable to meet his eye. "I knew you'd want to go to them. You weren't ready…needed to recover from those injuries."

"They're not that bad," he said gently.

She shook her head. "Mebbe it's not that. You've seen what it's like here. Mebbe it was just good to have someone to talk to who wasn't a complete stupe. And I'm too old, too tired and just plain too scared to join up with the rebels."

"So how you know where they are?" Jak asked.

Martha shrugged. "You know I like to move about here, be free. Or at least pretend I'm free. I see them, and I see where they move their camp. Don't talk to them, and make sure they don't see me. Just don't want to get involved."

"But if you show us where they are, you're getting involved now," J.B. murmured gently. "You sure about this?"

She snorted. "Hell, no. But mebbe I've got a reason to get involved. If they take you to the house of pain that the whitecoat sector runs, then how could I live with myself if I just let you go?"

J.B. nodded. "Let's do this, then. I figure that mebbe I know what this is taking, and I appreciate it."

She grinned lopsidedly and tickled behind the ear of her mangy dog. "Let's go then, before my nerve goes."

The night outside was still and quiet as J.B. extinguished the lamp and the three of them left the shanty. Martha led them quickly through the maze of dirt tracks, pausing only when a sec patrol became distantly audible. They detoured and took shelter behind a row of tumbledown huts as a three-man patrol ambled by, almost disinterested in what was around them. J.B. felt they could have been standing in plain view, and the sec men wouldn't have seen them. When they were out of sight, and the three had started off once more in the opposite direction, he voiced his disbelief.

"You were right about Schweiz, Jak. No sec chief with any real idea would stand for that kind of shit."

"If they're that bad, what does that make those of us who won't stand up them?" Martha asked of him. "Mebbe the same kind of learning that makes us like this makes them that way, too."

J.B. pondered this. "That could be to our advantage…all of us," he added.

They were now past the shanties and out into the undergrowth. Martha led them surefootedly through the mangrove until they could hear distant sounds of combat. Jak and J.B. exchanged glances: it was hand-to-hand, but was intermittent. There was also something familiar about it.

In a few short moments they were at the edge of a clearing, where a sight greeted them that gladdened the heart. A group of rebels was gathered in a circle, watching the fighting in their midst. As the three intruders emerged, they spun, hands reaching for blasters. The circle broke open, revealing four figures in the middle. Two of them were all too familiar.

Jak's face broke into a grin for the second time that night, a grin of relief as much as amusement.

"Hey, Ryan, teach these rebels fight, but better teach 'em triple red, first!" he exclaimed.

Chapter Sixteen

Ignoring the bristling rebels, who were momentarily in confusion at this intrusion, Ryan and Krysty broke through the ranks to greet Jak and the Armorer. They were curious as to what had happened to Doc and Mildred, and Jak swiftly filled them in on his activities, and the contact he had made with Mildred and Doc a short while before. He finished by telling how he had chanced on J.B., before the Armorer took over, detailing both what had already happened, and what was likely to happen to him within the next twenty-four hours.

"Fireblast and fuck," Ryan cursed. "I was hoping that we'd have more time than that, but I guess it's not going to happen that way."

He and Krysty outlined how they had come to be in the rebel camp. The truth was—and Ryan had no compunction in being brutally blunt in front of their newfound allies—that the rebels weren't in good shape. Because of the nature of the sector system, they had little idea of tactics or strategy, and no practical experience of combat. It had only been a few nights that Ryan and Krysty had been here, and although the rebels were willing to learn and were quick on the uptake, there was a hell of a lot of ground to make up before they could face armed sec.

"Not sure about that," Jak spit pithily before detailing the slack and well-worn habits that he had seen.

"Might just balance things a little," Ryan murmured. "It gives us a better chance, but—"

"Not much of one if no one in the ville decides to fight back. Just us and a few rebels?" Krysty added.

Martha, who had been listening up to this point but had been unwilling to give voice, glanced nervously at J.B. before speaking. Her voice trembled slightly, betraying her nerves.

"We—if I'm going to speak I might as well for all of the people like me who haven't had the guts to escape—might just find some of that strength if we could see that there were others fighting. And mebbe if that occupied the sec and we didn't look like we were going to get blasted at the first chance."

"You say you haven't got guts," J.B. said, turning to her, "but you led me and Jak here. You knew the rebels might shoot first and ask who we were after, but that didn't stop you."

"But that's these guys," she answered, gesturing to the gathered rebel force. "They're not the sec. They're not under Arcadian."

"But they are just men," J.B. answered her. "More than that, they're men who haven't had to really do the job for a long time because of the way the baron makes you all feel. If they were any damn good, you think that you could move about like you do? You think that Jak could have found out what he did, and seen what he'd told us about?"

"I guess not. But—"

"No," J.B. interrupted, "they've ruled you for so long

because you were scared. No need for that now. You want to break out? Now is probably the only option you'll have. Because if we go up against the sec and lose, then they'll be much stronger and come down harder in the future."

She considered that for a moment. When she answered, it was obvious that she still had some trepidation. "I guess you're right. Facing it ain't easy, though, and I don't know how easy it's going to be to get people in our sector to do anything."

"Just have to face that one when it comes," J.B. said. "Which might be sooner rather than later." He turned to Ryan and Krysty. "I figure it's going to happen in the morning. No matter what it actually is. I'm guessing it's Andower, but I might get lucky."

"Hope so," Ryan said.

He looked at Martha. "You're our link, you realize that? The only way we can know immediately if anything happens is if you come to us. Can you do that?"

She was trembling even as she thought about it, but one look at J.B. reminded her why she had come this far. "Yeah. I can. I have to, I guess."

J.B. embraced her. "It'll be all right. If I make it hard for them, then I can tie up the sec, make it easier for you to slip out here."

"We'll be ready. Right?" Ryan questioned the rebels around him. There was no such fear from them. This chance was what they had been waiting for.

"What about Millie and Doc. And you, Jak?" Krysty asked.

Jak shrugged. "Easy move in darkness. Daylight be problem but know ville better now—and vids. Figure mebbe J.B. makes trouble, then sec need pull out position. Not all sectors have anyway. Move where I am, then I find way out dark or light."

Ryan nodded. "Then that's the way it'll have to be. I'm not totally happy—there are too many places where it could break down—but I guess it's all we've got at such notice."

"We've been in worse," J.B. said with a wry grin, "or at least, you have. Not sure about me, but I'll take my chances."

Ryan grunted. "We'll give you every chance we can make," he said shortly. His sense of responsibility didn't sit easily with J.B. being directly on the firing line, and not himself. "You can always join the rebels. We could, too," he added, indicating Krysty.

J.B. shook his head. "No. This way we get the spark needed to fire it up a little. Besides, there's Millie and Doc. If we don't go back tonight, then Arcadian will take his anger out on them. And we couldn't do a thing."

"You're right," Ryan said softly. "Guess this is the only way." He looked at the lightening skies above them. "We should split up now, and get ready for the day ahead. It's going to be a bastard."

J.B. barked a bitter laugh. "You can say that again."

THE LAST FEW HOURS of darkness passed uneasily for the Armorer. He was tense, knowing what was to come, but powerless to act until the first move against him had been made. Every fiber of his being told him to make a preemptive strike. He had weapons, and it would have been simple to leap in ahead of the baron's men and

force their hand. Yet the plan, such as it was, relied on
his being taken as the catalyst.

He paced the dirt floor of his shanty, cursing to
himself, willing the sun to rise faster. He knew that he
should sleep, yet no rest would come to his restless
mind. Martha waited for him. She sat on the dirt floor,
the dog asleep across her knees while she gently stroked
his mangy hide. Like her, the dog was a misfit who had
seen his best days retreat behind him at speed. He didn't
have much to look forward to except her comforting
him. In the same way, she felt she had nothing to look
forward to except the comfort of keeping out of trouble.

Or at least, that had been how she had felt until she
had met J.B. Was it the last fall stirrings of lust, or
perhaps a deeper emotion? Or was it that she saw in the
Armorer something of how she had been when her body
had first started to fail her, and she had been sent to this
sector? She had said nothing to him, as she was now
ashamed of her association with Andower and his experiments. But once she had been a research chemist on
plant cell stimulation. The reason she knew the mangrove so well was because she had been responsible for
much of the modified plant life within, and the planning
of the germination. That had been before her hands had
started to knit with arthritis, and accidents in the lab had
made her dispensable. Back then she had closed her
mind to the experimentation outside her own sphere.
Coming to live in this sector, and how she was forced
to survive here, made her more than aware of the human
cost.

And now there was a way out. She was terrified. But
that nagging conscience would let her do nothing else.

Light crept through the shutters. Still she watched him pace up and down, wondering if she should explain to him why she couldn't let him down, even though it may make him view her in a different way.

No. None of that mattered. Only that she play her part, and he play his.

Light flooded the room as J.B. pulled back the shutters. He turned to her.

"Won't be long now. You know what to do."

She nodded. "Wait for them to come. See where they take you. Then get the hell out of there and head for the rebels."

"Exactly."

"But what about your friends? And Jak?"

"They're looking for signs. Jak's in a heavily patrolled sector. He'll see any movement. And I'll make sure there will be."

She stood up slowly and painfully, moving the dog as it opened one questioning eye.

"You be careful," she said simply, standing in front of him.

He smiled slowly. "I won't take any more risks than are necessary," he answered.

She shook her head. "That's no kind of an answer. But the only one, I guess." She kissed him gently on the cheek before beckoning the dog to follow in her wake as she walked out into the morning. She didn't want to look back because of the tears misting her vision.

J.B. watched her go, wondering what motivated her. She had been kindness personified to him since he had arrived, yet she seemed to want or ask nothing of him. Around her, the sector slowly came to life. The few people passing greeted him in their way. He was accepted here, and that, too, was down to her.

He knew without question that he would never know. There wouldn't be time.

He turned back into the hut. His bags with grens and ammo were there. His knife and the mini-Uzi were primed. He could just start a firefight and hope for the best. No, they would just blast the hell out of him and that would be it. If any revolt were to spread, then he had to be seen traveling through sectors, and he had to make a stand at a position where he could make the maximum impact, and so draw the most sec to him.

Now he just had to hope that they would be so naive as to let him take his weapons with him. They had been so far, relying on numbers. He had to give them no grounds to suspect that he would fight back.

So it was that when a sec party of five approached his shanty, he was ready, his face fixed in a mask of impassivity.

The party, watched by a curious and gathering crowd of sector dwellers, halted outside the shanty, and one of them detached himself.

"Dix, you know why we're here?"

"Not exactly," J.B. said, appearing in the doorway with his bags already slung across him, the knife and the blaster secreted where they were hidden but easily accessible. He had no wish to remind the sec of their presence. He added, "I just know that I got word I was moving to another sector."

"Something like that. It's time for you to move on to where you can be of some use," the sec man said without a trace of irony.

"Where?" J.B. asked. He could see Martha and her dog lurking on the fringe of the crowd, and was hoping that this opening would give him an opportunity to get word to her on where as much as when.

"Somewhere you'll be more useful," the sec man re-iterated with an annoying lack of clarity. "You'll find out soon enough. Just come with us."

J.B. nodded, and fell in with the sec crew without another word. Through the crowd, he could see Martha turn away, moving furtively into an alley between two shanties that saw her disappear from view, the mangy dog trotting at her heels. In his thoughts, he wished her luck and speed in reaching her destination. The sooner the rebels knew that it had begun, the better it would be.

Meanwhile, he had his own progress on which to focus. The crowd followed him at a distance while the sec escorted him from the sector. He could hear them at his back. As opposed to the confusion and hostility that had greeted his arrival, there was now a ground-swell of discontent that he was being moved. He had become one of them. It may just serve him well.

As he came to the area where they would cross into a new sector, he passed Curtis's hut. The sector leader stood outside, fully clothed for once, smirking as the Armorer was taken past him. There was no sign of the two young women who fed Curtis's desire. To outside eyes, the sector leader would appear to be a model of propriety. It was a small thing to consider, but J.B. would enjoy events wiping the smirk from his face.

They crossed into another sector, then passed through this one at triple speed before crossing into another. J.B. recognized the route from his previous journey out. These two sectors were on the way to the center. Two things crossed his mind. The first was that he might have been wrong in his assumption, and he was being taken to Arcadian. That would be sweet. What better place to kick-start the revolt? Lurking behind that was the question of whether or not they were passing through the sectors where Jak or Millie and Doc were quartered. If so, then chance would be aided. One thing for sure: Jak had spoken of heavy patrols in his sector. Here, there were only a few patrols, and the sector prior to this had seemed to be free.

Mentally, J.B. was running myriad possibilities, working out a game plan for each one if he could. So it was with a sudden start that he realized they had changed direction and crossed into another sector. Here, it was quiet. There was no one on the streets, and yet sec patrols could be seen on street corners, fairly heavy security for somewhere that seemed to be deserted. J.B. felt his heart sink. There was only one place this could be, and it seemed as though he would be forced into doing things the hard way.

He began to prepare himself as they approached a building whose porticoed arch led into a square. In the middle of the square a small, wizened, white-coated man peering at him myopically stood waiting between two heavily built and equally heavily armed guards.

"Ah," he said as J.B. was led to him, "Mr. Dix. Yes…" He halted the sec party with a gesture and, still flanked by his personal guard, walked through them to examine J.B.

The Armorer stood impassive, not wishing to give anything away. The whitecoat walked around him, making small noises of pleasure and affirmation to himself. He grasped J.B. by the chin and turned his head so that he could get a better look at him, squinting up at the Armorer's face. His grip was surprisingly strong, and it was all J.B. could do to prevent himself from wincing in pain as the viselike fingers tightened on his jaw.

"Yes… As I thought," the whitecoat said softly. "Perfect apart from the sight defect. A good specimen…" He let go of J.B.'s jaw, leaving the Armorer numb and with a temptation to shake his head to restore feeling. "Well, my friend," the whitecoat said, "it would be a shame to let you fester with that pervert Curtis when your problem is such a simple one."

J.B. didn't think he had a problem, but he let that go. However, what he heard next made his mouth dry up and make any protest impossible.

"It's a simple procedure. We have some perfect specimens we can use for transplant. Don't worry, my dear boy, we'll soon have a pair of perfect eyeballs popped in there."

He slipped his hand into one of his bags, his imperfect eyes flickering side to side. He ignored the blaster and the blade, thanking anything and anyone that they hadn't thought to relieve him of his weapons. He sought a gren and thumbed the pin. He would have to act quickly if he wasn't going to get blasted himself.

But then again, he would have to act quickly, no matter what.

MARTHA COULD FEEL her heart pounding as she walked quickly to the wooded areas that ringed the sector. She was hoping that the lack of vid cams here, and the crowd that had gathered around J.B.'s departure, necessitating a redeployment of regular sec patrols, would make her task easier.

She paused, looking around. There seemed to be no one who had noticed her slip away. Certainly no one in view around here. She tried to listen for any sound, but all she could hear was the nervous and irregular pounding of her own heart. As she paused, so the dog stopped at her feet and looked up, whining softly as her unease communicated itself to him.

"Don't worry, just keep to heel," she said softly, petting him as he took a last look around.

The mangy hound was at her heels as she scurried into the mangrove, picking her way toward the area where she had stood with J.B. and Jak the previous night…only a few short hours before, though it seemed an eternity right now.

She broke into a run, gasping for breath and moving blindly as panic overtook her. The dog barked at her heels. She had no idea where she was going, now, only that—

Her flight was arrested by a man who stepped from behind a tree and caught hold of her, clapping a hand over her mouth to stifle the scream she couldn't contain. But the dog didn't growl. It took a moment, but she recognized the man from the meeting the night before. She had reached her destination. He unclamped his hand as he sensed her breathing return to normal.

"It's started," she gasped between breaths. Then her vision began to swim, and she was aware of the dog yelping in fear as she fell backward and all went black.

IF J.B. HAD BEEN GIVEN the time to think about it, he would have wondered at the strangeness of a man's psyche. He thumbed the pin from the gren, holding down to give himself as much time as possible, and carefully extracted the object from his bag. He thought he caught a puzzled expression on the faces of Andower's guards, but he could have been mistaken. He shuffled his feet as the whitecoat made to grasp his chin again.

"Don't worry, Mr. Dix, we'll soon have you seeing better than ever. It won't hurt a bit…well, not a lot," Andower said, misunderstanding J.B.'s action.

Good. Every fraction of a second was precious. J.B. took advantage of this misunderstanding by stepping back, thrusting backward through the sec guards. Surprised by his actions, they let him pass through. He turned and ran, hoping that he had guessed right.

"My dear man, running won't help. There's nowhere to go. We can easily bring you back— Hello, what's that?"

Andower's words were prompted by the object he saw roll at his feet. Unused as they were to any opposition, the sec had slow reactions, which was exactly what the Armorer had counted upon. Not only were they slow to react to his bursting through them, they also failed to notice that he had let something roll at his feet.

He didn't dare to look back: no time. He had his eyes set on the portico. No blasterfire from behind him, though he was certain he could hear the cocking of blasters ready to fire. They would aim to wound, not chill. He was sure of that, although he didn't trust their aim. No, it was something far more deadly that he sought to escape.

"Move," he heard someone yell. Getting Andower out of the way? There probably wasn't—

The shock wave threw him forward, pitching him into the gap made by the portico. He used the momentum to carry himself through, rolling as he did so that he could push himself to one side, and avoid the channeled blast of air through the hole. The disturbed air threatened his eardrums, even though he let his jaw hang loose. Under the explosion, there was the symphony of breaking glass as the force of the blast shattered every window in the square. Rising above it all were the high-pitched screams of men torn to shreds by the shrapnel in the gren.

Had Andower been shuffled out of the way in time? The end of the whitecoat would be a good thing in itself. But there was no time for him to think about that now. Heaving and rasping to get air back into his lungs, J.B. sought cover as he fumbled the mini-Uzi from its place of concealment. The street was still empty, but it wouldn't be for long. He needed somewhere to dig in, and then hope for the best.

Martha and Jak…

As SHE CAME AROUND, Martha could hear voices barking orders, many of them, shouting over each other. The dog licked her face, happy that she was waking as it was upset and confused by the activity around, whining softly. She petted it to reassure it, then sat up. She had been moved to the rebel camp by the man she had—literally—run into. All around, men and women of varying ages were preparing their weapons. A man came over to her. She recognized him as one of the men she had seen talking to Ryan and Krysty just a few hours before.

"Where did they take him?" he asked without preamble.

She shook her head. "I don't know which sector. He tried to get them to give it away, but they didn't. I just know that they took him. I came straightaway. They couldn't have gone far."

As she spoke, a distant rumble echoed over the mangrove. A crooked smile crossed the face of the man standing over her.

"He wouldn't let them—that's a fucking gren. Can't remember the last time… Come on," he yelled, turning away.

In a blur of activity, she found herself swept up by the onrush of the rebels. Adrenaline pumping, the dog still at her heels, and unarmed, she found herself joining them as they ran through the woods, spreading out as it became thinner, moving into the outer areas of Sector Eight and finding that the shanty ville was already in uproar. Previously passive citizens who had been milling around in the wake of J.B.'s departure, and then stirred by the blast, were being beaten back into their homes by the sec patrols. The first volleys of blaster-fire from the rebels cut into the sec. Now, not knowing whether to stick to their task or fight back, their attention divided, the patrols found themselves in an alien position.

The unarmed dwellers picked up rocks and started to fight back. When the sec patrols turned on them, they found themselves under volleys of fire. Some fell as they were hit. Dwellers picked up the weapons, fired up by events, and joined the onrushing rebels. Martha picked up a handblaster. She had only ever seen them used, and had never handled one. But she had a personal mission.

As the sec was driven back, they approached Curtis's quarters. The sec chief was standing outside his hut, incoherently yelling orders to his men, grasping a longblaster that he held across his chest, more as a talisman than an offensive weapon.

Martha threaded through the crowd until she was almost in front of him. In the confusion, he didn't even register her until she had raised her blaster at him. The look of shock on his face was priceless. So much she wanted to say that to him before firing, but he started to level his blaster and there was no time. She fired three times, the kick making her old shoulders and wrists jar with pain.

One shot missed. The second took off the right side of his face, tearing through his eye socket and splintering the surrounding bone. The third was lower, and ripped into his thorax. He was thrown backward into the arms of the two fat women, who screamed as his blood pumped over them.

Martha stood stock-still for a moment, shocked by what she had done, yet also glad. It was the dog, pawing at her with a preternatural sense, that brought her back to reality.

With the mangy hound at her heels, she moved toward the onrushing rebel group. Safety in numbers: relative, sure, but all she had now in this new uncertainty. And she felt different, like they may soon be free, even if it took their lives.

"SCHWEIZ. WHERE IS that moron? I want him here now!" Arcadian strode back and forth across the plush carpet in his quarters. He could no longer take standing in the radio room, listening to the reports as they came in. First the man Dix tries to chill Andower and make a break; then the rebels invade the eighth sector and the dimmies who live there join them.

The gren blast could be heard to some degree across the whole of the ville: that was what had first alerted the baron to the evolving problem. Outside, in the central sector, there was now unrest as the populace clamored to know what was happening. Schweiz had panicked. The sec force was trying to quell a riot that was rapidly of their own making. Sending them in hard had been a poor piece of judgment.

"Sir, I need to see you." The sec chief, looking flustered even behind his shades, appeared in the doorway.

"It's the other way around, surely?" the baron asked with ice dripping from his tone. "I wanted to see you. What are you doing about the rebels and Dix? And why are you trying to punish the people outside instead of keeping them calm and informed?"

"It's best they know nothing, sir. Not until we have stopped the revolt."

"Revolt?" Arcadian went puce and his voice rose in both octaves and decibels. "You complete fuckwit. The people of this sector are the elite. This is what all citizenry aspires to. You don't try to beat them into submission and ignore the real problem. And what revolt? A few rebels who have the element of surprise. A swift retaliatory action and—"

"But the manpower, sir. They have numbers and it's going to take time, and—"

"And you panicked. You're a great disappointment to me, Schweiz," Arcadian said sadly. He shook his head. "I never thought it would come to this." Without warning, he reached into his robes and extracted a small handblaster. Schweiz was openmouthed. In all the time he had been sec chief, Arcadian had always proclaimed that he wouldn't carry a blaster. The baron read his expression. "This?" he said, indicating the blaster. He shrugged. "A man has to have something to fall back on."

With which he raised it and loosed one shot. Schweiz's eyes were wide-open in shock, visible as the shades tumbled from his nose. A trickle of blood from the single wound in his forehead trickled down to the line on the bridge where those shades had once rested, before he tumbled backward.

The baron stepped over his corpse, sucking his teeth at the mess the blood was making on his carpet. He strode to the radio room and seized the transmitter from the hands of his radio op.

"Listen here. This is your baron speaking. All sec on the east side to head for Sector Eight. Contain and eliminate the rebels. West side, I want you to head to the surgery area and eliminate the man known as Dix. I don't care how. I want these problems stamped on now."

He handed the transmitter back to the openmouthed radio op. "But sir," he said finally, "that leaves everything else wide-open."

Arcadian dismissed him with a wave of the hand. "Doesn't matter. Hit the bastards hard enough, and the teams will be back before anyone even notices they've gone. This will soon pass."

JAK HAD BEEN LUCKY. Pulaski had, that very morning, told him and three others that they were to be the subjects of a nocturnal assault course test. As such, they were excused for the day and ordered to rest for the forthcoming exercise. It was exactly what Jak could have wished. Rest be damned, he was restless and waiting for action. And now he was free to act when the time came.

The first indication had been the blast. Jak had heard it, as had most people scattered across the ville. But unlike the majority, he was able to pinpoint where the sound had originated. As he hung out of the window at his quarters, watching intently the streets below, he could also smell it in the air—the explosive in the gren and the warm smell of roasted flesh, caught in the blast. He could also see the streets emptying of sec patrols as they rushed past, out of their usual patterns, toward the sector where the blast had originated.

He also realized something that had been staring him in the face all along, and he cursed himself for being a stupe.

All along, there had been a view that the vid cams were there for the baron to keep track of what and where his people were at any given time. Now that this emergency had occurred, you would have expected the cams to move out of synch, and to follow the movement on the streets.

But they didn't. They merely moved in the same old patterns.

Jak had assumed that the cable feeds ran inside the poles on which they were mounted. But what if there were no cable feeds? Thinking back, they had seen many things at the baron's central administration building, but never once had they seen a room with vid monitors. Also, the way in which he had discovered people moved freely at night, albeit with practiced caution, was unlikely. Surely, even by chance, some would have been caught and sec procedures changed?

Jak realized that the vid cams were another of the baron's mind games. He didn't have the tech, but he had the psychology to make his people believe he had that tech, and that he was watching them all the time, so constraining their actions.

Jak cursed again, then cracked his grim white visage with a grin.

Maybe he had been in the dark—literally and figuratively—before. Now that he was in the light, this would make his task so much easier.

He hurried from his quarters, leaving the building by the front this time. He had no time to waste, and nothing now to prevent him from making the best time by whatever means.

And from the distant sounds of fighting that reached him, it wasn't a moment too soon.

THAT CHANGE WAS in the air was apparent to Mildred and Doc, even though they had no idea of what had occurred the night before, and even though their sector had no official sec parties that could be withdrawn.

They heard the distant blast, and there was an indefinable something that altered in the mood of the ville around them.

At the time, they were in the square where the chess games took place, watching yet another interminable and impermeable game being played on the large board in the center.

"It's not surprising they play stupid games like this if there isn't anything else to do," Mildred remarked. "I know I sure as hell would go crazy after a few months in here. Come to that, I'm not sure that I'm not anyway."

"Let me assure that you are not, my dear Mildred," Doc purred with a malicious grin.

Mildred chuckled. "Coming from you, that sure as hell isn't an assurance."

"Perhaps not," Doc murmured, "but all jesting aside, I fear that your desire for something else to occupy you may soon be about to bear fruit."

"Yeah, I can feel it, too. And that explosion was no accident. That was a gren, unless I can't tell what they sound like anymore."

"I would concur with that." Doc looked around them at the vacant lot. "I note that there are a number of people absent. Those I would associate with those in control of this sector, rather than those who are inmates like ourselves."

"I don't like you using that word about us, Doc, but I guess it's right. And I guess you are, too. I wonder what's going down."

"I suspect we will find out soon enough."

Doc's words were prophetic. Within a few minutes

he was astounded to see Jak approaching from the other side of the quadrant.

"What are you doing here in daylight? And how—"

"No time," Jak said brusquely before rapidly taking them through the events of the previous night, and his realization that they weren't being watched after all.

"So we could have just walked out at any time," Doc said sadly.

"If you could avoid sec," Jak added. "But sec were shit, anyway."

"Never mind that crap," Mildred snapped, "what are we going to do about John?"

"We need get Ryan and Krysty. They know some who join us."

"There are some here," Doc said, his eyes immediately scanning the area for Cloris or Hamilton.

"Good," the albino stated. "Need to move fast."

Doc caught sight of the pair he sought. They were clustered with others he recognized, in agitated discussion. "Come," he said simply, moving toward them and beckoning Mildred and Jak to follow.

They approached the group, which was absorbed by its own arguments. As the companions closed on them, they could hear snatches of the conversation. Hamilton and Cloris were attempting to rally the others into a fighting force. "There will never be a better time. There may never be another time," he heard the woman tell them.

"I fear she is correct," Doc said, approaching them without any niceties. "Our friend has come from another sector, and he has this to tell you."

He beckoned to Jak, whose eyes scanned them and

saw little to inspire in the way of fight, but who none-theless repeated his words of a few moments earlier. When he had finished, Doc appealed to them.

"I know you find the prospect of fighting a difficult one. Arcadian and his cohorts have traded on this, and have ingrained it for that reason alone. But I fear you have no choice, now. If you do not join with those who are rising around you, you risk being classed with your oppressors and swept away with them."

Hamilton looked at all three of them in turn. "A per-suasive argument, but one that takes no account of one small fact. We have no idea—any of us—how to rise up. What do we do?"

For a moment the three companions were non-plussed. While a revolution brewed around them, they were faced with potential allies who had no idea what to do next. It was obvious, given their background, yet perplexing.

"Find sector leaders, chill or take prisoner. Any weapons, take. Anyone opposes, chill. All move on center eventually, take down baron. Follow them. Simple," Jak rapped out after a moment's thought.

"That's it?" Hamilton asked.

"Do it. Rest follows," Jak shrugged. "We need go," he added to Doc and Mildred.

"Look, the lad has put it in simplistic terms, but he is right," Doc said quickly. "You need to take control of this sector. I do not think anyone outside the sector leaders will oppose you, and there was little in the way of armament here that I could see. Weight of numbers will carry it. This can be relatively nonviolent, but you must join with other sectors."

They group looked nervously, one to another.

"We don't have much choice," Hamilton said doubt-
fully. "We'll do our best."

"That, my friend, is all any of us can ever do," Doc
said, grasping him by the arm. "Now, I really must go."

With a last look back at Cloris, whose eyes met his
for a second and somehow assured him that, despite
Hamilton's doubts, they would manage, Doc hightailed
it after Jak and Mildred, who were already moving
away.

"Wait," he yelled.

"Hurry up, dammit, there isn't any time to waste,"
Mildred yelled back, the crack in her voice betraying
her concerns.

The sector beyond the board area was deserted. Most
of the dwellers were gathered around the vacant lot. Of
those who led them there was no sign. They moved
without fear and with a minimum of caution across the
sector and the wasteland between. Once across, they
entered a sector that neither of them knew. Its purpose
was a mystery to them, but the fact that it had been sec-
controlled was made obvious by the way in which the
dwellers were rebelling. Some had blasters, others im-
provised weapons. They were breaking windows and
smashing the interiors of some buildings. A mob was
gathered around what had to have been the sector
leader's building, and the lampposts and vid posts were
festooned with what at first appeared to be ragged
bundles. It was only when they drew near that they
could see that these were corpses—the sector leader and
his staff, clothes ripped where they had been flayed
until they chilled. If that hadn't worked, then hanging

them by their necks would have finished the job. The building behind the corpses began to bellow smoke and orange flame as the fires started within began to spread.

The mob surged away from the fire and turned in direction until it was able to move toward the center of Arcady. Jak, Mildred and Doc weren't known here, and suspicious glances came their way from some of the mob. Now wasn't the time to try to convince them that they were on the same side. Moving away as those suspicious faces were swept from them by the tide of humanity, they moved into the deserted side streets.

"This way…" Jak led Mildred and Doc through a maze of streets that were littered with debris, but were otherwise deserted. Within a short time, they were crossing over into another sector. "This is where Ryan and Krysty were," Jak panted as he ran. "Mebbe still here."

Instinct told him to head for the center of the sector. If any pattern at all could be discerned, it would be that the sector leaders would be the first targets. The sounds of a rabble told them that this was correct, and within a few streets they were at the edge of a brawling mob.

Those who lived in this sector were partly slave and partly master. Their duties were sometimes divided, and so now were their loyalties. Standing on the edge of the mob, it was hard to tell who was on which side. To just wade in would have been futile. But this mob impeded them, and it was impossible to see if their companions were in the midst.

A sudden burst of blasterfire rent the air, and brought the fighting to a halt, even though some pockets took longer to subside. Standing on the steps of the central building, a young man held a SMG above his head.

"You know me," he yelled, "and you know him." An older man was thrust out onto the steps, his hands bound behind his back. "Alex doesn't run this place anymore," the young man yelled. "None of us do. We're free. So I suggest we stop fighting among ourselves and take down the coldheart bastard who started this. To the palace…"

The air was filled with yells of agreement, excitement and plain confusion. Yet as the young man descended the steps, the old man left, now strangely forgotten; in his wake, the crowd began to move.

Mildred, Jak and Doc cut through the throng. They had spotted the unseen hand that had thrust the old man out into view.

"You'll never get away with this. Arcadian won't let you ruin his plans," they heard the older man say as they approached. A familiar voice answered.

"Not our fight to get away with, old man. And I figure Arcadian won't have a say in anything before too long."

"Ryan," Jak yelled. The one-eyed man and Krysty emerged from the building, blasters in hand.

"Am I glad to see you," Krysty said warmly.

"Hell, yeah," Mildred agreed. "But we're one short, and he's in big trouble if Jak's right."

Chapter Seventeen

J.B. unleashed another burst of fire from the mini-Uzi, then ducked. A blast of random fire from a number of weapons exploded in the air, pitting the brickwork around him, tearing out chunks that rained down on him and covered him in a choking dust that made his eyes stream and clogged his lungs. This had been going on for long enough to make him realize that his cover was poor, and he needed to move soon. His own fire was almost as random, as it was getting harder to see well enough to pick targets.

He was lucky that he had been able to get this far. It was only the poor quality of the sec that had enabled him to find this space. Yet, ironically, it was their poor aim that would force him into the open regardless of their accuracy.

He had rolled away from the gren blast and come up running. A quick look around had shown him there was nothing except the blank facades of buildings all around. He could have tried to get into one, but that would have left him exposed by the maze of corridors and his lack of knowledge. Further exploration had been strangled at birth by the sudden fire from behind him. The gren had drawn nearby patrols to him. Cursing his luck, he had dived for a brick shelter that he hoped would give him cover and access to a building. Despite his misgivings, it was now the only option other than the open of the street.

Fate was kicking him in the balls. The brick shelter had been originally built as a garbage storage area, and he found himself hemmed in, with nothing but a blank wall at his back.

The bastard coldhearts were obviously trying to reduce the brick to rubble and dust in their eagerness to drive him out, blinding and choking him in the process.

Then it came to him. The drain cover he had walked over, seen when he was placing the gren. Dark night! It had to be the one Doc had talked about. If only he could reach it. The dust in his throat and in his eyes was the answer. Not that he could create such a smoke-screen in such a way, but…

Rummaging in his bag, he found a gas gren. Keeping a good supply of ordnance and relying on a stupe sec force used to blind obedience was a winning combination, and the sense of impending doom that had settled on him now began to lift.

His only problem would be launching the gren, as it would mean coming out into the open for a moment. Given their lack of marksmanship, this was perhaps less of a risk than it would have been in other circumstances. He had only reached a couple of hundred yards from the portico, and now that seemed an advantage rather than the drawback of a few moments before.

Should he wait for a lull in the fire? As the noise and dust gathered around him, he figured he was best just going for broke. The gren was tear gas, and so he quickly tied a kerchief around his face after soaking it from his water bottle. The water was stale and brackish as the bottle had been neither needed nor heeded since their arrival, but that didn't matter. It would serve its purpose.

Counting to ten, steeling himself, and knowing that he had one chance and little time, J.B. released the pin from the gren, stepped out and tossed it into the air before stepping back until he heard it detonate.

The firing ceased as the sec forces gathered close by were hit by the cloud of tear gas. Checking to ensure the mini-Uzi had a fresh load, J.B. hit the sidewalk at a run, firing into the crowd of choking, blinded men to clear them. He didn't—couldn't—think about them firing back.

Through the portico and into the square, his eyes streaming, his nose filled with staleness but little gas, J.B. could see that there were no sec here, only the unidentifiable remains of those caught by the original frag blast. A crater in the middle of the square showed where the gren had blown. Just off-center was a dark hole. The drain cover had been blown off by the blast. It sure as hell saved him precious time in wrenching it off.

J.B. was down the ladder leading to the underground complex in less time than it took him to whip the kerchief from his face and wipe the tears from his eyes. He hit the bottom at a run, headed toward Arcadian's palace.

He could only hope that he wouldn't find himself alone there.

"SIR, IT DOESN'T LOOK good," the radio op said nervously. The baron had been hovering over his shoulder for some time, making him sweat as the messages came in. In both sectors where the sec had been deployed, there had been nothing but setbacks. The men in Sector Eight had fallen back and were being driven toward the center sector at a speed that almost had them falling over their own asses. Meanwhile, Dix had seemingly vanished into thin air after decimating the sec in that region. Andower was gone, and the sec that had been detailed to the sector were now in disarray as those inmates of the sector who still had the will and were able were now emerging into the daylight.

"Sir, what should I do?" the radio op reiterated, turning to the baron. "Sir, if we do nothing, then the other sectors, now that they have no one to keep them in line—"

Arcadian grunted and waved his hand dismissively. "They are no threat. They think we can see their every move. Beside which, most of them are happy. Why would they wish to join this futile rebellion? No, draw the sec back here to quell those who are on the march. The rest will be able to look after themselves for a while. They recognize the greater good when they see it."

That, thought the radio op, is just what I'm worried about. Particularly if they think like I do.

"FIREBLAST. I—" Ryan stopped dead, the others in his wake. The sight that greeted the companions was one that almost defied belief, even after all the things they had seen.

The street ahead of them was quiet, now. The sec men who survived had pulled back, and all that remained were the chilled corpses of those that J.B. had blasted on his way into the square. Except that some, it was clear, had needed more than the fire of the Armorer to end their lives.

This had come from those who now shuffled aimlessly around among the debris, men and women who had spent too long at the mercy of Andower and his experiments. Blank-eyed, dripping blood from wounds that were open, experiments that hadn't quite worked, they wandered in random directions. Some were psychological victims, their only outward signs of damage being the slack jaw and blank stare. Others, horribly, were victims of the good doctor's experiments. A woman with wings stitched to her back flapped them in a desultory manner while nibbling on something that may have been a dead sec man's ear. One man had an extra arm grafted to the center of his chest, the flesh hanging gray, dead and gangrenous. Another had an extra leg over which he was stumbling.

"Perversion. There is worse than this, and thank heavens it cannot be seen," Doc muttered savagely.

"We can't let them—" Mildred began.

"No," Doc cut in preemptively. "Let them slip away. It's for the best."

"But they're innocent victims," Mildred said softly.

"True. But what life for them? Besides, have you forgotten that J.B. needs us?"

"John looks like he's doing okay on his own," she answered. "You're right, of course. Prolonging suffering is no answer."

"Then I suggest we try to follow John Barrymore's trail," Doc stated.

"Not hard." Jak sniffed. "Figure he's headed back the way you did." He moved ahead toward the portico, stopping only to indicate the carnage in the square. The others followed, pushing away the shambling hulks that came close. The creatures flinched in the face of live opposition, revealing the treatment by which they had been conditioned.

"To Arcadian's palace," Krysty whispered as she looked at the dark hole in the center of the square. "What was that old saying about frying pans and fires?"

"John all over." Mildred sighed. "Guess he's going to need all the backup we can give him."

THE ARMORER CLIMBED the stairs at the end of the long corridor, his heart pumping and his eyes now clear. He knew that behind the door at the top of the stairs was the high hall of Arcadian's palace. He was in the heart of the beast, and he knew that there would be a heavy sec presence. He would need to come out blasting. In his mind, he ran over as much detail of the hall as he could, trying to select the best cover that would be available.

It was only when he reached the landing and tried the door that he realized that events may have run ahead of him. The noise that penetrated the thick oak of the door led him to believe that a search for cover may not be necessary.

MARTHA FOUND HERSELF swept up with the mob as it moved out of the eighth sector and surged toward the center of Arcady. Miraculously, the mangy hound wound around her, never losing sight, and not succumbing to the fighting that sporadically broke out.

This had decreased as they had moved into adjacent sectors. The sec forces were on the run, heading back toward the center. Their only fire was defensive, attempting to cover their rear guard, but too wild to really do any harm. Those in the sectors they had passed through had been initially confused, but had soon decided which side of the fence they came down upon. A few attempted to fight the rebels, driven by fear of what would happen if they joined with them. But they were small in number, and were soon either beaten or succumbed to the mass. Most found themselves swept up by the hysteria and the promise of a new future.

The mob of which she was a part converged with one that came from another part of the ville. For a moment, as they crashed into one another, it seemed that combat would ensue. But recognition of fellow rebel factions led to a joyous union as they swept toward the center. Joy: that was exactly what she could feel from them, and within herself. A giant weight that had been crushing them was being cast off, and it felt good. What might come after was scary, as it was unknown. That really didn't matter right now. In fact, now was really all that counted.

As they moved into the central sector, there were more sporadic outbreaks of fighting. Some of those who felt themselves fortunate to have made it to this level were unwilling to risk that status. Again, they were few. Most realized that status was a thing of the past. Or were just caught up in the moment. It didn't matter. All that mattered was that the rebel forces were now in the ville, led by a young man brandishing an SMG, exhorting them onward.

Toward the palace, which was now in their sights.

J.B. PAUSED AS HE WAS about to shoot through the lock on the door. There were sounds from behind him, running feet down the corridor. Echoing, hard to distinguish. He quickly descended the stairs and headed for the nearest door. It was locked, of course. Cursing, he pulled out his knife and forced the blade into the doorjamb, pushing the steel against the lock until it gave, the door springing open. The jamb showed some damage, but he doubted that the oncoming forces would pause to note the splintered wood. They were moving at too great a speed.

He slid into the room, closing the door behind him. He waited, blaster poised. They would pass, he would step out and shoot the living shit out of them. He was in no mood to ask questions.

As they clattered past, a smile crossed his features.

He pulled the door open and stepped out, hearing Mildred say, "Fuck it, he can't have come this way. The bastard door hasn't been touched."

"That's 'cause I was waiting for you. Been wondering when you'd turn up," he said with a wry grin, relishing the looks on their faces as they turned to him.

ARCADIAN STOOD at the head of the stairwell, looking down on the ragged remains of his sec force as they held out against the rebels. Part of him knew that it was a hopeless task. They were outnumbered, and the mob pressed forward with their greater numbers regardless of the cost. Yet he still believed that if his men could hold the mob at bay until the wave of hysteria subsided, then he could make them see reason. Whether this was delusion or not, there was no way he would surrender his dream lightly.

Any hopes of holding out were put to rest by one simple action. A burst of SMG fire reduced the oak door to splinters, and a gren tossed into the lobby exploded almost before the baron had a chance to react. He had only just thrown himself to the floor when it detonated, reducing his precious artifacts to matchwood and dust. As he lay, stunned, he could hear the chatter of blasterfire in rapid bursts, picking off those sec not claimed by the gren.

Slowly, like a man walking through a bad dream, he rose and walked down the staircase. He could see Ryan Cawdor and his people being greeted by the rebel forces as they surged through the doors of the building.

"Why?" he kept repeating, passing through a crowd that parted in surprise that he should walk among them so plainly. He walked up to Ryan and a young man who he vaguely recognized as a sector worker. "Why?" he asked again. "All I wanted was to make a better world. You could see that, surely? What was so wrong with that?"

"You can't make one," Ryan replied flatly. "Not because it's your desire. It has to be everyone."

The baron made to answer, but it was as though his question and Ryan's answer had broken the spell. The mob surged forward, and the baron was lost in a sea of arms, grabbing hands mauling at him. He was swept back as the crowd parted and a section began to move out and into the street, taking the baron with them.

"The labs—"

"Andower. Him, too—"

"Make him see what he's done—"

"Let him feel it—"

It was obvious what was about to happen. Ryan started to move, but found himself stayed by Tod, the younger man's SMG placed across Ryan's torso. The one-eyed man glared at him. No one told Ryan Cawdor what to do.

"You can't let them do that," he said. "At least chill the fucker cleanly, or you're no better."

"Why?" Tod questioned. "Let them. Call it payback."

"He's right," J.B. said. The Armorer's tone was cold.

"But—"

"Ryan, this isn't our fight. Let them deal with it their way. They've got to make this ville again. 'Sides which, it could have been me going through that, and that coldheart fucker wouldn't have stopped it for anything."

"Your man speaks the truth," Tod intoned. "Let it go at that."

He turned and left them, following the last remnants of the crowd as they ebbed and flowed toward the lab sector.

"God alone knows what they'll find, and what they'll make of it." Doc sighed. "Perhaps it's best we leave them to it."

Ryan looked around at the shattered palace. They stood alone. As always, just the six of them. And Tod had been right: this wasn't their fight. No one came out of this with any glory to robe themselves.

"Must be plenty of wags undamaged," he told them. "We need to find one, get supplies to replace the ones that we lost when they took us, and get the fuck out of here. This is no place for us."

Their silence was all the agreement he needed.

The Executioner®
Don Pendleton's
DEEP RECON

Mercenaries trade lives for guns in the Florida Keys...

When a BATF agent's cover is blown during a gunrunning bust in the Florida Keys, Mack Bolan is sent in to find the leak within the Feds—before more lives are lost. With highly trained ex-Marines manning the guns, it's kill or be killed. And the Executioner is ready to take them up on their offer....

*Available June
wherever books are sold.*

TAKE 'EM FREE
2 action-packed novels plus a mystery bonus

NO RISK
NO OBLIGATION TO BUY